Their Frontier Family

Center Point
Large Print

**This Large Print Book carries the
Seal of Approval of N.A.V.H.**

Their Frontier Family

Lyn Cote

CENTER POINT LARGE PRINT
THORNDIKE, MAINE

The text of this Large Print edition is unabridged.
In other aspects, this book may
vary from the original edition.
Printed in the United States of America
on permanent paper.
Set in 16-point Times New Roman type.

ISBN: 978-1-61173-709-7

Library of Congress Cataloging-in-Publication Data

Cote, Lyn.
Their frontier family / Lyn Cote. — Center Point Large Print edition.
pages cm
ISBN 978-1-61173-709-7 (Library binding : alk. paper)
1. Quakers—Fiction. 2. Unmarried mothers—Fiction.
  3. Illegitimate children—Fiction. 4. Families—Fiction.
  5. Moving, Household—Wisconsin—Fiction. 6. Domestic fiction.
  7. Large type books. I. Title.
PS3553.O76378T44 2013
813′.54—dc23
                                                    2012049267

To my hard-working and insightful editor,
Tina James

As far as the east from the west,
so far hath he removed
our transgressions from us.
—*Psalm 103:12*

Therefore if any man be in Christ,
he is a new creature: old things are passed away;
behold, all things are become new.
—*2 Corinthians 5:17*

Chapter One

Pennsylvania, April 1869

"Harlot."

Sunny Adams heard the harsh whisper across the nearly empty general store, knowing she was meant to hear it. Her heart clenched so tightly that she thought she might pass out. Two women at the door looked at her, lifted their noses, then turned and left the store, rudely jangling the little bell above.

She bowed her head, praying that she wouldn't reveal the waves of shame coursing through her. Though she wore the plain clothing of the Quakers, a simple unruffled gray dress and bonnet, she hadn't fooled anyone. They all saw through her mask.

A man cleared his throat. The storekeeper wanted her out. Could she blame him? While she shopped here, no "decent" woman would enter. She set down the bolt of blue calico she'd been admiring, hiding the trembling of her hands.

Feeling as if she were slogging through a cold, rushing flood, she moved toward the storekeeper. "I think that will be . . . all." She opened her purse,

9

paid for the items Mrs. Gabriel had sent her into town to purchase. Outwardly, she kept her head lowered. Inwardly, she dragged up her composure like a shield around her. Trying to avoid further slights, she hurried across the muddy street to the wagon. Approaching hooves sounded behind her but she didn't look over her shoulder.

Just as she reached the wagon, a man stepped out of the shadows. "Let me help you up," he said.

She backed away. This wasn't the first time he'd approached her, and she had no trouble in identifying what he really wanted from her. "I don't need your help." She made her voice hard and firm. "Please do not accost me like this. I will tell Adam Gabriel—"

"He's a Quaker," the man sneered. "Won't do anything to me. Just tell me to seek God or something."

And with that, he managed to touch her inappropriately.

She stifled a scream. Because who would come to her aid if she called for help? A prostitute— even a reformed one—had no protectors.

"I'm a Quaker," a man said from behind Sunny, "but I'll do more than tell thee to seek God."

Sunny spun around to see Noah Whitmore getting off his horse. Though she'd seen him at the Quaker meeting house earlier this year, she'd never spoken to him.

The man who'd accosted her took a step back.

"I thought when you came back from the war, you repented and got all 'turn the other cheek' again."

Noah folded his arms. "Thee ever hear the story about Samson using the jawbone of a jackass to slaughter Philistines?" Noah's expression announced that he was in the mood to follow Samson's example here and now.

Sunny's heart pounded. Should she speak or remain silent?

The rude man began backing away. "She isn't the first doxy the Gabriel family's taken in *to help*." The last two words taunted her. "Where's the father of her brat? She's not foolin' anybody. She can dress up like a Quaker but she isn't one. And we all know it."

Noah took a menacing step forward and the man turned and bolted between stores toward the alley. Noah removed his hat politely. "I'm sorry," he said simply.

"You have nothing to apologize for," she whispered. "Thank you."

His pant legs were spattered with mud. He looked as if he had just now gotten back from the journey that had taken him away for the past few months. She'd noticed his absence—after all, it was a small church.

But honesty prompted her to admit that Noah had always caught her attention, right from the beginning.

Noah wasn't handsome in the way of a

charming gambler in a fancy vest. He was good-looking in a real way, and something about the bleak look in his eyes, the grim set of his face, always tugged at her, made her want to go to him and touch his cheek.

A foolish thing I could never do.

"Is thee happy here?" Noah asked her. The unexpected question startled her. She struggled to find a polite reply.

He waved a hand as if wiping the question off a chalkboard.

She was relieved. *Happy* was a word she rarely thought of in connection with her life.

She forced down the emotions bubbling up, churning inside her. She knew that Mrs. Gabriel sent her to town as a little change in the everyday routine of the farm, a boon, not an ordeal. *I should tell her how it always is for me in town.*

But Sunny hadn't been able to bring herself to speak of the insults, snubs and liberties she faced during each trip to town—not to the sweet unsullied Quaker woman, Constance Gabriel. The woman who'd taken her in just before Christmas last year and treated her like a daughter.

Sunny then realized that Noah was waiting to help her up into the wagon and that she hadn't answered his question. She hastily offered him her hand. "Yes, the Gabriels have been very good to me."

Two women halted on the boardwalk and

stared at the two of them with searing intensity and disapproval. Sunny felt herself blush. "I'd better go. Mrs. Gabriel will be wondering where I am," Sunny said.

Noah frowned but then courteously helped her up onto the wagon seat. "If thee doesn't mind, since I'm going thy way, I'll ride alongside thee."

What could she say? He wasn't a child. He must know what associating with her would cost him socially. She slapped the reins and the wagon started forward. Noah swung up into his saddle and caught up to her.

Behind them both women made loud huffing sounds of disapproval.

"Don't let them bother thee," Noah said, leaning so she could hear his low voice. "People around here don't think much of Quakers. We're misfits."

Sunny wondered if he might be partially right. Though she was sure the women were judging her, maybe they were judging him, too. Certainly Quakers dressed, talked and believed differently than any people she'd ever met before. She recalled now what she'd heard before, that Noah had gone to war. For some reason this had grieved his family and his church.

"You went to war," slipped out before she could stop herself.

His mouth became a hard line. "Yes, I went to war."

She'd said the wrong thing. "But you're home now."

Noah didn't respond.

She didn't know what to say so she fell silent, as well.

Twice wagons passed hers as she rode beside a pensive Noah Whitmore on the main road. The people in the wagons gawked at seeing the two of them together. Several times along the way she thought Noah was going to say more to her, but he didn't. He looked troubled, too. She wanted to ask him what was bothering him, but she didn't feel comfortable speaking to him like a friend. Except for the Gabriels, she had no friends here.

Finally when she could stand the silence no longer, she said, "You've been away recently." He could take that as a question or a comment and treat it any way he wanted.

"I've been searching for a place of my own. I plan to homestead in Wisconsin."

His reply unsettled her further. Why, she couldn't say. "I see."

"Has thee ever thought about leaving here?"

"Where would I go?" she said without waiting to think about how she should reply. She hadn't learned to hold her quick tongue—unfortunately.

He nodded. "That's what I thought."

And what would I do? She had no way to support herself—except to go back to the saloon. Sudden revulsion gagged her.

Did those women in town think she'd chosen to be a prostitute? Did they think her mother had chosen to be one? A saloon was where a woman went when she had nowhere else to go. It wasn't a choice; it was a life sentence.

As they reached the lane to the Whitmore family's farm, Noah pulled at the brim of his hat. "Sunny, I'll leave thee here. Thanks for thy company. After weeks alone it was nice to speak to thee."

We didn't say much—or rather, you didn't. But Sunny smiled and nodded, her tongue tied by his kindness. He'd actually been polite to her in public. At the saloon, men were often polite but only inside. Outside they didn't even look at her, the lowest of the low.

With a nod, Noah rode down the lane.

Sunny drove on in turmoil. A mile from home she stopped the wagon and bent her head, praying for self-control as she often did on her return trip from town. If she appeared upset, she would have to explain the cause of her distress to Constance Gabriel. And she didn't want to do that. She owed the Gabriel family much. She'd met Mercy Gabriel, M.D., the eldest Gabriel daughter, in Idaho Territory. Dr. Mercy had delivered Sunny's baby last year and then made the arrangements for Sunny to come here to her parents, Constance and Adam, and try for a new start.

But she couldn't stay in this town for the rest

of her life, no matter how kind the Gabriels had been.

"I have to get away from here. Start fresh." Without warning the words she'd long held back were spoken aloud into the quiet daylight. But she had no plan. No place to go. No way to earn a living—except the way she had in the past.

She choked back a sob, not for herself but for her daughter. What if the type of public humiliation she'd suffered today happened a few years from now when her baby girl could understand what was being said about her mother?

Noah's questions came back to her, and she felt a stab of envy that the man was free to simply pick up and start again somewhere new on his own. Sunny did not have that luxury. *What am I going to do?*

Noah slowly led his horse up the familiar lane, to the place he called home, but which really wasn't home anymore. Sunny's face lingered in his mind—so pretty and somehow still graced with a tinge of innocence.

Ahead, he saw his father and two of his brothers. His brothers stopped unloading the wagon and headed toward him. Not his father. He stared at Noah and then turned his back and stalked to the barn.

This galled Noah, but he pushed it down. Then he recalled how that man on Main Street had touched Sunny without any fear. It galled him to his core, too. She had no one to protect her. The man had been right; the Gabriels would not fight for her. The idea that had played through his mind over the past few months pushed forward again.

His eldest brother reached him first. "You came back." He gripped Noah's hand.

"I'm home." *For now.* His other brothers shook his hand in welcome, none of them asking about his trip, afraid of what he'd say, no doubt.

"Don't take it personally," his eldest brother said, apologizing for their father's lack of welcome with a nod toward the barn.

"It is meant personally," Noah replied. "He will never forgive me for disagreeing with him and going to war." Noah held up his hand. "Don't make excuses for him. He's not going to change."

His brothers shifted uncomfortably on their feet, not willing to agree or disagree. They were caught in the middle.

But not for long. Meeting Sunny in town exactly when he'd come home and seeing her shamed in public had solidified his purpose. She needed his protection and he could provide it. But would she accept him?

Feeling like a counterfeit, Sunny perched on the backless bench in the quiet Quaker meeting for another Sunday morning of worship she didn't understand. She sat near the back on the women's side beside Constance Gabriel, who had taught Sunny to be still here and let the Inner Light lead her.

But how did that feel? Was she supposed to be feeling something besides bone-aching hopelessness?

Little Dawn stirred in her arms and Sunny patted her six-month-old daughter, soothing her to be quiet. *I've brought this shame upon my daughter as surely as my mother brought it onto me.* She pushed the tormenting thought back, rocking slightly on the hard bench not just to comfort Dawn, but herself, as well.

The door behind her opened, the sound magnified by the silence within. Even the devout turned their heads to glimpse who'd broken their peace.

He came. Awareness whispered through Sunny as Noah Whitmore stalked to the men's side and sat down near, but still a bit apart from, his father and five older brothers. Today he was wearing his Sunday best like everyone else. His expression was stormy, determined.

Dawn woke in her arms and yawned. She was a sweet-tempered child, and as pretty as anything with reddish-blond hair and big blue eyes. As Sunny smiled down at her, an old, heartbreaking thought stung her. *I don't even know who your father is.* Sunny closed her eyes and absorbed the full weight of her wretchedness, thankful no one could hear what was in her mind.

18

Noah Whitmore rose. This was not uncommon —the Quaker worship consisted of people rising to recite, discuss or quote scripture. However, in her time here, Noah had never risen. The stillness around Sunny became alert, sharp. Everyone looked at him. Unaccountably reluctant to meet his gaze, she lowered her eyes.

"You all know that I've been away," Noah said, his voice growing firmer with each word. The congregation palpably absorbed this unexpected, unconventional announcement. In any other church, whispering might have broken out. Here, though, only shuttered glances and even keener concentration followed.

Sunny looked up and found that Noah Whitmore was looking straight at her. His intent gaze electrified her and she had to look away again.

"I'm making this announcement because I've staked a homestead claim in Wisconsin but must accumulate what's necessary and return there while there is still time to put in a crop." Still focusing on her, he paused and his jaw worked. "And I have chosen a woman who I hope will become a wife."

A wife? Sunny sensed the conspicuous yet silent reaction Noah's announcement was garnering. And since Noah was staring at her, everyone was now studying her, too. *He couldn't . . . no, he—*

"Adam Gabriel," Noah said, his voice suddenly gruffer, "I want to ask for thy foster daughter

Sunny's hand in marriage. And I want us to be married now, here, today."

Ice shot through Sunny. She heard herself gasp. And she was not the only one. She couldn't think straight. Noah wanted to marry *her?*

I couldn't have heard that right.

Adam Gabriel and Noah's father, Boaz, surged to their feet, both looking shocked, upset. A few other men rose and turned toward Noah.

White-haired Solomon Love, the most elderly and respected man at the gathering, stood. He raised his gnarled hands and gestured for the two fathers and the others to retake their seats. Adam sat first and then, grudgingly, Noah's father.

Sunny could do nothing but stare at the floor, frozen in shock as Noah's impossible words rang in her head.

Noah inhaled, trying to remember to breathe. Though this was the reaction he'd expected, his emotions raced like a runaway train.

Solomon moved to the aisle and faced Noah. "I understand why thee is in a hurry to get thy crop in, yet taking a wife is an important decision. It cannot be made lightly, hurriedly." The man's calm voice seemed to lower the tension in the room.

"This isn't a hasty decision," Noah said, finding he was having trouble getting his words out.

"When did thee court Sunny?" Solomon asked politely.

Sunny tilted her head, as if asking the same question.

Noah looked down. Everyone here knew that the woman he'd courted over a decade ago—and who had rejected him when he went off to war— sat in this very room, now the wife of another man. And how could he explain how Sunny had attracted him from the first time he'd seen her here at Christmas last year? She'd drawn him because he sensed another soul that had lived far beyond this safe haven.

The war had never penetrated the peace here. An image of soldiers, both blue and gray, lying in their own blood flashed in his mind. The gorge in his throat rose. He made himself focus on here. On now. On her.

"I haven't approached Sunny," Noah continued, keeping his voice steady. "In her circum- stances . . ." His voice faded. Then he looked Sunny straight in the eye. She still looked stunned. He hoped she wasn't going to resent this public declaration. After meeting her in town upon arriving home, he'd thought this over carefully. He'd decided the best way to spike scurrilous, misguided gossip was to propose publicly.

He cleared his throat and chose his words with care. "I didn't want her to take my interest wrongly." That much was true. He'd first seen the way she was treated in town long before he'd left for Wisconsin. "But I think she'll make me a good wife. And I'll try to make her a good husband."

Noah turned his gaze to Solomon Love, wanting to give all his reasons. "I could have just gone to Adam Gabriel's house later to ask, then taken her to the justice of the peace." Noah paused and bent his head toward her as if acknowledging he would have needed her agreement. "But I didn't want to do it like that. I didn't want to do this the world's way, or away from the meeting."

"Like last time? When thee ran away and enlisted?" his father retorted, obviously unable to keep his ire undercover—even here.

Noah stood his ground with a lift of his chin. His father wasn't going to ruin Noah's plans. Or hurt Sunny's feelings.

Solomon cleared his throat. "Marrying should be about thee and the woman thee wishes to marry. 'Therefore shall a man leave his father and his mother, and shall cleave unto his wife,' " Solomon said in a tone that effectively capped a lid on any further public cleaning of the Whitmore family closet.

Boaz glared at Noah still, but shut his mouth tightly.

Noah didn't relax. He glanced at Sunny. She still looked frozen. He hoped he hadn't done this all wrong. Concern tightened into a ball in his midsection.

Solomon's wife, Eve, a little silver-haired

sparrow of a woman, rose and leaned on her cane. "I think we should all pray about this now. And, Solomon, we are old and forget the passion of youth. There is no reason to prevent Sunny and Noah from marrying today and leaving for Wisconsin tomorrow with the blessing of this meeting. As long as this is what *the two wish*. And if they have sought God's will and have become clear, we should not try to prevent this marriage. Which I believe," Eve said, her quavering voice firming, "would be of benefit to both."

"Good counsel, wife, as usual." Solomon beamed at her. "Noah, will thee sit and let us pray for thee and Sunny that thee both have clearness about this?"

"I will." Noah sat, suddenly very weary. He glanced at his father, who still managed to bristle though he neither moved nor spoke.

Every head bowed, so Noah lowered his and waited . . . He hadn't kept track of how much time had passed until he heard Sunny's baby stirring and whimpering. Then he realized that the service had gone on much longer than usual. Others were also becoming restless. Noah tried to sit as if he were at peace, but his nerves jittered. Homesteading he'd seen proved hard enough for a man with a wife. He needed Sunny even though he hadn't thought of marriage after the war. He was offering her a fair deal. He needed a wife and she needed the protection a husband could provide. If Sunny refused him, he'd be forced to go alone.

Solomon stood again, his joints creaking. "We are past our time. Noah Whitmore and Sunny, if it meets with thy approval, my wife and I will meet with thee here at two this afternoon to seek clearness about this."

Noah rose. "I'm willing and I thank thee."

All eyes turned to Sunny. She flushed scarlet.

Constance touched Sunny's arm. "Is thee willing to meet for clearness?"

Sunny nodded, her eyes downcast.

Constance stood. "Our foster daughter is willing."

Noah nodded his thanks.

Then, as if released from a spell, the congregation broke up. They would head home to eat a cold dinner with no doubt a heated discussion of Noah Whitmore proposing to the latest soiled dove the Gabriels had taken in. Noah wished he could change that, but he'd discovered that human nature could rarely be denied.

Outside the meetinghouse Noah approached Sunny, his broad-brimmed Quaker hat in hand. "I know my proposal shocked thee. If thee is not interested in marrying me, just say so."

She looked up at him and then glanced around pointedly, obviously letting him know that too many people hovered nearby. "I am unsure. I will come at two."

He bowed his head and backed away. "At

two." Just then the woman he'd loved walked past him. She nodded and gave him an unreadable look. He felt nothing for her now. She didn't understand him. She hadn't understood why he'd gone to war. And he certainly was no longer the man she'd contemplated marrying ten years ago.

He turned his gaze to Sunny. She was so pretty and so quiet. He didn't know what had caused her to become a prostitute, but she wanted to change, wanted a new start, just like he did. They were well suited in that regard.

Solomon's Bible quote repeated in Noah's mind. *Therefore shall a man leave his father and his mother, and shall cleave unto his wife: and they shall be one flesh.* Declaring his proposal had sharpened his need for Sunny to go with him.

He could only hope that she would seize her chance to start anew. And in the process, possibly save him—from himself.

Sunny paused on the step. She'd never entered the meetinghouse by herself. April sunshine had been tempered by the cool breeze from the west. She pulled her shawl tighter.

Dawn had lain down for her long afternoon nap so Sunny had come with empty arms here—to make a decision that would change both their lives forever. Should she accept Noah's proposal? The thought of marrying chilled her, robbing her of breath.

She couldn't think why he would want to marry her. Why *any* man would want to marry her.

She opened the double door and stepped inside. There in the middle of the Quaker meetinghouse on two benches facing each other sat Eve and Solomon Love, and Noah Whitmore, the man who had said in front of everybody that he thought she would make a good wife.

Fresh shock tingled through her. His thrilling words slid from her mind into her heart and left her quaking. *What do I know about being a wife?*

Sunny tried to conceal her trembling, the trembling that had begun this morning. She walked as calmly as she could manage toward the bench where Noah sat. Without looking directly at him, she lowered herself onto the same bench as he.

Sitting so near him stirred her—and that alarmed her. She had never felt attraction to any man. Was Noah's recent kindness to her the cause? She faced the Loves, who had been good enough to speak to her since she'd come here. Very few of the Quakers—or Friends, as they called themselves—had made the effort to get to know her. They'd been kind but distant. She couldn't blame them for avoiding her. They were holy, she was stained.

Eve smiled at her and, reaching across the divide, patted her hand. "Sunny, thee does not know about the clearness meeting. It is how

Friends try to clear their thinking and make sure that they are within God's will."

Unsure of what she should say, Sunny merely nodded. She concealed her left hand in the folds of her gray skirt. In the hours since this morning she'd chafed the flesh beneath one thumb from fretting, a childhood habit. She'd been forbidden to suck her thumb or chew her nails, so when upset, she'd taken to scratching, worrying at her hand. She resisted the need to do it now.

"Noah," Solomon asked, "please tell us again what thy plans are and why they include Sunny."

"I have staked a claim on a homestead in western Wisconsin. Very near the Mississippi River." Noah's words were clipped. "Planting time is near. I need to return as soon as possible."

Sunny's emotions erupted—fear, worry and hope roiled inside her at Noah's words.

"That sounds as if thee is committed to leaving us for good." Solomon's voice was measured and without judgment.

Noah nodded.

"Why have thee chosen to ask Sunny to be thy bride and go with thee?" Eve asked.

Sunny nearly stopped breathing. Her throat muscles clenched with fear.

Noah propped his elbows on his knees and leaned forward as if thinking.

Many questions tumbled through her thoughts, but she could not make her mouth move. Was

Noah asking out of pity? Was she in a position to say no to him even if it was? The memory of the man who had inappropriately touched her several days ago slithered through her again, as if he were here leering at her. *Dear God, no more.*

In spite of her inner upheaval, Sunny made herself sit very still as silence pressed in on all of them. She drew in a normal breath. Yes, she could refuse this proposal, but she had Dawn to think of. Would life with Noah be better for Dawn than life alone with her mother? Would he be a loving stepfather for Dawn?

"Noah?" Eve prompted.

"How does a man choose a wife?" Noah asked in return. "I need a wife and want one. I only know that Sunny has attracted my attention from the first time she came to meetings. I've watched her with her little girl. She seems sweet and kind."

It seemed to be a day for Sunny to be stunned. No one—no one—had ever praised her like this. A melting sensation went through her and she wished that the backless bench would give her more support. She tightened her posture.

"That is a very clear reply," Solomon said.

"Sunny, is thee ready to take a husband?" Eve asked.

Sunny swallowed, thinking of how he'd praised her. "I am." She paused, then honesty forced her to bring up the topic she did not want to discuss. "I have a past."

28

Noah gave a swift, stark laugh. "I have a past, too."

"It is good to be honest with one another," Solomon said, tempering the emotions with a glance.

"I have a daughter," Sunny said, each word costing her. She pleated her plain gray cotton skirt.

"I know, and I'm willing to take responsibility for her," Noah said, glancing toward her.

Sunny measured his tone. He sounded sincere. Nonetheless she had overheard a few words about his own family. And she must speak for her child. "Your father has been known to show temper."

"I'm nothing like my father," Noah said as if stung.

Sunny absorbed this reaction. The bad blood between the two had been plain to see even in her short time here. Maybe not getting along with his own father would make him a more considerate parent, could that be?

"I'm sorry I spoke in that tone to thee," Noah apologized. "I promise I will provide for your daughter, and I will protect her. I'll try to be a good father."

Noah had just promised Dawn more than Sunny's own unknown father had ever done for her. She nodded, still hesitant. "I . . . I believe you."

"I have watched thee all my life, Noah," Eve said. "And thee has not had an easy time. Losing thy mother so young, that was hard. And thy broken engagement when thee went off to war. But thee cannot change the past by merely moving to a new place."

Sunny wished Eve would explain more. Who had Noah loved and been rejected by?

Noah sat up straight again. "I know that. But I cannot feel easy here. My father doesn't need me. My five brothers are more than enough to help him." Though he tried to hide it, hurt oozed out with each word.

"Thy father loves thee," Solomon said. "But that does not mean that a father and son will not disagree."

Noah's expression hardened.

Sunny sensed his abrupt withdrawal. Noah Whitmore had been kind to her in public, protected her, something hardly anybody had ever done for her. He'd asked her to marry him and said she was sweet and kind. He offered her marriage and protection for Dawn. But could he love her?

How could she ask that? Did she even deserve a man's love?

She touched his sleeve. He turned toward her. When she looked into his eyes, she fell headlong into a bottomless well of pain, sadness and isolation. Shaken, she pulled back her hand and lowered her gaze, feeling his piercing emotions as her own. What had caused his deep suffering?

She had met other veterans. Was this just the war or something more?

What had happened to Noah Whitmore?

"I want to start fresh—" Noah's words sounded wrenched from him "—and take Sunny and her little girl with me." Noah claimed her hand, the one she'd just withdrawn from him. "Sunny, will thee be my wife and go west with me?"

Noah's hand was large and rough but so gentle, and his touch warmed her. Then she did something she had barely learned to do—she prayed.

Dear Father, should I marry Noah Whitmore?

She waited, wondering if the Inner Light the Quakers believed in would come to her now, when she needed it so. She glanced up into Noah's eyes and his loneliness beckoned her, spoke to her own lonesome heart. "Yes," she whispered, shocking herself. Her words pushed goose bumps up along her arms.

Noah shook her hand as if sealing a contract. She wondered how this new beginning, complete reversal had all happened in less than one unbelievable day.

"We will make the preparations for the wedding to take place during this evening's meeting," Solomon said, helping his wife to her feet. "May God bless your union with a love as rich and long as Eve's and mine."

The elderly man's words were emphasized by

the tender look he gave his spouse, who beamed at him in turn.

Oh, to be loved like that. Sunny turned to Noah and glimpsed stark anguish flickering in his dark, dark eyes.

Maybe Noah, born and raised among these gentle people, was capable of love like that. Am I?

But what could I possibly have to offer in the way of love?

I've never loved any man. The thought made her feel as bleak as a cold winter day. Would she fail Noah? Men had only ever wanted her for one thing. What if that was all she was able to give?

Chapter Two

The weekly Sunday evening meeting became Noah and Sunny's wedding. Two single straight-backed chairs had been set facing each other in the center of the stark meetinghouse. Noah sat in one with his back to the men.

Outwardly he'd prepared to do this. He had bathed, shaved and changed back into his Sunday suit—after Aunt Martha had come over to press it "proper" for his wedding. While she'd fluttered around, asking him questions about his homestead, Noah's brothers had been restrained and watchful. Only his eldest brother, Nathan, had asked about Wisconsin and had wished him congratulations on his wedding. His father grim, silent and disapproving. Nothing new there.

Now Noah—feeling as if he were in a dream—watched Constance Gabriel, who was carrying Dawn, lead Sunny to sit on the straight-backed chair set in front of the other women. His bride managed only one glance toward him before she lowered her eyes and folded her hands. Since he couldn't see her face, he looked at her small, delicate hands. Tried not to think about holding them, tenderly lifting them to his lips. Sunny brought out such feelings in him. He wanted to protect her and hold her close.

While away this year he'd thought of her over and over. He'd barely spoken over a dozen sentences to this woman yet he knew he couldn't leave her behind—here among the sanctimonious and unforgiving.

A strained, restless silence blanketed the simple, unadorned meetinghouse. Fatigued from tension, Noah quelled the urge to let out a long breath, loosen his collar and relax against the chair. Without turning his head, Noah knew his father sat in his usual place beside Noah's five brothers. He felt his father's disapproving stare burn into his back like sunlight through a magnifying glass.

Finally, when Noah thought he could stand the silence no longer, Solomon rose and came to

33

stand beside him. Eve rose and came to stand near Sunny. Noah held his breath. There was still time for his father to cause a scene, to object to the wedding, to disown him again. Noah kept his eyes focused on Sunny.

"Sunny, Friends do not swear oaths," Solomon said, "but we do affirm." Then he quoted, " 'For the right joining in marriage is the work of the Lord only, and not the priests' or the magistrates'; for it is God's ordinance and not man's; and therefore Friends cannot consent that they should join them together: for we marry none; it is the Lord's work, and we are but witnesses.' "

Noah's heart clenched at the words *the Lord's work*. Where had the Lord been when sizzling grapeshot had fallen around him like cursed manna? Cold perspiration wet Noah's forehead. He shoved away battlefield memories and tried to stay in the here and now, with Sunny.

Solomon continued, "When thee two are ready, my wife and I will lead thee through the simple words that will affirm thy decision to marry."

Sunny looked up then.

Noah read her appeal as clearly as if she had spoken—*please let's finish this.* "I'm ready if Sunny is," Noah said, his voice sounding rusty, his pulse skipping.

Sunny nodded, her pale pink lips pressed so tight they'd turned white.

Noah gently took her small, work-worn hand in

his, drawing her up to face him. He found there was much he wanted to tell her but couldn't speak of, not here or maybe ever. Some words had been trapped inside him for years now. Instead he found himself echoing Solomon's quiet but authoritative voice.

"In the fear of the Lord and in the presence of this assembly of Friends, I take thee my friend Sunny to be my wife." He found that she had lifted her eyes and was staring into his as if she didn't quite believe what was happening. "Promising," he continued, "with God's help, to be unto thee a loving and faithful husband, until it shall please the Lord by death to separate us." Noah fought to keep his voice from betraying his turbulent emotions.

Sunny leaned forward and whispered shyly into his ear. "Thank you."

Unexpectedly, his spirit lightened.

As Sunny repeated the Quaker wedding promise to Noah, her whole body shook visibly. When she had finished, he leaned forward and pressed a chaste kiss upon her lips. The act rocked him to the core. For her part, Sunny, his bride, appeared strained nearly to breaking. Was marrying him so awful? Did she think he'd be a demanding man? He would have to speak to her, let her know . . .

"Now, Sunny and Noah," Solomon continued, "thee will sign thy wedding certificate and I ask all those attending to sign it also as witnesses."

At Solomon's nod, Noah took his bride's arm and led her to a little table near the door. A pen, ink and a paper had been set there for them. At the top of the paper someone had written in large bold script, "The Wedding Certificate of Sunny Adams and Noah Whitmore, April 4, 1869 at the Harmony, Pennsylvania, Friends Meeting."

Noah motioned for her to go first, but she shook her head. "Please," she whispered.

He bent and wrote his name right under the heading. Then he handed her the pen. She took a deep breath and carefully penned her name to the right of his, her hand trembling.

Then Noah led her to the doorway. By couples and singles, Friends got up and went to the certificate and signed under the heading of "Witnesses." Then they came to her and Noah and shook their hands, wishing them well. All spoke in muted voices as if trying to keep this wedding secret in some way.

Adam and Constance Gabriel signed and both of them kissed Sunny's cheek. "Thee will spend thy wedding night at our house, Noah, if that meets with thy approval," Constance murmured, still cradling Sunny's baby.

"Thank thee," Noah replied. He'd known better than to consider subjecting his bride to a night in his father's house. He'd been planning on taking Sunny to a local inn but this would be better, easier on her, he considered, as a thought niggled at his conscience. Should he have confessed to Sunny his limitations before the wedding? That their marriage would not be the usual?

One of the last to come forward to sign the wedding certificate was his father. He stomped forward and signed briskly. Then he pinned both of them with one of his piercing, judging looks. "I hope thee know what thee are doing."

Sunny swayed as if struck. Noah caught her arm, supporting her. All the anger he'd pressed down for years threatened to bubble over, but to what purpose? *I will not make a scene.* "Thank thee, Father, for thy blessing."

His father scowled and walked past them. Then one by one his brothers signed, shook his hand and wished him the best. Finally his eldest brother, Nathan, signed and leaned forward. "God bless thee, Noah and Sunny. I'll miss thee. We all will. Please send us thy post office address. Though separated, we will still be a family."

Noah gripped his brother's hand and nodded, not trusting his voice.

"We will write," his bride said, offering her hand. "I will try to be a good wife to your brother."

Noah turned away and faced the final few well-wishers, suddenly unable to look at Sunny. *I promise I'll take care of thee, Sunny, and thy little one. Thee will never want and thee will never be scorned. But I have no love of any kind to give. Four long years of war burned it out of me. I am an empty well.*

It was done. Sunny had become a wife. And now in the deep twilight with Noah riding his horse nearby, she rode in the Gabriel's wagon on the way home to their house. The wedding night loomed over her. How did a wife behave in the marriage bed? Nausea threatened her.

Oh, Heavenly Father, help me not shame myself.

She wished her mind wouldn't dip back into the past, bringing up images from long sordid nights above the saloon. Why couldn't the Lord just wipe her mind clean, like he'd taken away her sins?

That's what she'd been told he'd done, but Sunny often felt like her sins were still very much with her, defining her every step of the way.

After arriving at the Gabriel home, she managed to walk upstairs to the bedroom she usually shared with the youngest Gabriel sister. She now noted that fresh white sheets had been put on the bed for tonight, her last night in this house. She stood in the room, unable to move.

Constance entered. "Thee will want to nurse Dawn before bed."

Sunny accepted her child, sat in the rocking chair and settled the child to her.

Constance sat on the edge of the bed and smiled. "We are very happy that thee has found a good husband."

Sunny didn't trust her voice. She smiled as much as she could and nodded.

"Each man and woman must learn how to be married on their own. It cannot be taught. I have known Noah from his birth. He was a sweet child and is an honest man. Adam and I had no hesitation in letting thee marry him."

Sunny heard the good words but couldn't hold on to them. She was quaking inside.

"The only advice I will give thee is what is given in God's word. 'Submitting yourselves one to another in the fear of God.' And 'Let not the sun go down upon your wrath.' "

Sunny nodded, still unable to speak, unable to make sense of the words. Then the sweet woman carried Dawn away to spend the night in their room. Before Constance left she said, "When thee is ready, open the door for thy husband."

As Sunny went through the motions of dressing for bed, she experienced the same penned-in feeling that had overwhelmed her at fourteen when her mother had died. A week later, penniless and with no friends in the world other than her mother's, Sunny had taken her mother's place upstairs in the saloon. At this memory Sunny's stomach turned. That horrible first night poured through her mind and she fought the memories back with all her strength.

That was the past. Living away from the saloon, surrounded by the Gabriels' kindness, had begun softening her, stripping away the hard shell that had protected her from the pain, rejection and coarse treatment she'd endured.

It won't be like that. This is Noah, who called me sweet and kind and who has married me. Being with him will feel different. But how could he want her after she'd been with so many others?

From across the hall, Sunny heard Dawn whimper. She quieted, waiting to see if her child needed her.

Dawn made no further sound and Sunny took a deep breath. A new image appeared in her mind —her little girl in a spotless pinafore running toward a white schoolhouse, calling to her friends who were smiling and waving hello.

Marrying Noah Whitmore had given her daughter the chance to escape both the saloon and the stain of illegitimacy. And they would be moving to Wisconsin, far from anybody who knew of Sunny's past. Dawn would be free. Hope glimmered within her. *I've done right.*

She slipped on her flannel nightgown and then opened the door. Before Noah could enter, she slid between the sheets, to the far side of the bed. Waiting.

A long while later Noah entered and without a word undressed in the shadows beyond the flickering candlelight.

Sunny's heart thrummed in her temples. Harsh

images from her past bombarded her mind but she tried to shut them out.

Noah blew out the candle in the wall sconce.

She closed her eyes, waiting for the rope bed to dip as Noah slid in beside her.

"Sunny, I don't feel right about sharing a bed with you tonight. We're nearly strangers."

I used to lie down with strangers all the time. She clamped her lips tight, holding back the words, afraid that he would realize he'd made a terrible mistake in marrying her.

"I'll bunk here on the floor. Just go to sleep. We've a long day tomorrow. Good night, Sunny." He lifted off the top quilt and rolled up in it on the floor.

"Wh-why did you marry me?" she asked as confusion overwhelmed her.

He turned to face her, scant moonlight etching his outline. "It was time to take a wife."

"You know what I was."

"Yes, I know. You lay with men who paid you. Did you ever kill anyone?"

The question shocked her. "*No.* Of course not."

"Well, I have. Which is worse—lying with a stranger for money, or shooting a man and leaving him to bleed to death?"

Stunned at his bleak tone, she fell silent for a long moment, not knowing what to say.

In the dark she moved to the edge of the bed and slipped to the floor. In the dim light she

41

reached for his hand but stopped just short of taking it. "That was war. You were supposed to kill the enemy."

He made a gruff sound, and rolled away from her. "Good night, Sunny."

Her heart hurt for him. She longed to comfort him, but he'd turned his back to her.

Late into the night she stared at the ceiling, thinking about his question, about how he'd sounded when he'd spoken of war. Would they ever be truly close, or had too much happened to both of them? Was it her past that had made him sleep on the floor? Or was it . . . him? *Oh, Lord, can I be the wife he so clearly needs?*

"It's not much farther!" Noah called out, walking beside the Conestoga wagon, leading his horse.

Sunny, who was taking her turn at driving the wagon behind the oxen, waved to show him she had heard his first words to her in hours. Dawn crawled by her feet under the bench. Boards blocked the opening to the side and rear. She hoped her idea of "not much farther" matched his.

Beyond the line of trees with spring-green leaves the wide Mississippi River meandered along beside them, sunlight glinting on the rushing water, high with spring rain and snow-melt. Frogs croaked incessantly. After several weeks of traveling all she wanted was to stop living out of a wagon and arrive home, wherever that was.

The unusually warm April sun, now past noon, beat down on Sunny's bonnet. She'd unbuttoned her top two collar buttons to cool. The air along the river hung languid, humid, making perspiration trickle down her back. A large ungainly gray bird lifted from the water, squawking, raucous.

"I'm eager for you to see our homestead," Noah said, riding closer to her.

"I am, too." *And scared silly.*

Too late to draw back now.

Several weeks had passed since they'd wakened the morning after their wedding and set off by horseback to the Ohio River to travel west by riverboat. In Cairo, Illinois, Noah had purchased their wagon, oxen and supplies. Then they'd headed north, following the trail on the east side of the Mississippi. Noah pointed out that the trail was well-worn by many other travelers, and told her that French fur trappers had been the first, over two hundred years ago. She'd tried to appear interested in this since it seemed important to him. She'd known trappers herself. They weren't very special.

"It will take work to make our claim into a home," Noah said.

She gave him a heartening smile and ignored her misgivings. This was her husband, this was her fresh new start—she would have to make it

43

work no matter her own failings. "I'll do my best."

He nodded. "I know that."

Sunny blotted her forehead with the back of her hand. Then she saw a town appear around the bend, a street of rough buildings perched on the river's edge.

"That's Pepin," Noah called out.

"Thank Heaven," Sunny responded, her spirit lifting.

Dawn tried to stand and fell, crying out. Sunny kept one hand on the reins and with the other helped Dawn crawl up onto her lap.

"Is she all right?" Noah asked.

"Fine. Just trying to stand up."

"She's a quick one."

Usually silent Noah was almost chatting with her. *He must be happy, too.*

Noah always slept in the wagon bed at the end near the opening, evidently protecting her but always away from her. But just last night he called out, "Help, help!" She'd nearly crawled to him. But he'd sat up and left the wagon and began pacing. She hadn't known what to do. Sunny was beginning to believe he slept away because of his nightmares. Because of the war perhaps?

She wondered if his lack of sleep made him silent. Whenever she spoke, he replied readily and courteously. Yet he rarely initiated conversation, so today must be a good day.

Soon she pulled up to a drinking trough along

the huddle of rough log buildings facing the river—a general store, a blacksmith, a tiny government land office and a wharf area where a few barges were tethered.

And a saloon at the far end of the one street.

Buttoning her collar buttons, Sunny averted her face from the saloon, deeply grateful she would not be entering its swinging doors. Ever.

A man bustled out of the general store. "Welcome to Pepin!" he shouted. "I'm Ned Ashford, the storekeeper."

Noah approached the wagon and helped her put the brake on. Then he solicitously assisted her descent. Only then did he turn to the storekeeper. He shook the man's hand. "Noah Whitmore. This is my wife, Sunny, and our daughter, Dawn."

He was always careful to show her every courtesy, and every time Noah introduced her and her baby this way, gratitude swamped her. For this she forgave him his tendency to pass a whole day exchanging only a sentence or two with her.

Maybe it wasn't the sleepless nights. Some men just didn't talk much—she knew that.

But she could tell that he was keeping a distance between them. Their marriage had yet to be consummated.

She didn't blame him for not wanting her. Sudden shame over her past suddenly lit Sunny's face red-hot.

"You just stopping or staying?" the friendly storekeeper in the white apron asked.

"I have our homestead east of here claimed and staked." Noah sounded proud.

Our homestead—Sunny savored the words, her face cooling.

"I thought you looked familiar. You were here a few months ago. But alone."

"Right." Dismissing the man's curiosity, Noah turned to her. "Sunny, why don't you go inside and see if there's anything you need before we head to our homestead. It will be a while before we get to town again."

The farther they traveled, the more Noah dropped his use of "thee" in favor of "you." Noah appeared to be changing his identity. *I am, too.* And the sheer distance they'd come from more populated places heartened her. The farther north they went the fewer people there were. That meant the chances of her running into anyone who'd met her in a saloon were slimmer. A blessing, but now, Noah was saying they would be living far from this town?

Trying to quell her worries, she smiled and walked toward the store's shady entrance. The storekeeper beamed at her and opened wide the door.

A memory flashed through her of the store-keeper in Pennsylvania who had wanted her out of his establishment. She missed a beat and then proceeded inside, assuring herself that no one here would ever call her a harlot or touch her in a way that made her cringe.

Only Noah knew the truth about her past, about Dawn's illegitimacy. Wisconsin was far from Idaho Territory where Dawn had been born and she couldn't imagine meeting anyone from her old life.

Yes, only Noah could ruin her here.

But he'd never do that. Surely he would never betray her, now that she was his wife . . . would he?

She took a shaky breath. "I don't know if I need anything, Mr. Ashford. But it is good to get out of the sun and see what your fine establishment has to offer."

Mr. Ashford beamed at her. "Pepin County is growing every day, now that the war is over and men are looking for a place to settle their families. Of course in the 1600s the Pepin brothers first arrived—Frenchmen, you know. The river made it easy to get to."

As Sunny scanned the large store, Mr. Ashford's seemingly inexhaustible flow continued. "Now you go just a few miles east and you'll be in the forest and not much in the way of settlers. Your man was smart to homestead here in Wisconsin." The words *your man* warmed her to her toes. She'd always had *men,* not one who'd claimed her as his own.

"No soddy house for you. With all the trees

hereabouts, he can build you a nice snug cabin and have firewood aplenty. 'Course that makes it harder to clear land for a crop. But . . ." The man shrugged.

Sunny suddenly sensed Noah and turned to see him just inside, leaning against the doorjamb, silently urging her to come away. This wasn't the first time that he'd let her know he wanted to keep his distance from others.

Today she could understand his urgency. It was time to go see their land. "Your store is very neat and well-stocked," she said as she reluctantly made her way toward Noah.

Mr. Ashford beamed at her again.

"Does thee . . ." Noah stopped and began again. "Do you see anything you need, Sunny? I want to get to our homestead with plenty of time left to set up camp for the night."

Still hesitant to leave this cool, shady place, Sunny considered once more. "No, thank you, Noah. I don't need anything."

Noah peeled himself from the doorjamb. "Store-keeper, I'll need a bag of peppermints."

Sunny turned to him, her lips parted in surprise.

"My wife has a sweet tooth." One corner of Noah's mouth almost lifted.

He'd noticed her buying peppermint drops in Cairo, and savoring one a day till she'd run out.

The storekeeper chuckled as he bagged peppermint drops and then accepted three pennies from Noah.

"Shall we go, wife?"

She smiled, stirred by Noah's thoughtfulness. "Yes. Good day, Mr. Ashford."

"Good day and again, welcome to Pepin!"

Noah helped her back onto the wagon bench and lifted Dawn up to her. Then he handed her the bag of candy, which she slipped into her pocket as she felt a blush creep over her cheeks.

Noah led them down the main street and then to a bare rocky track, heading east away from the river, away from town.

Just before turning onto the track, Sunny glanced back and saw a woman dressed in red satin come out of the saloon and lean wearily against the hitching rail. Sunny averted her eyes, her heart beating faster. But she couldn't afford to show any pity or sympathy with this woman.

I must remember which side of the line I belong on now.

She'd studied how decent women behaved and hoped her masquerade would hold up well. The happy image of Dawn in her white pinafore running toward school and friends bobbed up in her mind again.

She wouldn't fail Dawn, no matter what.

Because of the roughness of the track, they progressed slowly, cautiously, through the thick

49

forest of maple, oak and fir. This forest had probably never felt the blade of an ax. Noah marveled at the huge trees and with each landmark, his excitement gained momentum. All those nights when he'd lain alone, sometimes in a tent, sometimes under the open sky, listening to the sounds of war playing in his mind. How long had he dreamed of having a place of his own? How long had he dreamed of having a wife to bring to it?

Longer than he could say.

Why did he continue to leave his wife alone at night? His lovely wife, with her soft voice and shy smiles. The truth was, he could not bring himself to touch her. What right did he have? The faces of men he'd killed continued to plague his nights, waking them both. His lungs tightened painfully. How could he touch her when he felt that he belonged with the damned?

This marriage was out of practical necessity for both of them, nothing more, he reminded himself.

Finally the big pine, nearly three feet in diameter, loomed ahead of him, the rag he'd tied to a low branch fluttering in the breeze. In the distance he heard the creek rushing with melted snow runoff. He turned to Sunny, feeling the closest thing to joy that he could remember in years. "Our land starts here."

Sunny reined in the oxen and looked around at the dense forest. "The storekeeper wasn't joking when he said there'd be a lot of trees."

He nodded with satisfaction. "Enough for all our needs. Let's head closer to the creek, to our home-site. We'll make camp there."

Sunny glanced at the sun, now hovering just above the horizon, pink-orange clouds shimmering in the tiny slits between the dark wide tree trunks. "We'll need to hurry to get ready before sundown."

He tried not to take her lack of enthusiasm personally. But he couldn't help noticing that she'd sounded much happier in town.

"I already cleared a place for our house. And I can get started felling more trees for our cabin first thing in the morning."

She nodded. "I want to see it."

He led the oxen with his hand at their heads, enduring their slow progress as they shuffled their way through the undergrowth of the forest. Then the clearing opened before them. "Here it is."

Her watchful silence followed. He tried to see the clearing through her eyes but couldn't. "We want to be near the creek, but not so near that we get the mosquitoes that hang close there. And the house will be on the rise, so no spring flooding." He couldn't stop himself as he explained how he had chosen the site.

Sunny tied up the reins.

He hurried to help her down. She always seemed so frail, and he'd been surprised when she'd asked to learn how to drive the oxen, even though they were docile creatures. When she set her feet on their land, she gazed around assessing it. Then she looked to him. "You chose well."

He tried to stop his smile but couldn't, so he turned away. "I'll go draw us some fresh water and lead the oxen to the creek. They can drink their fill, and there's grass there for them to graze on. There's a spring here, too. We'll have a spring house—soon." The dam that held back his words had burst. He tried to stop before he revealed just how glad he was to finally be home.

"I'll gather some wood for a fire." She lifted Dawn, who was just beginning to fuss.

"You sit down and nurse her," he said as he unyoked the oxen. He saw her sitting on the step up to the wagon bench, settling Dawn to nurse, and he had to turn his head from the cozy picture they made.

Other men came back from the war and went on with their lives. What kept him from being a real husband to her? Why did he resist any attempt by her to get closer? There was a chasm between them he was responsible for and could not bridge. Was he truly protecting her from himself, from the horrible things that lived on inside him?

Or was he simply incapable of anything even resembling . . . love?

Chapter Three

In the morning Sunny awoke to Dawn's hungry whimpering. She stared up at the cloth covering of the Conestoga wagon, illuminated with sunlight, and stifled a sigh. She touched the rumpled blanket at her feet that Noah had slept upon— when he wasn't tossing with another awful nightmare. She heard him already outside, stirring up the cook fire. Lassitude gripped her.

Dawn began to cry and that moved Sunny. Noah had crafted a kind of hammock just inside the front opening of the canvas top. Sunny lifted her child down, changed her soaked diaper and then put her to nurse. The breeze blew warm and gentle.

Tears slipped down Sunny's cheeks. She clamped her eyes closed. Loneliness was stripping away her peace. Weeks had passed since she'd had a simple conversation with another woman. The faces of her mother's friends, her only friends in the world except for the Gabriels, came to mind. She'd left them all behind. How would she handle this loneliness, keep it from destroying her peace?

"Good morning, wife." Noah looked in from the rear opening.

Sunny blinked rapidly, hoping he wouldn't notice the tears. "Good morning," she replied, forcing a smile.

"I've got the coffee boiling." His words revealed little but the mundane. Didn't he ever long to sit with another man and talk of men things? Men came to saloons to do that, just to jaw and laugh. Not that she wanted Noah to go to the saloon in town.

But, Noah, why don't you want to talk with other men?

She patted Dawn, who wore the seraphic smile she always had when nursing. When Sunny looked up, she glimpsed a look on Noah's face that she hadn't seen before.

He looked away quickly.

She sensed such a deep loneliness and hidden pain in him. But she also keenly felt the wall he kept between them. "I'll be out soon."

"No rush. We have a good day. Perfect for felling trees."

Sunny tried to look happy at this news. He turned away and she heard him unloading tools from the storage area under the wagon.

This won't last forever. We'll go to town from time to time. I'll meet local women, become part of this community. Again she pictured Dawn dressed in a fresh white pinafore, running toward a little white schoolhouse, calling to her friends. And they were calling back to her, happy to see her.

I can do this. This is Dawn's future, not just mine.

After breakfast Noah picked up his ax and headed toward the edge of the clearing.

"Please be careful, Noah," his wife said.

Her concern made him feel . . . something. He couldn't put a name to it, but it wasn't bad, whatever it was. "I'm always careful with an ax in my hand."

She didn't look convinced, but in time she would be. He looked at her for a moment, at the way her lush blond hair flowed down her back as she brushed it, getting ready to pin it up for the day.

His wife was beautiful.

Turning away to shut this out, he studied the trees at the edge of the clearing and chose which one would be the first for their future cabin. He selected an elm thrice as tall and wide as he. He gauged where he wanted it to fall and took his position. He swung and felt the blade bite the bark and wood, the impact echoing through his whole body. He set his pace and kept a steady rhythm.

Finally at the right moment he swung and the tree creaked, trembled and fell with a swish of leaves. It bounced once, twice and shivered to a halt. Wiping his brow with a handkerchief, Noah grinned.

Sweat trickling down his back, he began to chop away the branches so he could roll the first fresh log aside and start on the next tree, a maple. Then he heard something unexpected. He stopped, checking to see if he'd actually heard it.

In the distance came the sound of another ax. And another.

Irritation prickled through him.

"Do you hear that?" Sunny asked from behind him. "Sounds like someone else is felling trees. Maybe they're building a cabin not too far away."

Hoping she was dead wrong, he glanced over his shoulder and glimpsed her smile as she listened intently. She'd obviously just walked back from the creek, a dishpan of washed breakfast dishes in her arms.

"Might be loggers. Or someone cutting wood for winter so it has time to cure before then." He turned back to the maple. "You need to keep back from me. When I take a swing, I don't want to hit you."

"I'll stay back. I'm setting up my outdoor kitchen and such," she said, moving away.

The sound of the other axes on the clean spring air echoed around his own swings, making it harder to concentrate and keep his own rhythm. He fumed. *I chose this site because it was miles from town and any other homestead. Whoever you are, go away.*

As if the logger had heard his thoughts, the distant chopping stopped.

He shook his arms and shoulders, loosening them. With renewed purpose, he swung his ax, eating into the corn-hued wood pulp, sending chips and bark flying.

In between swings he overheard Sunny singing to Dawn. He'd made the right decision. Sunny always kept cheerful, never complained and worked hard. They'd make do.

Noah was sizing up the third tree when something startled him.

"Hello, the wagon!" called a cheerful male voice.

Noah was puzzled for a second, then realized the greeting was a twist on the usual frontier salute of "Hello, the house," which people often said to let the inhabitants of a house know someone was approaching, giving them time to prepare to welcome rare visitors.

Just what Noah didn't need—clever company.

"Hello!" Sunny called in return. "Welcome!"

Her buoyant voice grated Noah's nerves. He lowered his ax, trying to prepare himself to meet whoever had intruded. With one swift downward stroke he sunk the ax into a nearby stump.

Two men, both near his age, were advancing on him, smiles on their faces and their right hands outstretched. He didn't smile, but he did shake their hands in turn.

He wanted to be left alone, but he didn't want people talking behind his back, thinking him odd. He'd had enough of that in the army and in Pennsylvania. In the army his Quaker plain speech had marked him as odd and back home, he was a Quaker who'd gone to war. He hadn't fitted in either place. And he'd given up trying.

"We heard your ax," the taller of the two said. "I'm Charles Fitzhugh and this is Martin Steward. We're your closest neighbors."

"I'm Noah Whitmore." Then he introduced the men to Sunny and Dawn, his wife and child. "Your claims must not be very far away." He clenched his jaw. He'd checked every direction but one—northeast—since he'd been told that no claim lay in those rolling hills.

"Mine's a little over a mile away on the other side of a hill—" Charles pointed northeast "—and Martin's another half mile farther from mine." The man grinned affably. "I've a wife and two daughters, and Martin's building his cabin to bring his bride to."

Martin's cheeks reddened at this announcement. He had a round face and brown hair in a bowl cut. "She lives south near Galena, Illinois."

"What's her name?" Sunny asked, waving the men toward the fire. She soon was pouring them cups of coffee.

Noah ground his teeth. Maybe it was time he made things clear to Sunny about not being overly friendly. He hadn't thought it necessary, based on her difficult past. He'd assumed she'd want to keep to herself as much as he did. Clearly he had much to learn about his wife.

Charles complimented Sunny on the coffee and then turned to Noah. "I'm helping Martin get his cabin up. Why don't we join forces and work together? Three men can get a cabin up in days. Since you've a wife and child, we'll come and help you first and then we can help Martin out. Get him married off sooner than later."

Martin's face turned a darker red.

Noah nearly choked, his reluctance shooting up into his throat. "I—"

"Oh, how wonderful!" Sunny crowed. "So neighborly." And she wrung each man's hands in turn. "Isn't that wonderful, Noah?" She turned, beaming toward him.

Noah wanted to object, to tell them he didn't want their help. But the words wouldn't come. Quakers—not even his father—wouldn't rudely rebuff any offer of help.

He nodded and folded his arms over his chest.

"I already told my wife that we were coming down to stay the day and get a load of work done." Charles grinned, apparently oblivious to Noah's reluctance. He and Martin handed Sunny their empty cups.

"I'll have lunch enough for all of us," Sunny promised. She quickly glanced at Noah. "I'll warn you though, I'm not much of a cook."

Noah turned away and the men followed him, discussing which tree to cut down next. Martin said he was good at squaring off and produced his adze, stripping bark from the already-downed trees.

Soon Noah and Charles were chopping the maple as a team. With each stroke of the his ax, Noah swallowed down his annoyance. Why couldn't people leave him alone?

Sunny must be made to understand exactly how he wanted the two of them to live. He needed to make that clear. Once and for all.

By the cook fire Sunny and Noah sat on logs across from each other. Supper eaten, she eyed him in the lowering sunlight, her nerves tightening by the moment. The instant their neighbors had appeared, she'd noted her husband withdrawing. No one else had noticed. But it had been obvious to her. Now he was clenching and unclenching his hands around his last cup of coffee, frowning into the fire. Why didn't he like such kind neighbors coming to help?

Rattled, she didn't know what to do in the face of his displeasure—whether to speak or keep silent. She couldn't imagine Noah lifting a hand to her but in the past men had. One—in a drunk rage—had broken her hand.

Fighting the old fear, she nursed Dawn and then put her down for the night in the little hammock in the wagon. Then she stood in the lengthening shadows by the wagon, unable to stop chafing her poor thumb. As she watched her angry husband, she felt her nerves give way to aggravation. Nothing had happened that should make any man upset.

Finally she recalled one of Constance Gabriel's few words of advice: "Do not let the sun go down upon your wrath." These words from the Bible must be right. But could she do it? Could she confront this man who'd only been her husband for a period of weeks?

A memory slipped into her thoughts. Constance and Adam Gabriel had been alone in the kitchen, talking in undertones. She'd overheard Constance say, "Adam, this must be decided."

So wives did confront husbands. Sunny took a deep breath.

"Noah," she said, "what's wrong?"

"I don't want people hanging around," he muttered darkly.

"Why not?" she insisted, leaning forward to hear him.

He sat silent, his chest heaving and his face a mask of troubled emotions.

"What is wrong, Noah? The men just came to help us."

"I don't want their help. I want to be left

alone. I don't want us getting thick with people hereabout. I picked this homesite far from town to steer clear of people. I've had enough of people to last me a lifetime. In the future, we will keep to ourselves."

His words were hammers. "Keep to ourselves?" she gasped. The happy image of Dawn in her white pinafore shifted to a shy, downcast Dawn hanging back from the other children who looked at her, their expressions jeering as tears fell down her cheeks.

"No." Sunny said, firing up in defense. "No." She came around to face him. "Why did you marry me if you wanted to be alone?"

Noah rose. They were toe-to-toe. His eyes had opened wide.

"Why don't you want to be neighborly?" she demanded, shaking.

He took a step backward. "I . . . I . . ."

"What if I get sick? Who will you call for help? If I get with child, will you deliver it alone? We have no family here. How can we manage without our neighbors?"

They stared at each other. Sunny shook with outrage at his unreasonable demand.

Noah breathed rapidly, too, as if he'd just finished a race. Finally he shook his head as if coming awake. "I don't want people here all the time," he said. "I just want peace and quiet."

"People have their own work to do." She

clamped her hands together, feeling blood where she'd chafed her thumb. "Once the cabins are built, Charles and Martin will be busy with their own work."

He let out a rush of air and raked his hands through his hair. "All right. Just remember I don't want people here all the time."

She wanted to argue, but sensed much more was going on here than was being said. "I will keep your wish in mind," she said, scanning his face for clues as to what was happening inside him.

He stood, staring at her for a moment as if seeing her for the first time. "I'm going to clean up at the creek." He grabbed a towel from the clothesline she'd strung earlier in the day and stomped off.

Sunny slumped against the wagon, calming herself, consciously shedding the fear and anger. He didn't want people around him. Maybe he didn't want her around him? Maybe he'd only brought her here to cook and clean. That would explain why he showed no interest in getting closer to her.

The thought made her angry all over again.

Climbing into the wagon, she checked on Dawn who slept peacefully in her little hammock. She'd be safe here. Sunny climbed down, grabbed another towel from the line and headed toward the creek, too. The unusual high temperature and humidity combined with the argument had left her ruffled and heated. Earlier she'd noticed a bend in the creek that was shielded by bushes where she could discreetly cool off.

Noah already splashed in the wide part of the creek, deep with spring runoff. In the long shadows she skirted around, barely glancing toward him. Within the shelter of the bushes, she slipped off her shoes and tiptoed over the pebbles into the cool water. She shivered, but in a good way. Soon ankle-deep, she was bending and splashing water up onto her face and neck, washing away the grime and stickiness.

The cool water soothed her, the sound of its rippling over the rocks calmed her nerves like a balm. She sighed as the last of her indignation drifted away on the current. She waded out onto the mossy bank and dried off.

At the sound of her name she turned and found Noah walking toward her. Night had come; moonlight glimmered around them. She braced herself, waiting for him to reach her. Had he come to start the argument anew?

He paused a foot from her. "I'm sorry, Sunny." The soft words spoke volumes of anguish.

She gazed at him, uncertain. Their disagreement had been over nothing—or everything—and she sensed that Noah was struggling just like she was. She recalled his words on their wedding night, when he'd asked which was worse, lying with strangers or killing them.

Amid the incessant frogs croaking around them, he whispered, "Sunny, I just need space, peace."

His voice opened the lock to her heart and freed her. "Noah," she murmured.

"But I want you to be happy here, too," he added.

His tenderness touched her, but she didn't know how to respond. They were still strangers.

In the silent darkness he helped her gather her shawl around her shoulders and then they walked to the wagon. Sunny tried to figure out what had happened this evening, what bedeviled her husband, and how she could bring him peace. She had no answers.

At the wagon she hoped he would follow her inside so she could comfort him. But, as usual, he let her go in and then he wished her good-night from the foot of the cramped wagon bed.

Sunny lay very still, wondering if Noah would have another nightmare tonight, and if he'd ever reveal what the dreams were about. She had a feeling his nightmares and his reluctance to be around people were connected.

And she was determined to find out how. She just needed to be patient. But patience had never been one of her talents. Someday they would have to talk matters out. Maybe when Noah's nightmares ceased?

Chapter Four

The next morning Sunny had a hard time speaking to Noah. Or looking at him for that matter. She stooped over the flickering flames of the cook fire. A stiff breeze played with the hem of her skirt. To keep safe as she was frying salted pork with one hand, she held her skirt with the other. She didn't know what was causing the awkwardness she felt with Noah.

In the pan the pork sizzled and snapped like the words she'd spoken to him last night. Was it the fact that she'd spoken up to him for the first time? Or had the awkward feeling come because he'd shown such tenderness to her when he'd escorted her into the wagon? Tenderness from a man was not something she was used to.

Yet today Noah remained silent as usual. And this morning that grated on her more than it did normally. How was she supposed to act when the neighboring men came today to help?

She remembered her resolution to get to the bottom of Noah's reluctance and she decided to speak up again.

"I expect our neighbors will be coming to help soon," she murmured.

Noah nodded. "Probably." He took another sip of the coffee, steaming in the cool morning air.

Sunny glanced down. Lying on her back on a blanket, Dawn waved her arms and legs and cooed. As always, her daughter brought a smile to Sunny's face.

"She's having a good time," Noah commented.

Sudden joy flashed through Sunny, catching her by surprise. This was not the first time he'd taken notice of Dawn and said something positive, but it still caught her off guard. Taking this as a hopeful sign for the future, Sunny managed to nod. She finished the pork and quickly stirred in what was left of last night's grits. She deftly swirled the pan till the concoction firmed. "Breakfast is ready."

She lifted the frying pan off the trivet and served up their plates. Searching for more topics to discuss, she said, "I hope we can get some chickens. I will need eggs."

"We will. It won't be much longer that we'll be living like tramps," Noah said, sounding apologetic. "Before you know it, we'll be in our cabin."

"I know we will," she said quickly. "You're working so hard. I wish I could help more."

"You do enough," he said gruffly. "After the cabin's up, I'll make us a nice table and some sturdy benches."

"You know how to make furniture?" Sunny bit into the crisp pork, trying to ignore the way his dark hair framed his drawn face. She wished she could wipe away the sleepless smudges under his eyes.

"Yes, I had an uncle who was a cabinetmaker. He taught me one summer."

"You know so much. And I can barely cook."

"You do fine."

Her heart fluttered at the praise. She clung to their discussion to keep her feelings concealed. "Mrs. Gabriel taught me what I know. But I wish I'd had time to learn more."

"You do well," he said, looking at her, his dark eyes lingering on her face.

Impulsively she touched his arm. "Thanks."

His invisible shutters closed against her once more. Her action had pushed him deeper into reserve. She concentrated on eating her own breakfast and not showing that she felt his withdrawal, his rejection.

She passed the back of her hand over her forehead, sighing. *Be patient,* she reminded herself. *Maybe he just needs more time.*

"Hello, the wagon!" Their neighbor Charles Fitzhugh's cheerful voice hailed them.

"Good morning!" Sunny called, checking to see how her husband was taking the arrival of the two men. However, when she glanced toward the men, she froze. A petite, dark-haired woman and two little girls accompanied them. Her breath caught in her throat.

Noah rose and with his free hand gripped first Charles's and then Martin's hand. "Morning. Just about done with breakfast."

"Mrs. Whitmore, this is my wife, Caroline, and our daughters, Mary and Laura," Charles Fitzhugh said.

Sunny bobbed a polite curtsy, her heart sinking. Her hand went to her hair, which she hadn't dressed yet. Fear of saying something she shouldn't tightened her throat. What if she said something a decent woman wouldn't ever say? Would they know instantly what she was? What she'd been?

"Don't mind me," Caroline Fitzhugh said. "I just came for a short visit and then I'll be going home. I knew it was early to be calling but I just felt like I needed a woman chat this morning."

Sunny nodded. She quickly smoothed back and twisted her hair into a knot at the base of her neck and shoved pins in to keep her bun secure. A woman chat, oh, yes—she'd longed for one, too. But after weeks of loneliness she must guard her overeager tongue, not let anything that might hint at her past slip out.

I can do this. I just need a touch of help, Lord.

Soon Sunny was washing dishes in the spring with Mrs. Fitzhugh down creek from her. Nearby, Caroline's little girls played in the shallows. Mrs. Fitzhugh held Dawn and dipped her toes into the water to Dawn's squeals of delight. Sunny's heart warmed toward this woman, obviously a good mother. But that sharpened the danger that she would let her guard down and give herself away.

Soon the two women were back at the campfire, sitting on a log and watching the children play with some blocks Mrs. Fitzhugh had brought in a cotton sack. Happy to gnaw on one block, Dawn watched the two toddlers pile the rest on the uneven ground. She squealed as she watched the blocks topple.

"You and Mr. Whitmore been married long?" the neighbor asked, accepting a fresh cup of coffee.

"Not too long," Sunny hedged vaguely. The sound of the men's voices and the chopping as they worked on yet another tree suddenly vanished as her heart pounded loudly.

Mrs. Fitzhugh smiled. "I just meant you look almost like newlyweds. It'll take a few more years to look like you've been married forever."

Sunny didn't know what to say to this. Was the woman suggesting that she and Noah hadn't been married long enough to already have a child?

"Where you from?" Mrs. Fitzhugh asked politely.

The woman's voice remained honest, not accusing or insinuating. Sunny managed to take a breath. "Pennsylvania. My husband came here earlier this year to find us a homestead while I stayed back with my family." That was true—the Gabriels had told her to consider them her family.

"I'm from eastern Wisconsin. Met Charles there."

Sunny knew that the woman wasn't asking her anything out of the way, but each question tightened a belt around her lungs. She looked toward the men and saw Noah send a momentary glance her way, his expression brooding.

"I'm . . . we're very grateful for your offer of help."

Mrs. Fitzhugh waved her hand, dismissing Sunny's thanks. "It's too early to plant and Charles isn't sure he will put in a crop this year. Kansas is calling him."

"Kansas?" Sunny gazed at the woman with genuine dismay. All the way to Kansas? Sunny thought of all the miles she'd traveled from Idaho to Pennsylvania and then here. "I'm not much of a traveler," she admitted.

Before Mrs. Fitzhugh could reply, another voice hailed, "Hello, the house!"

"Nancy! Is that you?" Mrs. Fitzhugh called out with obvious pleasure.

Soon another woman sauntered into the clearing —a big blonde woman obviously expecting a child, with a toddler beside her. While Caroline Fitzhugh dressed as neat as could be, this woman appeared disheveled but jolly.

"I was coming over to visit you, Caroline. And then I heard the axes and once in a while, on the breeze, a word that sounded feminine. I hope you

71

don't mind me stoppin' in." She looked to Sunny.

"No. No. You're very welcome," Sunny rushed to assure the newcomer though she wasn't sure she meant it. "Please join us." She waved the woman to one of the large rocks around the campfire and quickly offered her coffee.

Two women to talk to—a blessing and a trial.

"I'm Nan Osbourne. My man and me live over yonder." She waved southward. "Glad to see another family come to settle."

"Mrs. Whitmore and her husband are nearly newlyweds," Mrs. Fitzhugh said.

"Well, none of us are much more than that." Mrs. Osbourne gave a broad wink. "You got any family hereabouts, Miz Whitmore?"

"No. No. I have no family . . . near," she corrected quickly. She'd just told Caroline that she had stayed with her family. "And Noah's family is all in Pennsylvania . . . too." Picking her words with such care quickened her pulse.

"That's hard, leaving family," Mrs. Osbourne said, looking mournful. "I cried and cried to leave my ma."

"My mother has already passed," Sunny said, her words prompting a sudden unexpected twinge of grief. Or was it recalling she was all alone in the world? Why would she mourn Mother's death now, almost seven years after it? Was it because so much was changing? *I'm not alone now. I've got Dawn and Noah.* Gratitude rushed through her. Could this be proof that God was forgiving her? There was so much she didn't understand about God and sin.

"I got news." Nan Osbourne grinned. "We got a preacher in town now."

"Really?" Caroline Fitzhugh brightened with excitement.

Sunny tried to keep her face from falling. A preacher? In the past more than one had shouted Bible verses at her, calling her a harlot and predicting her damnation. The fires of hell licked around her again. She touched Dawn, her treasure, smoothing back her baby fine hair, and the action calmed her.

"The preacher's goin' to preach this Sunday right in town. He says around ten o'clock," Nan announced.

"That's wonderful. I've been missing church." Caroline sighed.

Sunny tried to appear happy as her peace caved in.

"I think it's wonderful that he's goin' to preach out in the open like a camp meetin'. Then even them who don't want to hear the gospel will."

Sunny posed with a stiff, polite smile on her face. Was the woman talking about the people who'd be just waking upstairs at the saloon? Of course she was. Once more Sunny wished so much that she could help another woman get free of that life.

But I can't. I've got to make this new start work for Dawn.

"You'll be comin', won't you, Miz Whitmore? You and your man?" Nan asked.

Crosscurrents slashed through Sunny. *I want to go. I want You to know, God, how thankful I am for this second chance.* But would the preacher see right through her? Would Noah want to go? *Let* her go?

A thought came. Should she mention that Noah had been raised Quaker? He'd almost stopped using "thee." Did that mean he didn't want to be considered a Quaker anymore?

Both women were gazing at her expectantly.

Sunny breathed in deeply. "I'll discuss it with him. I know I want to attend. Do you know what kind of preacher he is?"

"I didn't ask," Nan said. "Out here on the frontier, preachers are so rare we can't be choosy about them. He struck me as a good man."

Sunny nodded, hoping she hadn't asked the wrong thing. "I'll speak to Noah. But unless he forbids me, I'll be there."

Both women looked startled at this announcement.

Sunny cringed. She'd said the wrong thing, hinting that Noah might not be a Christian. And she couldn't let that simmer and turn into gossip. She leaned forward to give some explanation. "Noah was raised Quaker. I wasn't.

So I don't know if he'll . . ." Words failed her.

Caroline patted her hand. "I understand."

"Quakers were against slavery," Nan said stoutly. "They did a lot of good with helpin' slaves get free."

Sunny gave a fleeting smile, tension bubbling inside.

"Nan and I will pray that you get to come to the meeting," Caroline said in a low voice. Nan nodded vigorously. And Sunny knew she'd made progress on making friends this morning. Her mood lifted—for a moment.

What would Noah say about going to the Sunday meeting? And her telling these friendly strangers that he'd been raised Quaker?

In the last rays of twilight Noah sat by the fire, his stomach comfortably full. Sunny didn't know how to cook many things but what she did cook tasted good. Exhausted from felling trees all day, Noah realized he'd discovered a few muscles he hadn't known about—and they were not happy with him.

He held a narrow block of wood in his hand, whittling it into a new handle for a small ax. During this quiet time Sunny was acting funny—opening her mouth as if to speak, then closing it, and worrying her thumb by picking at it and hiding her hand behind her skirt. Why, he didn't know. Or want to ask. Last night had been enough honesty.

"How many more logs do we need for a cabin?" his wife asked.

She sat by the fire nursing Dawn who seemed fussier than usual. The firelight highlighted the gold in Sunny's hair. Once again, he realized he had married a pretty woman. Everything about her was so soft and this world was so hard. He wondered what it might be like to hold her.

"Noah?" she prompted.

"Sorry. My mind was wandering." He shut his mind to a surprising image of holding Sunny close, a daunting thought. He shaved some more from the wood. "Another day and we should have enough for a cabin. Then Charles and Martin will help me lift the logs into place."

"I'm so grateful to them."

His hands were beginning to tremble with fatigue as he whittled. "Who was that other woman who stopped by?"

"Nan Osbourne. She and her husband live nearby. She seems very nice. From her accent, I'd say she was from south of here."

Noah nodded. Sunny's continued pensiveness piqued his curiosity. In spite of himself, he asked, "What did she have to say?"

Sunny startled as if caught doing something she shouldn't. "We just talked about recipes and they told me about the people who live hereabouts."

Noah examined the handle he was crafting, running his thumb over it. Sunny was definitely holding something back. But he was too tired to risk asking for more. He didn't have the energy to be irritated by hearing something he might not like. So he hesitated. Sunny also had a way of stirring him. She was now. But he couldn't act on this. He found it impossible to make a move.

The bottomless well of sorrow and dark things roiled up within. Sunny made him long to feel normal again. But he'd seen too much, done too much that was unforgivable. Repressing this, he rose while he still could stand. "I'm going to go to bed now. I'm worn out."

"I'll bank the fire. You go ahead, Noah. I should have seen how tired you were." She rose and briefly touched his arm. "Go on."

Her innocent touch made him ache with loneliness. He moved away, obeying her. Noah shucked off his boots and then hoisted himself onto the hard wagon bed and rolled into his blankets. His last thought as he fell asleep was that Sunny deserved better than him.

A few days later Sunny stepped inside their new cabin. She hadn't anticipated how it would make her feel. *This is my home, our home.* She'd never lived in a real house, never dreamed she would. She wanted to hug the walls and do a jig on the half-log floor that Noah had insisted on laying. A dirt floor might be all right in the summer but not in the winter, he'd said. Dawn whimpered in her arms and struggled to be put down. Sunny bent and set her on the floor.

"I'm glad this is done," Noah said from behind her.

She turned around and nearly hugged him, but his expression held her off. "Me, too. It's a wonderful home." During this bright moment the way Noah always held himself apart chafed her. Would it always be this way?

"Hello, the house!" Caroline Fitzhugh called out. "We came to see your new home."

Whisking Dawn up into her arms, Sunny stepped outside to see that Caroline and her family and the Osbournes had come to celebrate. Charles Fitzhugh carried a fiddle and the women each carried a covered dish.

"Oh, I have nothing prepared!" Sunny exclaimed.

"We're makin' this party!" Nan called out cheerfully. "We won't stay long, just wanted to see your fine new cabin and congratulate you."

Sunny said all that was proper but when she turned to Noah, it was as if he'd slammed all the shutters and locked the door against their company. She gave him an understanding smile but he stood like a tree, not responding by even a flicker of an eyelid. She went up on tiptoe and acted as though she were kissing his cheek in order to whisper, "They won't stay long. Don't spoil their happiness."

He glanced down at her, stony-eyed. Dawn

began to cry and Sunny jiggled her in her arms.

Then he gave Sunny a tight-lipped nod. "Welcome to our new home." Sunny sighed silently with relief. "Come right in."

Nan had brought her husband, a tall lanky man with curly blond hair. He, along with the other guests, admired the large cabin with its roomy loft and lean-to for the animals.

Sunny was a bit embarrassed because Dawn continued to fuss. She tried to distract their company by talking about future plans. "Noah is going to dig me a root cellar. And build a spring house," Sunny said, caught up in the flush of showing her new home. She tried to check herself, knowing that Noah was scrutinizing, gauging each word.

"You're going to have a right nice place here all right," Nan said. "You must be plannin' to stay here."

"I plan to stay longer than five years to get title to the land," Noah said. "I traveled all over northern Illinois, eastern Iowa and southern Minnesota. I decided this land was the best I'd seen."

His loquaciousness shocked Sunny. Maybe Noah was feeling a bit of pride and happiness. Remaining cautious, she kept her mouth shut and let Noah do the talking.

"Well, you haven't tried to plow yet," Mr. Osbourne said wryly. "You'll find that Wisconsin's best crop is rocks."

"As long as they don't sprout and grow new ones, I'll do fine," Noah responded.

His voice was pleasant enough but Sunny sensed his disdain for a man put off by rocks. Dawn chewed on her hand and whimpered.

Mr. Fitzhugh drew his bow over his fiddle. "I'll play one song and then we all got to get back to our own work."

"And we'll help carry stuff from your wagon to your door," Nan said. "That'll lighten your load."

Before Sunny could speak, Mr. Fitzhugh began to play a merry tune, the kind that beckoned clapping. Sunny hadn't heard music for so long. She had loved to dance in the saloon—it was the only fun she'd ever had there—and she was a good dancer. But Quakers didn't dance.

Dawn again wriggled to be put down. Sunny obliged and then tapped her toe to the cadence and couldn't stop her smile from widening.

Dawn stared at the violin, distracted from her fussing. Noah bent down and swung her up into his arms and Sunny's heart skipped a beat. Noah held Dawn by her waist and swung her gently back and forth to the tune. Dawn squealed with laughter. Then Sunny reached over and showed Dawn how to clap her hands. The three of them together, like a happy family. It was like a moment sent from Heaven.

But of course the song ended. Everyone clapped for Charles's fiddling, shook hands and the two couples started to leave. Just as Sunny was relax-ing her guard, Nan turned and asked, "Have you and the mister decided whether you're comin' to meetin' this Sunday?"

Sunny's breath caught in her throat. "I've been meaning to discuss that with Noah," she managed to say.

"Meeting?" Noah looked askance.

"Yes, we got a preacher, a real nice old one who's come to live with his son's family in his declining years," Nan explained. "He's preachin' at ten o'clock in front of the general store."

"Can we pick you up in our wagon?" Mr. Fitzhugh invited. "We'll be passing right by your place. Even though I'm thinking we'll be heading to Kansas soon, I wouldn't want to miss preaching."

Sunny waited to see what her husband would say. She didn't meet his eye—she couldn't.

"I'll think on it," Noah said at last.

The other two couples tried to hide their surprise at Noah's less than enthusiastic response.

"I don't think he'll be preachin' anything that would go against you being a Quaker," Nan said.

Sunny's face burned. She knew she'd done the wrong thing by not telling Noah what she'd done.

"I'll keep that in mind," Noah said, his jaw hardening.

I'm in for it now. Sunny stood at her husband's side and felt waves of sick worry wash over her. Dawn began fussing again, chewing one of her little fists. Sunny knew Noah wouldn't raise a hand to her but he could freeze her with a glance. *Oh, Lord, help me reach him. Help me make him understand why I told them that he'd been raised Quaker. Lord, I want to do what is right. Help me explain this to him.*

Sunny couldn't get Dawn to hush. Night had fallen and she'd tried everything in vain—nursing her, bathing her, rocking her. Now she paced the rough new floor. What could she do to soothe her child?

As she paced, she scanned her new and very empty home. Earlier Noah had helped her arrange pegs in the wall to hang clothing and pots and pans. The only furniture was the rocking chair that the Gabriels had given them money to buy as a wedding present, a three-legged stool and a chest near the door which held their linens.

Her bedroll sat against the wall. Noah had put his up in the loft. Their continued nightly separation was a constant twinge in her side. Would he never forget that she was damaged goods?

Noah entered the cabin. Since the two couples had left, he had not said a complete sentence to her. Sunny wished Dawn would stop crying—the incessant sound had tightened her nerves like a spring. Sunny sat down and tried again to get Dawn to nurse so she would fall asleep as usual.

Noah stood watching Dawn fight Sunny.

"I'm sorry," Sunny apologized. "I think it's her mouth. She wants to nurse but I think it hurts her." As she tried to soothe the inconsolable baby, Sunny felt like crying herself.

Noah turned and went to a smaller chest he'd moved just inside the door. He lifted out a small bottle Sunny instantly recognized—whiskey. Dawn wept in pain, Sunny was frantic and Noah was going to get drunk? Sunny burst into tears.

Noah came and knelt in front of her. "Here. See." He opened the bottle and the all too familiar, unpleasant smell wafted to Sunny's nose. He tipped the almost full bottle and then stuck his little finger into the amber fluid. Then he slipped the little finger into Dawn's surprised mouth.

"What are you doing?" Sunny gasped.

"I saw a woman do this once when I was traveling. She said the whiskey numbs the gums. And the few drops of alcohol will soothe the baby. The woman said it was an old remedy for a teething child. See how red and swollen Dawn's gums are?"

Sunny felt like an idiot. Teething. Of course. Constance Gabriel had mentioned that the baby would teethe and it would hurt. Noah dipped his little finger in the bottle once more and then ran it around Dawn's swollen gums again. "That should be enough, just enough."

They both watched Dawn. In a few minutes she fell back exhausted, resting against Sunny.

"Thank you," Sunny said.

"Wish I'd thought of it earlier." He rose, capped the bottle and stowed it away. "This whiskey's just for medicinal purposes. I never cared for strong drink."

He turned and faced her. "I did get drunk a few times in the army," he confessed, "but never again. It doesn't help, just makes you sick and the next morning everything's as bad as it was before you got drunk. Only you've got a head-ache to boot."

Sunny nodded. She'd seen too many drunks in her life and the drink never did them any good. This was one of the rare times he offered some-thing of his past, himself. She took it as his way of easing her worry over Dawn, over the bottle of whiskey. Sunny felt fatigue replacing anxiety.

Of her own accord Dawn began to nurse. Within a few minutes Dawn fell asleep, her lips still quivering as if she were nursing.

Noah lifted the baby and put her in the hammock he'd suspended from the high ceiling.

His tender care of her baby snapped Sunny's reserve. "I'm so sorry, Noah," she said impetuously. "I didn't mean to tell the women anything about you being a Quaker. I'm sorry." Embarrassing tears welled up in her eyes. She turned away and wiped them with the hem of her apron.

Noah just stood beside Dawn, making the hammock sway gently.

"You haven't told me," Sunny said, even as she tried to stem the flow of words, "why you're not using *thee* anymore. And then they told me about the preaching this Sunday. And I didn't know what to say. They were looking at me, wondering why I wasn't saying right away that we'd be coming. So I said you'd been raised Quaker and I didn't know if you'd want to go to a different kind of meeting." She ran out of words and put her hands over her face. "I'm so tired," she whispered.

Noah pulled up the three-legged stool and sat beside her. His nearness made it possible for her to staunch her tears.

"Sorry," she whispered.

"When I enlisted in the army, I was put out of the meeting."

His tone sounded flat, unemotional. Yet Sunny sensed the words concealed a volcano of feelings. She waited, tense.

"When I came home, I just wanted to go back to my life, the way it was before the war. So I publicly repented of going to war and asked for forgiveness and was restored to the meeting. But of course, I couldn't go back to being who I was before the war. And at meeting, everybody still looked at me differently. Like I was . . ." He shrugged.

Like you were damaged goods. Stained. She knew how that felt. Awful.

"I've stopped using *thee* because I don't feel like a Quaker anymore."

She wanted to ask, *What do you feel like then? What do you have nightmares about?* But the words wouldn't come. Long silent moments passed as they sat together.

Noah rose and offered her his hand.

She let him help her from her chair, stunned by the fact that he initiated the contact. "We'd better get some sleep."

He nodded. "Good night, Sunny."

He climbed a ladder to the loft and left her alone in the sparsely furnished room, still reeling from the feel of his hand in hers. She slipped off her dress and apron and hung them on pegs as she realized she still didn't have the answer to the question that had been weighing on her for days.

Were they going to the Sunday meeting—or not?

Steady showers came the next day, forcing the three of them to stay inside though Noah went out to fetch wood for the fire. He'd wisely left some in the wagon to keep it dry. The unusual April heat had fled, replaced with a chill and damp air.

Though Sunny thought they had cleared things up, Noah was brooding once more, which did not encourage her to ask what he'd decided about the Sunday meeting.

Dawn still fussed some, but Sunny had made a "sugar baby," a tightly knotted rag with sugar inside. Dawn gnawed on it and it seemed to give her some relief.

Noah had brought in a few slender logs about four feet in length, obviously not meant for the fire. He stripped away their bark.

"What are you making?" she ventured.

"Legs for our table."

"I see." *I see that you've gone back to your usual dour self.* She lifted the pan of breakfast dishes and carried it out. She set it on a convenient stump. She'd let the rainwater rinse the soap from the dishes she'd scrubbed.

Inside again, she sat in her rocker and lifted a shirt from the mending basket, trying to ignore the unspoken question between them.

Noah methodically stripped the bark, making a neat pile of the shavings. Finally he rose from the three-legged stool. "I'll go see to the cattle."

He opened the door, letting in chilly moist air. "You can go to the meeting if you want. I won't be going." He shut the door behind him.

Sunny sat, staring at the needle in her hand. Dawn rolled on her back, watching her mother as if asking for Sunny's response to this. Should she go to the meeting without him or stay home, too? What did God want her to do as a good wife—stay home with her husband and wait till he wanted them to go? Or was she supposed to go because that was the right thing to do? What if Noah never wanted to go?

Chapter Five

Sunday dawned bright yet cool. Sunny wished her mood matched her name, but a heavy cloud weighed over her undecided heart.

She stood outside the door of their new cabin at the white enamel washbasin, set on a waist-high stump. She was washing her hands, preparing to go to meeting—without Noah. With closed eyes, she scrubbed her face and then bent over to rinse away the soap, shivering from the cold water and chill air.

She felt Noah push the linen towel into her wet hands. She accepted it and dried her face. Looking up, she met his dark eyes. She tried to read his expression, but couldn't. The shutters he'd put up once again concealed everything from her. The weight over her heart pressed down harder.

As he walked back into the cabin, Sunny realized this was just more evidence of Noah's constant courtesy. Distracted, she'd come out without a towel, so he'd brought her one. She held it in her hands, touched by his thoughtfulness.

Inside again, Sunny continued making breakfast. She still wore her old everyday housedress.

Did that make Noah think she wasn't going to the meeting in town?

Without thinking, she grabbed the handle of the cast-iron pot. Then yanked it back, scorched. She waved her hand and snapped her mouth shut so no ill words slipped out. She bowed her head. *God, please, I want to do what's right. Is going to the meeting the right thing?*

Of course no answer came. She used a quilted potholder and then stirred the oatmeal that had been simmering all night over the banked fire. After a sprinkle of fragrant cinnamon, she stirred in some sugar. "It's done."

As usual at meals, she sat in the rocker holding Dawn while Noah sat on the three-legged stool. Silence. She couldn't think of anything to discuss but the unanswered question plaguing her. She ate and the oatmeal sat on the top of her uneasy stomach. The sun was gleaming around the shutters and she must get ready if she was going. It was time.

Noah finished his oatmeal and rose. "Going to let the oxen out to graze."

Then she was alone. Dawn squirmed and Sunny let her down so she could crawl around on the floor. Dawn's teething distress appeared to have abated. She cooed and gurgled. As Sunny watched her daughter, she suddenly knew what she had to do. This wasn't just about Noah.

She stood and opened the chest, and drew out

the simple gray dress she had always worn to the Quaker meetinghouse. She also drew out a colorful paisley shawl she'd bought in Idaho. It would brighten up the drab dress. In the past, from a distance, she'd watched people go to church and they had all dressed up fine.

Within minutes she was ironing the dress and trying not to think too much about her decision so she wouldn't lose her breakfast to nerves. Before long she stood at the mirror, dressing her hair. The mirror was small so she couldn't see more than her head and neck. She smoothed her bodice and skirt, still warm from the iron. Then she lifted Dawn and quickly dressed her in a freshly pressed white dress.

Through the open door Sunny heard the jingling of a harness. Her ride to church was coming. Before she stepped outside, she tied her bonnet strings and collected a fresh handkerchief and a sugar baby in case Dawn fussed. Sweeping her shawl around her shoulders, she took a deep breath and carried Dawn outside.

Noah waited near the door, watching the Fitzhughs' wagon come nearer.

"You're sure you don't want to come?" Sunny murmured just for his ears. Her voice quavered. *Please, come.*

He shook his head but wouldn't meet her eyes.

Her stomach roiling, she waited for the wagon to draw up to her. She exchanged greetings with the neighbors. The Fitzhughs were obviously trying not to stare at Noah, who was obviously not dressed for church. She approached the wagon and handed Dawn up into Caroline's arms.

"We can't persuade you to come with us?" Charles asked Noah with an encouraging smile.

"God doesn't want to see me," Noah said in a sour tone. However, with his usual courtesy, he had come to help Sunny climb up onto the bench.

She turned and leaned close to his ear and whispered, "I'm doing this for Dawn—and for us."

She sat beside Caroline and accepted her daughter back. She didn't dare look at Noah. The wagon started up, creaking and straining.

Though her heart beat like she'd run a race, Sunny knew in her soul that she was doing the right thing. She could feel it. She couldn't wait for Noah to come to terms with whatever troubled him. Life passed quickly day by day, and she must do what was needed.

Noah stood stock-still, watching his wife, perched stiffly on the wagon bench, disappear among the trees. Sunny's whispered words tightened around him like bonds. *Us.* She'd said *us.*

All at once the unseen chains holding back the past released. Cannon roared in his ears and men, horses, screamed. Noah staggered as if he'd taken a blow. He sat down hard on a nearby stump. A whirlwind swept through him, an inner storm of anguish. He bent his pounding head into his hands and swallowed down dry heaves. How could the simple words at parting stir up the past and swamp him so?

When he was able, he forced himself to his feet. "I have work to do," he said to the surrounding silence. His feeble words vanished in the air. He was alone—completely.

He headed to wide boards he'd split from an oak. "Dawn will want to sit on that three-legged stool soon. I better have a place for me to sit."

Why was he speaking out loud when no one could hear him? Was he losing his mind? Did he think he was chasing away the past? Determined to overcome the weakness, he stood one of the wide boards on end and ran his trembling hand over its rough surface. From the fine grain of the wood, he figured that the oak must have been over a hundred years old. He sucked in the cool breeze, trying to keep his inner hurricane at bay.

He'd constructed two sawhorses and now he lay the first board across them and began stripping the bark from the sides. Then he unearthed his plane from his tool chest and began planing the wood smooth for the tabletop. The slow rhythm steadied his nerves. But each time he guided the plane over the wood, sending up a ribbon, he heard his wife's whisper again. *I'm doing this for Dawn—and for us.*

He couldn't make sense of this. Did she mean that she wanted Dawn to be raised a Christian? Did she think that taking a baby to church would accomplish this? Did she want *him* to be a churchgoer? What did that mean to her? His father had attended meeting every Sunday, but had it changed, softened his hard heart? He slid the plane in a steady rhythm while images of Sunny's face slid through his memory.

The total lack of human presence crowded in on him. Though he fought it, he recalled that awful unspoken, crushing tension that had pressed down on him and all his company as another battle loomed before them. He felt a phantom sensation—a soldier pinning a paper lettered with Noah's name and his company on the back of his collar. This was the only way soldiers could be identified if something happened to them in the upcoming carnage. The sense of impending death blasted him once again.

The strength went out of Noah's legs. The plane fell from his hands and he slid to the ground. Leaning on an elbow, he gasped for breath. Why was this happening to him?

He looked upward, letting the sun warm his face. Then he shuddered violently once and let gravity take him down to the moist earth, to the wild grasses. Near his hand he noticed a tiny violet. He touched the petal and it made him think of Sunny—soft and delicate.

Why had she married him, a man so inadequate in every way?

As the wagon neared town, Sunny's heart was now racing at the prospect of being in a meeting with proper people who thought she was just like them. Could she pull this off?

"Just a perfect day for the meeting," Caroline murmured.

"Let's hope the preacher doesn't put us to sleep standing up," Charles said with a quirk to the side of his mouth.

Caroline tapped his arm, scolding in a low voice, "Charles, the children will hear you."

Little Mary and Laura rode in the back, holding on to the side of the buckboard. Dawn, half asleep, lay in Sunny's arms, lulled by the rocking of the wagon.

From the corner of her eye Sunny watched the interaction between the husband and wife beside her on the bench. She'd never really been around many married folk. These two were more lively than Constance and Adam Gabriel, but was that personality? Or was it that the Fitzhughs weren't Quakers?

This brought her back to the fact that she had no idea how she was to behave or what she was expected to do at this outdoor meeting. She'd only been to the Quaker meeting and the Gabriels had told her that it was different than a regular church service. She'd never told them she had never been inside a church and wouldn't have known the difference. Sunny's stomach rolled into a ball.

What if she did something no "Christian" would do at a meeting?

The wagon broke free of the shelter of the forest, rocking down the bluff to the flat ground beside the wide blue river. She had never given thought to how many people lived hereabouts. Now she saw around twenty or so men and women in family groups standing in front of the Ashford's General Store.

Charles helped Sunny down and then Caroline. In turn, the Fitzhughs each lifted out a daughter from the wagon bed. Holding Dawn still half asleep on her shoulder, Sunny stayed a bit behind using them as a shield. Nan and Gordy Osbourne waved and gravitated toward them. Sunny gratefully concealed herself within this group of neighbors.

A constant buzz of conversation made audible the buzz of excitement running through this wilderness gathering. Sunny's stomach tightened another turn.

An old man, very thin and with long white hair pulled back as it had been worn in the olden days, and in an old-fashioned black suit, sat on a straight chair on the store's porch. Before she could get more than a glance at him, he pulled an old watch from his vest, glanced at it and then stood. He raised both hands and everyone turned toward him, hushing children, expectant.

Sunny braced herself and heightened her awareness so she wouldn't miss a cue or fail in some way.

"My name is Old Saul and don't call me Mister or Pastor. I'm going to be seventy-one this year and Old Saul or Preacher is good enough for me." He held up a thick, well-worn black book. "And God's Holy Word is enough for me to base my life upon."

A man in the rear said quietly, "Amen."

Sunny stared at the Bible, wishing she were better with letters so she could read it and make more sense of its words.

"And I won't fly under false colors. I was not always a preacher, but was a sinner. I won't tell you about my sins. And I won't ask you about yours."

Sunny trembled with relief. But her taut nerves didn't relax. An eagle flew overhead, casting its shadow over them.

"We all have sinned and fallen short of the glory of God. But John tells us, 'if we confess our sins, He is faithful and just to forgive us our sins, and to cleanse us from all unrighteousness.' "

At these words a fire burned through Sunny—a good fire, a cleansing fire. She was able to draw breath more freely.

"My prayer is that this meeting will give all of

you hope. That's what Christ is all about. If we don't have him, we have no hope."

"Amen," Sunny whispered reverently with many others the first time she'd spoken this aloud. She felt a pull toward this man and his good, plain words.

"I'm an old man and can't preach for long, so listen up!" Old Saul grinned at them. Something about him was working its way not only in Sunny but in those standing around her. Everyone was smiling and moving closer to catch every word.

"John goes on to say 'the darkness is past, and the true light now shineth. He that saith he is in the light, and hateth his brother, is in darkness even until now . . . because that darkness hath blinded his eyes. I write unto you, little children, because your sins are forgiven you for His name's sake.' "

Forgiven, Sunny repeated to herself. *Oh, could that be so?*

Old Saul was true to his word and spoke only a few more minutes. Then he introduced his son and daughter-in-law, who led the gathering in a few hymns. They sang a line and the congregation echoed it.

Sunny kept quiet at first but soon was singing along. She had missed music. Saloons most always had a piano and someone to play it. Sunny caught herself, glad no one could read these thoughts. She shouldn't be thinking of saloon music here and now.

As the hymn ended, Old Saul stepped forward and asked for prayer requests. People spoke up where they stood. And the old preacher prayed for each. Then he led them in the Lord's Prayer, which Sunny had never heard before. It struck her as lovely.

When the meeting was over, Sunny followed everyone as they lined up to shake the old man's hand and greet his family. When it came her turn, she lowered her eyes and curtsied, mimicking softly what she'd heard others say. "Thank you for the preaching."

"Look up."

Sunny did, startled. Frightened.

"I like to see a pretty woman's face," Old Saul said, grinning. A few around them chuckled.

Sunny blushed warmly.

"Now don't take that wrong. I'm not flirting with you."

More people chuckled. Sunny wished she could slip back into the shelter of the crowd.

"Your husband didn't come with you?" Old Saul lifted a bushy white eyebrow.

Sunny was mortified, and couldn't think of a word of reply.

"No, sir, he didn't," Charles spoke up behind her. "He's a good man, though."

"I have no doubt," Old Saul said. "I'll come visit him if I'm able, Mrs. Whitmore."

Sunny inhaled sharply. Noah would think

she'd set him up, which surely would cause trouble.

"Don't worry, ma'am. I'll let him know it was my idea, not yours," the preacher assured her as if he'd read her caution.

Sunny tried to smile as she stepped aside to let Charles and Caroline take their turn greeting the old man. She stood back and watched, wondering what Old Saul would have said if she—or another woman—had come out of the saloon in a red satin dress to listen to him. Did he mean what he said about all having sinned? Or did he believe that some sins—like living upstairs at a saloon—couldn't be forgiven or forgotten?

On the next day, midmorning, axes echoed in the forest clearing. Sunny walked toward the sound, her baby in her arms. Dawn squirmed, wanting down. "No, honey, we're going to see where Martin will bring his bride. We're almost there."

To distract Dawn she began to sing a silly song about a girl named Susannah. Dawn stared at her, an endearing look in her wide blue eyes.

"Yes, your mama can sing silly songs if she wants to."

Dawn crowed.

Sunny wished she felt as cheery as she was acting. When she'd arrived home, Noah had not asked about the Sunday meeting, but had merely talked a bit to Charles who'd given him a gentle scold. Noah had just half smiled and shaken his head.

She had been feeling such a bleak sense of separation from Noah, even though she was glad she'd gone to church. How could she reconnect with him? How could she make him understand why she'd done it?

Weighed down with this heavy burden, she followed the narrow track made by wagon wheels that had crushed the wild grass. Four men labored in the clearing. Nan's husband, Gordy, had joined the effort to build Martin's cabin.

Under the blue sky, she paused to watch the four of them working together. Noah was chopping in rhythm with Charles Fitzhugh while Gordy and Martin worked on another tree across the clearing from them.

Sunny waited at the edge of the green woods. She didn't want to startle the men during such dangerous work. In fact, she didn't really want to be here. But she'd been drawn to seek out Noah, to bring something warm for the men to drink as a kind of peace offering. The distance she felt between her and Noah made her feel lost and scared. Maybe she shouldn't have gone to the preaching in town after all.

She shook the thought from her head—she was glad she'd gone. It had been . . . important.

When she'd arrived home yesterday she'd wanted to share about the white-haired and kind-eyed preacher who called himself Old Saul. She'd come home aching to let it all out but Noah had silently warned her away. He'd barely spoken six words to her all afternoon and evening. Her husband had gone deep within himself, even more than usual. At first she thought it was anger at her, but that didn't feel quite right. It was more like Noah was angry at himself.

Or perhaps . . . God?

"Timber!" Charles shouted. Their tree fell. Sunny stepped back farther into the shelter of trees, breathlessly watching the felled tree bounce and bounce, branches whipping back and forth. The ground under her feet shook. Finally it lay on the ground, shuddering still. Her husband and Charles moved to it and began stripping the branches off with hatchets.

How did they have the courage to do this terrifying work? Shaking her head, she ventured into the clearing. "I brought fresh hot coffee!" she called, holding up a jug wrapped in old cloth.

Her voice was drowned out by another voice.

"Timber!" Gordy yelled.

Sunny stepped back within the forest again. The second tree creaked, cracked, plummeting to the earth. It bounced, once, twice—and headed straight toward Noah and Charles.

Sunny shrieked, threw the jug down and ran forward heedlessly. "Noah!"

The huge log bounced high and sailed over

Charles. Then it began dropping. In a rush of branches and leaves, it clipped her husband.

He fell.

"Noah!" she shrieked again. Sunny's heart pounded as she pelted toward her husband, now lying on the ground. Dawn began to cry as Sunny clutched her tightly.

The logged tree careened on till it slammed into the trees ringing the clearing. It dropped then—hard.

Sunny fell to her knees beside her husband. He lay, gasping, on the still dewy grass. He clutched his left shoulder as a moan was wrenched from him. "Is it broken?" she asked.

"Can you move your shoulder and arm, Noah?" Charles asked, standing at her side, leaning over.

Noah looked up at him as if dazed. Then with teeth clenched in a grimace, he slowly rotated his left shoulder and flexed his elbow and wrist. "It didn't . . . break anything."

Still shuddering with fright, Sunny hugged Dawn to her.

"Man, if you hadn't ducked, it would have taken your head clean off," Charles said, sounding amused.

"Good . . . I ducked then," Noah breathed rapidly, catches in his voice signifying pain.

Men. Joking at such a time.

Sunny set Dawn down and reached out for Noah's hand. She examined him and saw that the log branches had whipped the side of her husband's face, leaving streaks of gouged skin and blood. His sleeve had been nearly torn off at the shoulder. She pulled the cuff, ripping off the sleeve to expose the lacerated arm. Fortunately none of the cuts looked deep but blood oozed up.

"Martin? You have a spring, don't you? Would you bring me fresh water and a clean cloth for bandages?" Sunny asked.

"Right away. I got a big bottle of iodine, too." The younger man hurried away to his tent.

"My woman sent along a jar of arnica ointment to share when we're done for the day." Gordy turned and ran to a bag, which hung from a tree branch nearby. He returned with it and handed it to Sunny with a roll of cloth bandages. "Her grannie makes it with that herb. It's real good for bringing down swelling and bruises."

Soon Sunny was washing away blood from Noah's face and arm. Then, from a scared-looking Martin, she took the bottle of iodine. She steadied herself to cause her husband pain. She noted Noah bracing himself to withstand it.

Dr. Mercy in Idaho had taught her that infection could kill and that iodine fought infection. So she tipped the bottle at the top of Noah's shoulder and trickled the brown liquid down over his lacerated face and bleeding upper arm.

Noah gasped and gritted his teeth. Sunny knew it burned like fire. The men stood by solemnly, enduring the pain with him. When she'd anointed every cut, gouge and scrape, she began to rub the arnica ointment into the bruised skin around his shoulder joint.

"Rub it in good," Gordy urged. "That might help keep the shoulder from swelling so much he can't move it."

Sunny obeyed and then wrapped the cloth bandages around Noah's arm. When Martin handed her a large square of muslin, she fashioned a sling. And when all the doctoring was done, she bent her head down, feeling waves of weakness. And sheer terror. *He could have been killed. I could have been widowed today.* But she had done what a wife was expected to do. She'd taken care of Noah. That steadied her.

"I think we should back it down to just two of us felling and the other two stripping," Charles said. "Logging is unpredictable. Don't want anybody else hurt today."

"I could use a drink of something," Noah said.

Ignoring her light-headedness, Sunny found the jug she'd dropped in the grass. The jug's lid had held. She unscrewed it and poured out a cup of coffee for Noah. "I have enough for all. Martin, do you have mugs?"

Soon the four men sipped the still-hot coffee. Then Charles helped Noah to his feet, holding on to him, steadying him.

"My right hand and arm are okay," Noah said,

still breathing in gasps. "I can help with the stripping. It'll keep my mind—"

Sunny supplied silently, *off the pain.*

"—busy," Noah finished.

Sunny wanted to object. Noah needed to lie down and rest, help his body heal, not stress it with work. But she knew better than to voice this. Men didn't show weakness. And Noah wouldn't appreciate her coddling him in front of other men.

She hardened herself and kept quiet. "I'll be back with lunch later."

"No need, Miz Whitmore," Gordy said. "My Nan is bringing stew and biscuits over at midday."

Sunny merely nodded, tight-lipped. "That's nice of her. I'll drop by to see her then, too." The desire to show her husband some affection nearly swept her from her feet, but they didn't show affection to each other. "You men, be careful. I think you cost me a few years of life just now," she said, sounding as calm as she possibly could.

The men chuckled but she glimpsed in their eyes that the accident had shaken them, too. Well, good, maybe they'd be more careful. She lifted Dawn and told her to wave goodbye to the men.

Still shaking inside, Sunny headed for home. Stark, cold fear coursed through her but she set a steady pace toward home. One thought echoed in her head the whole way: *I could have lost him today.*

• • •

Noah sat on his stool in the cool faint light, his arm and shoulder still aching from his accident several days ago. He'd slept like the dead from fatigue though the pain awakened him occasionally. As they ate breakfast, Sunny sat in the rocker nearby.

"When Martin's cabin is done and he goes south to claim his bride, I'll finish our table and benches," Noah announced.

"You're helping Charles and Gordy finish work on Martin's cabin today?" she asked.

He tested his arm. "Yes, and I think I can leave off the sling soon."

Sunny glanced at him. "I'm glad you're feeling better. And there has been no infection."

"That iodine nearly burned me to death," Noah said, making an attempt at humor. He could tell Sunny was trying to hide her concern.

"Dr. Mercy Gabriel, Constance's daughter, taught me about cleaning wounds."

He nodded. "You did good."

His words of praise clearly made her happy. A beautiful smile lit up her face and Noah had to look away. He sipped his coffee, focusing on how glad he was that he would be able to work a full day again without showing weakness.

Sunny had been right about being neighborly. He wanted to go to Martin's today. It was a good feeling to want to be with other men. The time spent laboring at Martin's place had restored something in Noah. He hadn't thought it possible, but he'd liked working together as he and his brothers had labored together on their dad's farm. He didn't want to lose it.

"I can't understand why Charles plans to take his family to Kansas. Everything a man needs is here," he said.

Sunny sighed deeply. "I don't understand it, either. But it's a free country."

"I like to be where there are trees."

"Me, too. I lived on the plains and didn't like the . . . emptiness. They made me feel—"

Noah stopped her. "Look."

Dawn had been crawling on the floor. But now near him, she was trying to get on her feet. Noah watched, fascinated as the baby tried to pull herself up on the rim of his stool.

"Should be walking before long," Sunny said, sounding proud.

"We'll have to watch her then. You heard them last night."

Sunny tilted her head. "Last night?"

"The wolves were howling at the moon. I spoke to you. You let me know you heard them, too."

"I don't remember. I must have been talking in my sleep."

When he saw the fear in Sunny's eyes, he regretted telling her. "I don't want you to be upset. Just keep an eye on Dawn when she starts walking. We need to remember we aren't living in town. And I've seen bear scat, too."

Sunny nodded solemnly. "I'll remember." She looked at him. "I've been walking over to Martin's place by myself."

"That's okay. Bear will steer clear of humans. Wolves usually don't bother an adult but I think a child alone might be different."

Sunny nodded. Then Dawn's knees weakened. She plopped down and squawked her displeasure.

Noah smiled. The baby added life to their quiet cabin. Watching Dawn made him think of the coming Sunday. When he'd seen the tree heading for him, in the face of death he'd realized how glad he was to be alive. And then watching Sunny hurry to care for him . . . Whether he lived or died hadn't mattered to anybody for so long. He must care for her, too.

I'm doing this for Dawn—and for us. Sunny's words suddenly began to make sense to him. His wife was wise, much wiser than he. He inhaled deeply and felt himself calming. Now he knew what he should do, but could he actually do it?

Chapter Six

Outside, Noah stood before the mirror hanging on a peg by the door. With his almost-healed arm free of the sling, he carefully shaved his face with his honed razor. He'd moved the mirror out here so he could see himself clearly in the crisp morning light. He needed to shave . . . because he was going to attend Sunday meeting this morning.

Fear that he might not be able to make it through the meeting clutched his stomach with cold hands.

He was aware that his wife was eyeing him and holding back the obvious question. He wanted to tell her but somehow he couldn't say the words, *I'm going to meeting*. Once he'd come to under-stand Sunny's reason for attending, he'd faced the truth. *I have to do this for Dawn, and for Sunny—and for myself.*

He rinsed away the soap and then wiped his damp face with a towel, inhaling the bracing air. "Sunny?" He cleared his clogged throat. "Will you press my dress shirt and suit?"

"Right away, Noah." She scurried into the cabin.

He heard her open the chest, which kept their better clothing clean and safe. He should have told her yesterday so she wouldn't have had to iron on Sunday. The old ways still clung to him—no work on First day, what Quakers called Sunday. He gazed into the limitless blue above the tall treetops, drawing strength from the serenity around him.

Finally he went inside and stood watching Sunny finish ironing his trousers. Her hands were deft and watching her was a pleasure, carrying his mind away from what he must do today.

Dawn crawled to him, grabbed his pant leg and tried to haul herself up to stand. Glad of the distraction, he reached down and swung her up into his arms. She crowed, exultant. He jiggled her and she crowed again. Such innocence. A fierce protectiveness surged within him. This child depended on him. He murmured silently, *I won't fail you, child.* Not like his father had failed him. His heart clenched into stone.

Dawn patted his chest with her soft tiny hand, easing in some indefinable way the tightness there. He picked up the child's little pink palm and kissed it. Then he lifted her high overhead, again causing her to squeal with joy.

"Thank you," Sunny said, "for keeping her busy."

When he glanced at his wife, she had looked away. Her soft hands moved over the dark cloth. Steam rose from the dampened fabric. The heavy iron slid along the cloth, pressing the wrinkles and creases flat and fresh. If only humans could lie on an ironing board and have their imperfections ironed out.

He lowered Dawn to his chest, clasping her close, and stepped outside with her. He walked to a nearby pine tree and took her hand and stroked her palm across one needled bough. The little girl's face showed intense concentration and awe. "Those are pine needles," he murmured. "Pine needles."

All of a sudden the child collapsed against him. He realized she was hugging him, an unexpected boon. And for what? The only gift he'd given her was lifting her to touch a pine tree.

Sunny stepped outside. "Your clothes are pressed." She looked at her daughter hugging him still.

Their gazes linked, connecting them in some powerful way. "She's so bright. Everything's a wonder to her," he managed to say.

Sunny nodded, then walked to him. She held out her hands for the child so he could go dress.

He didn't want to relinquish the little one—he didn't want to go inside and dress to face this thing he must do.

Dawn made the decision for him. She turned and launched herself at her mother, who caught her. "If you dress now, Noah, I'll have time to do my hair and finish—"

He nodded mechanically, cutting off her

appeal. He'd made his decision, but every step toward the goal jolted him. "Right away."

Soon they were both attired in their First day best, standing at the end of their track, waiting for the Fitzhughs to arrive. Noah's heart beat like train wheels racing over iron tracks.

The jingling harness announced the wagon and then their friends came into view amidst the trees. Charles beamed at him. Noah merely nodded, holding in his inclination to turn back home.

"We're so happy to see you, Noah," Caroline said.

Noah ducked his head politely. He led Sunny to the rear and helped her and Dawn up. Then he hoisted himself onto the wagon bed beside her. Charles chirruped to the team and they took off with a lurch and bump.

In front of the store, Noah lifted Dawn into his arms and accepted and returned greetings. He glanced at the chattering people gathered around. Sunny stood beside him. He wished he'd said something to her, but her presence was both a comfort and an accusation. Why couldn't he explain things to her?

Why couldn't he explain *himself* to her?

A brisk breeze blew off the river. He shielded Dawn as best he could. The little girl squirmed to be let down and he knew the same urge—to get down and go about his business, not stand here waiting, dreading.

An old man arrived in a wagon with a couple and two teenage boys. With what looked to be his son's help, the old man got down from the wagon bench. From the crowd's reaction, Noah knew this must be the preacher. At once the man's frailty and strength touched Noah.

The preacher was thin with age but his hands told the tale of years of labor. People around him called out greetings. The old man lifted a gnarled hand in reply and then took the seat that Ashford the storekeeper brought out for him.

Noah felt the crowd move forward, carrying him and Sunny closer than he wanted to go. Then the old man smiled broadly—and it was like he drew them all to him. Feeling the strain of being with others, Noah gathered the invisible bonds that held him together. He didn't belong here, but he'd come so no one would single out his family as strange or different.

He'd thought that was what Sunny's words had meant. However, now that he'd arrived, it was clear that wasn't what she'd meant at all. The past which he'd bottled inside him strained to be released. He tightened his control, clenched his teeth against it. *I faced cannon and sabers and cavalry horses. I can stand down this man.*

Sunny watched her husband, had watched him all morning. What had made him decide to come to this gathering? His presence caused her to be even more nervous than she had been last Sunday. Would he remain her silent Noah or had he come to say something? All around her, everyone was smiling. Though nervous, Sunny forced herself to do the same.

Dawn squirmed in Noah's arms. Sunny reached over and gently took the child and set her down. Noah didn't object—in fact, he didn't look toward her at all. He looked to be in pain. Sunny touched his arm.

He glanced down.

She smiled up at him, trying to let him know that everything was all right.

He gazed at her and gave the slightest nod. Then, he drew her hand into the crook of his arm.

At first, Sunny was shocked. Then she felt herself beaming with pride at this show of oneness. This man, the handsomest here to her mind, was not ashamed to claim her here in front of everyone. No other man had ever done so. When Dawn pulled herself up using Sunny's skirts, Sunny felt for the first time that the three of them stood together, a family.

The son and daughter-in-law of the preacher began to lead the gathering in a hymn. Though aware that Noah remained silent beside her, Sunny sang along as best she could. Then the son and his wife moved to the side, sitting down on the bench outside the store.

Suddenly Sunny was shocked to see that during

the hymn singing, Dawn had somehow left her side and crawled up to the porch, and was now in the process of hauling herself up—using the trouser leg of the preacher!

Sunny's hand flew to her mouth as she gasped. "Dawn!"

The old preacher reached down, grasped the little hands and helped the baby stand up.

Sunny rushed forward through the couples. "I'm so sorry—"

Old Saul held up a hand. "No need to be sorry. Jesus said, 'Suffer the little children to come unto me, and forbid them not: for of such is the kingdom of God.' What a sweet little girl." He patted Dawn's back and the little girl crowed.

Sunny paused, unsure what to do.

"Just let her be," the old preacher reassured her. "She's doing no harm." He closed his eyes and began to pray for Dawn, for her family, for this town.

Sunny calmed and drifted back to Noah. Dawn remained at the preacher's feet, alternately crawling, cooing and dragging herself up to stand. Old Saul watched her with evident pleasure. "Jesus loved little children. He loved them, no doubt, because the world had not yet twisted them, harmed them." He touched Dawn's bright curls lightly.

"How many of us," he continued, "wish we could shed the sorrows and worries of this life and be like children, playing until we are exhausted and then falling into deep sleep without night-mares or cares to wake us?"

Noah stiffened beside her. Sunny moved a few inches closer to him. He still had the night-mares, and he still had not told her about them. She wanted to slip her hand back onto his arm, but he was very far away—she could see that in his eyes. The preacher went on speaking about repentance, forgiveness and becoming as innocent as children again. Then they sang another hymn, which Sunny thought beautiful. *Amazing grace, how sweet the sound that saved a wretch like me. I once was lost but now I'm found, was blind but now I see.*

Then they lined up to shake Old Saul's hand but more to hear his words, different for each of them as if he knew just what to say. Sunny wished this didn't make her nervous. But surely the man would have little to say to her now that her husband had come. They were a couple just like all the others.

When her turn came, she shook his hand and smiled. Old Saul beamed at her and mentioned how he'd enjoyed her little girl's part this morning.

Then Noah accepted the older man's gnarled hand, shook it and with a murmured phrase, tried to step back. Old Saul gripped his hand, keeping it. He didn't say anything, just looked up into

Noah's eyes a long time. Then he said, "I served under Old Hickory, Andrew Jackson, at the Battle of New Orleans."

Noah didn't move or speak for a few moments. Finally when he nodded curtly, Old Saul released his hand.

And with relief Sunny stepped aside for the Osbournes to take their turn, Noah by her side. Sunny wished she could make sense of the older man's words. She knew that there had been a president named Andrew Jackson, but what about the Battle of New Orleans? She regretted once again her lack of schooling.

But more worrying was the edginess she sensed from Noah. She realized that the time might be nearing for her to confront Noah as she had after Charles and Martin had come and logged that first time.

Going to meeting had stirred him up again, just like that day. She didn't want to make him face what was bothering him, but she needed to know why he'd come to the meeting this morning. She needed to understand him.

And perhaps there were some things he needed to understand about her, as well.

A few days later Noah cleared his throat at the end of supper. "We should go over to the Fitzhughs now."

"Oh?" Sunny looked up. The weather had been

cool and gloomy all day so the door was shut. Only faint light filtered in around the closed shutters. They would put glass windows in before fall, Noah had promised.

Today's weather matched Noah's mood. She hadn't gotten up the courage to ask Noah why he'd gone to worship. But maybe it wasn't the right time. Noah had had the worst nightmare of all last night, and she could see he didn't feel like talking.

"The Fitzhughs are leaving in the morning for Kansas."

Noah's words crushed her spirit. For a moment she couldn't speak. Caroline had been her first friend here. Was losing Charles's cheerful presence one cause of Noah's renewed edginess? The Fitzhughs had been the ones to bring Noah and her into the community. Was losing them hitting Noah hard, as well?

"Oh, Noah, I thought they might wait till Martin's bride came. Or change their minds about leaving."

"Charles is itching to head west in time to find a place and plant a crop." Noah's tone was dark.

Heavyhearted, Sunny rose, shed her apron, donned her bonnet. Then she thought of something and knelt by the door to open the chest. After she tucked the small gift into her pocket, she picked up Dawn and stepped outside. Noah shut the door behind them, pulling out the latch string.

"I'll carry Dawn," Noah said.

Three deer leaped across the path ahead of them. How graceful they were.

"Plenty of game hereabouts." Noah followed the game with his gaze. "We'll eat well."

His commonplace observation sat at odds with the turmoil she sensed in him. Last night he'd had such a nightmare that he'd wakened Dawn. He climbed down from the loft and paced outside till, exhausted, Sunny had fallen asleep. She'd hoped the Sunday service would have helped. What would help Noah?

The two of them walked the trail in silence. The trees cast long shadows and from the nearby creek, peepers—little frogs—peeped all around them. And then they were at the Fitzhughs' place.

The Osbournes had come as well as Martin. They all gathered outside the entrance to the small one-room cabin.

"I wish you'd stay long enough to meet my girl Ophelia," Martin said. "I wrote her about our neighbors."

"When you tie the knot, you write us, Martin," Caroline Fitzhugh said, looking down.

Sunny recognized the tremor in Caroline's voice. She recalled that Caroline had family in Wisconsin. What was Charles thinking taking his family all the way to Kansas? Why, there still were Indians and buffalo out there.

Martin nodded glumly. "You've been such good neighbors."

"Well, Martin, you tell Ophelia," Nan Osbourne said stoutly, "she'll still have me and Miz Whitmore nearby."

"That's right," Sunny agreed quickly.

The men moved apart, talking. The women gravitated to each other. Sunny set Dawn down to play with the other children. She didn't know what to say so she let the other women do the talking. Finally the sun lowered enough for Noah to say they needed to head home.

Sunny shook Charles's hand and then hugged Caroline farewell. She pushed the length of the blue ribbon she'd brought into Caroline's hand. "For your girls. To remember us by."

"That's real nice," Nan said, standing at Sunny's elbow. Nan's voice trembled as if tears threatened.

The visitors all walked together to the wagon trail. There, Martin turned the other direction and parted with a wave. Together, the Whitmores and the Osbournes walked westward down the track in the waning light, subdued and quiet. Nan leaned close just before she and her husband turned off toward their place. "My time is getting near. Can my husband come and get you when I need help?"

Shock shot through Sunny. "Of course I'll come. But I've only been to my own birthing."

"Gordy will head into town to bring out the storekeeper's wife," Nan explained further. "She's had ten herself and said she'd be glad to come help me. But while Gordy's gone, I'll need somebody to sit with me just in case."

"Gordy," Noah spoke up, "you come and fetch Sunny. Then *I'll* go to town for you. You should stay with your wife."

Noah's quick offer of help encouraged Sunny. He wasn't as withdrawn today as she had first thought. Then recalling the nightmare he'd suffered last night cast a veil over her hope. The dreams seemed to be getting worse, not better.

"Thanks, Noah. Thanks." Gordy shook his hand and the Osbournes waved and headed toward their place.

With Dawn already heavily asleep on Sunny's shoulder, they reached the cabin just as the last rays of sunshine flickered through the trees and disappeared. Noah shut the door behind them. Sunny laid Dawn in her hammock.

Noah turned to climb up the ladder to the loft to leave her to dress for bed alone as usual. The Fitzhughs moving on still lowered her mood. But Noah's offer of help to the Osbournes kept repeating in her mind.

Noah had not wanted to get "thick" with their neighbors but he obviously couldn't go against his own good nature. Hope bobbed within her and she decided to speak.

"Noah." she paused, then went on, feeling as if she were venturing out onto new ice, "I'm concerned about your nightmares." There, she'd said the word neither of them had ever spoken.

"I didn't mean to wake Dawn last night." His voice was gruff.

"That isn't my concern." She found she didn't have the words she needed. Exactly what was she trying to say? "You're my concern." The words startled her. But should they? This was her husband. And he needed something. But was it something she could offer?

"I can't help having them." He started up the ladder to the loft.

She went after him. "Don't leave me. Let's talk. Maybe if we talk—"

"Talking is just words," he barked.

"Words can be important. We spoke words and we became husband and wife. God spoke words and the world was created. Can't we talk about your nightmares? Maybe it would help." The last sentence wobbled from her lips.

" 'Maybe it would help,' " he mocked. "Words can't change what happened." He hurried up the last rungs.

"Noah—"

"Let it be, Sunny," he growled.

"Noah, I can't let it be. We need to talk this out. It can't hurt and it might help." She wasn't really sure about the first part.

He came down the ladder, carrying his blanket and pillow with him. He headed for the door.

Panic shot through her. Was he leaving her? "Where are you going?"

"I'll sleep in the wagon." He stalked to the door.

She hurried after him. "No, Noah—"

He shut the door in her face.

Leaving her caught between fear and frustration, she wanted to go after him, but fear held her back. What if he left her and Dawn? She'd only tried to be a good wife, but she'd failed. She slumped into the rocker, shaking inside. Those moments stand-ing together as a family at Sunday worship, had they just been an act? Had they made no progress toward becoming a real family? Had she done more harm than good tonight? Pushed him further from her?

Weary from lack of sleep, Noah inhaled the morning air, scented with pine. The chill each morning was lessening. Spring was drifting toward summer. He'd need to break ground soon to plant in time to harvest. Sunny and Dawn had gone over to Nan's early this morning. They were sewing some dishcloths and potholders for Martin's bride.

Noah remained behind alone, working on his table and thinking of the argument he and Sunny had had last night. She had made him so angry, and yet he could tell it was because she was worried. Still, he didn't like being pushed.

He'd felt something else last night, too. He'd wanted to reach for her, to grab her and pull her into his arms. He thought about taking her arm Sunday morning in town, showing possession. Something was changing between them. No matter how much he tried to convince himself that theirs was a marriage of practicality, he couldn't deny that there was something else happening. Was that why he'd spent the sleepless night, tossing and turning in the wagon?

The sound of an approaching harness jingling wafted to him on the breeze. Crosscurrents sawed through his mind. He wanted to be left in peace; he wanted whoever it was to stop.

The wagon came jouncing over the track through the trees toward his cabin. Noah froze in place. The preacher had come to call.

And Sunny wasn't here to handle the social niceties and keep the preacher busy, away from him. Noah stiffened himself. He had done all right in town on Sunday, not letting his real feelings show. He could handle this. He had to. He didn't want to be the local oddity—again.

He bent his reluctant mouth into a smile of greeting. "Preacher!" he called out in false welcome. He put down his tools and walked over to the wagon.

The preacher stopped well into the clearing. He laid his reins down, turned and scooted to the edge toward Noah. "Will you help an old man down?"

Noah offered both hands and let the preacher

take hold and ease down rope steps that had been hung on the side of wagon. "I thank you," the older man said on solid ground.

Noah felt his jaw tightening. He smiled broader to loosen it.

"I won't stay long. I can see you're working. Show me your place."

The simple request had an odd effect on Noah. This was the first time he'd ever been able to show anybody what he and Sunny had accomplished already and in only a little over two and a half weeks. As Noah led him to the cabin, the older man leaned on Noah's arm.

"Charles Fitzhugh and Martin Steward helped me get my cabin up."

The older man stepped inside and tapped the log floor with the toe of his boot. "I do like a good foundation."

"Martin and Charles helped me lay the rock foundation underneath the whole. We stirred a slurry of rock, sand and water and poured it all over the stones as mortar. This cabin will stand, not shift or sink."

The older man nodded. "You built yourselves a nice big cabin. It will do for the large family I hope you and your pretty wife will be blessed with."

Noah felt the strain return, wrap around him. Would he and Sunny ever have a family? Not as things stood between them now, they wouldn't.

He hated to be reminded of his failing. When would he be able to reach for her? How could he break through to where he wanted to be? His stiff smile slipped. Sleeping outside hadn't helped.

"You've already been blessed with that pretty little girl. Do you know how lucky you are?"

Lucky wasn't a word he'd use to describe himself. And he'd argued with Sunny. And wakened Dawn with that nightmare. Noah felt the preacher studying him. "Dawn is a joy," he said at last.

The older man went to the stone fireplace. "This is fine stonework. Who taught you how to build a fireplace without mortar?"

"I had a grandfather who was a stonemason. He taught me to lay a hearth."

"You could make this a trade. There're a lot of people around here who would pay good money to have a hearth like this."

Noah shrugged. He had no interest in working for others.

"Keep that in mind, son. There might come a time when you need some cash money."

With a mere nod, Noah led the preacher outside and showed him the lean-to and the oxen grazing along with his horse. The preacher's easy words were calming to Noah. He worked hard to keep alert for any word-trap the man might set for him.

"Now I see that you also work with wood. You

are a man of many talents," Old Saul said as he noticed the table Noah was building.

Noah shrugged again, not offering any response. When would this man leave him in peace?

"Well, you let me stretch my legs. If you give me a glass of your spring water, I'll get back up on the wagon and go on to my next stop. I'm glad you showed me your place."

The older man was as good as his word. He drank his cup of water. Noah helped him to get back up onto his wagon bench and he turned the team and jingled away.

Noah had expected a homily, or stiff sermon, or some kind of prosy pap. Why had Old Saul come? Noah couldn't figure it out. Then he recalled the only comment the old preacher had said that didn't address the cabin and its furnishings had been about Dawn. *Do you know how lucky you are?* He imagined Dawn's hug and had trouble drawing a deep breath. *I don't feel lucky, but I am. I'm not alone anymore.*

The next morning Sunny stared across at Noah, sitting on the three-legged stool. Somehow, when she saw Noah's long, lean form stretched over the low stool, her heart ached for him. He looked vulnerable, haggard from lack of sleep. She supposed she looked the same way—they hadn't spoken much since their argument.

Once again she had to stifle words of comfort.

Noah, like most men, didn't want to admit to any weakness. At least he'd slept in the loft last night, not out in the wagon. Her stomach rumbled with anxiety and she caught herself worrying her thumb. It was already red and nearly bleeding again. Should she apologize for pushing him so hard to tell her about his nightmare? Should she explain why she wanted to know? That her curiosity was because she cared so deeply?

"Hello, the house!" interrupted her thoughts.

Glancing to each other, she and Noah both went to the door and he opened it.

Martin sat on his wagon bench. "I'm off this morning to get married." If the man could have smiled wider, his face would have split in two.

Sunny spontaneously clapped her hands. "Oh, wonderful!" She hurried forward, drawn to the man's palpable joy.

Noah scooped up Dawn and followed her. "How long will you be away?"

"About ten days or so. Ophelia has everything ready for our wedding and is already packed to come north."

Sunny chuckled. "We will make your bride welcome."

"I know you will. I wrote her already that we have good neighbors." The groom blushed.

"You travel careful." Noah stroked the neck of one of Martin's horses, a chestnut.

"I will. I've got the preacher's blessings—he stopped to see me yesterday."

"He must be making the rounds. He stopped here, too," Noah said.

Sunny swung around to look into Noah's eyes. He hadn't said anything about the visit. Why had the preacher come? Her nerves jittered.

"Seems like a good man," Martin replied. "Ophelia was happy to learn we got a preacher. She'd miss going to worship."

Sunny tried to look as if she felt the same way as Martin's bride. But she couldn't stop worrying about what the preacher had said when he'd visited. Had he come to ask questions about her? Did her past show in some way she didn't understand?

"Well, I'm off." Martin slapped the reins and turned his wagon. He responded to their enthusiastic goodbyes with a wave over his head. The creaking wagon retreated down the track.

Sunny did not want to start another argument, but she had to know. She clenched the hand she had worked raw. "You didn't say that the preacher had come."

Noah turned to her slowly. "He just stopped to look over our place. That's all."

"And he stopped at Martin's, too," Sunny mused. "Seems so."

Noah didn't seem angry, so she pushed on. "What did the preacher mean about Andrew

Jackson and the Battle of New Orleans? That couldn't have been in the War Between the States."

Noah offered her the child. "No, that battle took place in 1815 in the second war with England. I've got work to start now. We may have a table to eat off tonight."

Sunny accepted Dawn. She could tell Noah did not want to pursue the topic any further. Yet why had the preacher said those words to Noah? What did late President Jackson and a battle over fifty years ago have to do with Noah?

Sunny trailed Noah, no longer able to keep her curiosity in check. She hovered nearby as he unearthed his woodworking tools from the chest, trying to come up with the right words. She followed Noah to the area where his two saw-horses stood ready. He laid a board down and began planing it, making a rhythmic scratching sound, and sending up curls of wood shavings. Dawn squealed, reaching toward the curls.

Noah looked up. "Do you need something, Sunny?"

She chewed her lower lip. "I do, Noah. Tell me—why did you go to meeting?" Her voice quavered just above a whisper.

Noah paused in his work.

Sunny waited, Dawn straining to get down from her arms.

"Isn't it enough that I went?" he asked gruffly, beginning to plane again.

"Noah," she murmured coaxingly, "I just need to know you. Know why you changed your mind. Before when I asked you to go, you said . . . you sounded . . ." She couldn't think what more to say. She gave up and turned.

"I thought over what you said."

His words stopped her. She swung back around. "Something *I* said?"

"About doing it for Dawn, and for us. You were right. We don't want to stick out, be different. In the army I was the private that used *thee* and then back home, I was the Friend who had gone to war. I, *we,* will not stand out as the strange ones here. It just causes talk. We don't need that."

She paused, stunned at the amount of words that had just flowed from Noah's mouth all at once. And then his meaning burst over her. He'd gone to meeting for Dawn and for her, not just himself.

Sunny rushed forward and with Dawn between them, pressed herself against him. He didn't hug back. He still held his plane, but he bent his head forward, his chin grazing the top of her head.

They silently shared a moment of the most tender connection. Sunny blinked back one tear. And then stepped away. "I need to get busy baking some bread or we'll have none for supper."

"Sounds good."

Sunny hurried into the cabin. Part of her wanted

to stay with Noah and talk. So many questions she wanted to ask him. Why had he gone to war? Why had his father been so angry with him? What did he dream in his nightmares?

The moment of being close to Noah, not only physically but also as partners, two people pulling together for their family, had nearly lifted Sunny off her feet. But she couldn't press her luck. She'd felt dreadful, fearful, when she'd confronted Noah. She didn't want to spoil this feeling, this special first.

Soon Dawn played with some jar rings, clacking them on the wood floor. Humming, Sunny kneaded the soft, cream-colored bread dough, covered it with a clean cloth and then set it on the mantel to rise.

She still felt like a pot simmering and realized she needed to calm down. Noah was a complicated man. She didn't want to do anything that might disturb the progress they'd just made. An idea of how she might please him occurred to her. She smiled and set about her baking, still humming and now grating fresh cinnamon.

Chapter Seven

Noah concentrated on planing the table and two benches, but he couldn't banish the feeling of Sunny pressed against him. Her softness threatened to weaken him. He had to remain strong, keep himself in check. Her questions were getting more and more pointed, closer to things he himself didn't understand—it made it hard for him to talk to her.

The wood flowed under his plane. He paused to stroke the tabletop—time to start sanding it smooth and then he'd oil it. The thought of sitting at a table tonight, a real table, pleased him. It would please her, too. If he couldn't answer her questions, at least he could give her a table on which to serve her meals.

Later in the afternoon Noah first carried in the broad tabletop, standing it against the wall. Then he brought in the trestle and two substantial squared and footed table legs. While he put the base together, Sunny held Dawn. He felt her intense gaze on him. He then lay on his back on the hard floor under the table and fastened down the top, pounding in the wood bolts he'd whittled.

Dawn was making urgent sounds and straining

to get down to come to him. He got up and pinched her cheek. As he bent over his work, he hid a smile at her preference for him. The preacher's words about how lucky he was rang in his ears.

He stood back for just a moment, admired his handiwork and then ducked outside to bring in the benches.

"We have a table, Mrs. Whitmore." He couldn't keep the pride of workmanship out of his tone. But he stepped out of reach so she wouldn't hug him again.

"Oh, Noah, it's lovely." Sunny set Dawn down and stroked the tabletop. "The wood grain is beautiful and the table just fits our room."

"Should sit up to ten easy." More of the preacher's words came back to him about Sunny and he having a family large enough to fit their cabin. Hot shame at his inadequacy as a husband sent him swiftly out the door. "Got to water the stock," he said, excusing himself.

"I'm making cinnamon buns for supper!" Sunny called after him.

He caught the worry in her tone. She sounded afraid he was irritated with her. How could he tell her that wasn't true? The irritation, frustration, aggravation he felt—it was all directed at himself.

In the small sunlit meadow Sunny bent over the green leaves, moving them to reveal the tiny red berries hiding underneath. Only a few feet away Nan bent in the same posture. They were picking wild strawberries, and Sunny's mind was racing with ideas about what she could make with them. The cinnamon buns hadn't had the desired effect on Noah, but perhaps fresh strawberries would draw him closer.

"I'm so happy you let me know," Sunny said. "I love strawberries."

"Well, my auntie had a nice berry patch at home and hers were bigger, but these will do with some sugar on 'em."

Dawn and Nan's little boy, Guthrie, crawled among the plants and wild grasses, entertaining themselves. Careful not to bruise or crush the soft velvety berries, Sunny gathered and dropped them into a wood bucket she'd brought. Nan appeared to have such an easygoing life compared to Sunny's. And, of course, their pasts obviously separated them. This difference constantly niggled at Sunny.

Sunny had become accustomed to Nan's ways and that in itself made her especially wary. She continued to fear that she might, by some chance remark, reveal her past. She couldn't let herself get too comfortable with anybody or she might lose everything she'd worked for since leaving Idaho. She and Noah couldn't move on to make another fresh start. They had their cabin finished and they were becoming part of the community.

"Well, I can't bend over another second. I'll just have to sit and scoot," Nan declared with a bit of humor and a deep sigh. The woman's pregnancy was obviously drawing to a close. She eased herself down to sit among the wild vines and began picking in this new position.

"How are you doing?" Sunny asked with sympathy.

"I'm getting to that stage where I just want it over!"

Sunny recalled how she'd felt the last few weeks before Dawn had been born. The breeze through the high leaves overhead sounded something like laughter, a cheery, soothing sound. "I understand."

Nan sighed loudly again. "You only been pregnant once?"

"Yes." Sunny stilled within. Why had Nan asked that?

"This is my third time. I lost my first."

Sunny snapped upright. "Oh, Nan, I'm so sorry."

"I'm just tellin' you because it's got Gordy worried. My first delivery just . . ." The young woman fell silent. "It was bad. And the baby didn't survive. It was a little girl."

Sympathy swamped Sunny as she tried to imagine what that had been like. She chastised herself for thinking that Nan's life had been easy.

"Will you ask your man to stay with Gordy during my birthing? He'll need somebody to talk with. Even though Guthrie came out right, my husband's worried I'll have a bad time again."

Sunny moved swiftly to Nan, bent and hugged her shoulders. "Yes, of course. And you're going to be fine. Mrs. Ashford will know how to help. And I'll be there, too."

Nan squeezed Sunny in return. "I know and I'm praying every night for another safe delivery. My mom birthed thirteen and she only had trouble the first time. That's what I keep telling Gordy, but . . ." The young woman shrugged.

Sunny straightened up and moved back to where she'd been picking, thinking of how everyone seemed to have secrets, or private pain. Suddenly, she caught movement from the corner of her right eye. She glanced over and nearly screamed. "Nan," she whispered, shaking, "there's a bear at the edge of the clearing."

"Which way?"

"Over your right shoulder." What had Noah told her to do if she met a bear? *Had* he told her what to do?

"Don't act riled," Nan said soberly. "I'm going to stand up slowly and start talking so it'll know we're humans. They don't see very good."

"Okay." Sunny's knees weakened but she kept on her feet. She located Dawn nearby, crawling on the ground, pursuing a butterfly.

"Well, good afternoon, bear," Nan said conversationally. "I know you like berries, but we got here first. We'll leave you some—don't you worry. Sunny, I'm going to start singing now. Only humans do that. You sing along. 'You are my sunshine, my only sunshine.' "

Sunny tried to sing along but couldn't get her voice to work.

"Sunny," Nan said after a moment, "it's a mama bear with a cub. Are you good at climbing trees?"

Sunny didn't think she could budge, much less climb. "No."

"Okay, we'll just sing some more and back away real slowlike. Let her know we're not going to mess with her baby."

How could Nan sound so calm?

Sunny stared at the bear, trying to join the song, and took a few halting steps backward.

The bear paused as if listening and then rose a bit, sniffing the air.

"Oh, good, she's smelling us."

Sunny didn't know how this could possibly be good. But then the bear herded her cub away and ambled off into the woods.

Giving way, Sunny sank to the warm earth.

"Are you all right?" Nan walked awkwardly to her side.

Sunny stared up at the woman. "Weren't you scared?"

"Yes, but I've seen bear before. She's just naturally going to protect her young. We can understand that. We're mamas with cubs, too."

This simple statement of fact sent Sunny into a storm of laughter. Then Nan began laughing, too. The two children wandered over to watch their mothers collapse on the ground and laugh themselves silly. Yet, Sunny also experienced a new strength. She'd faced a bear and hadn't panicked or done anything foolish. And she could laugh about it.

"You what?" Noah demanded, stopping his coffee mug halfway to his mouth.

Sunny turned from the hearth where she was stirring tonight's stew. "I said Nan and me saw a mama bear and her cub when we were berry-picking this afternoon."

"Didn't I tell you to be careful of bears?" He realized he was gripping the handle on his mug so tight that if it had been china, he'd have snapped it.

"I was careful." Sunny looked puzzled. "Nan told me what to do and then the bear herded her cub away from us. It was really funny."

Funny? A mother bear with a cub—was there anything more terrifying than that? He imagined Sunny and Dawn ravaged and left for dead. He set his mug down with a clunk.

"You look upset with me," she said, her voice tentative.

He clasped his hands together, holding in the anger and terror that flashed through him. He wanted to rage at her, *You could have been killed. Dawn could have died.* He chewed the insides of his mouth, trying to release his rage, keep from upsetting Sunny. "I'm not angry with you. Just be careful, all right?"

"I did just what Nan told me to do. I'll be careful, Noah."

He nodded woodenly, still roiling inside. "Good. Good."

Sunny bustled around the kitchen, then halted.

"Noah," his wife said with audible hesitation, "Nan asked me to ask you a favor."

"Nan wanted a favor from me?" He couldn't think of what another man's wife would want from him.

Sunny didn't look up while scooping stew into bowls and getting them on the table. "Nan's first baby didn't survive the birthing." She glanced up and then down quickly. "She didn't have any trouble when she had Guthrie. But Gordy's still worried about this baby coming."

What can I do about that? He forced himself to calmly sip his coffee.

"Nan hopes you'll stay with Gordy while he's . . . while she's in labor. She thinks it will help him get through it easier." Sunny looked him full in the face then, and then bent to pick Dawn up.

Of course he'd rather refuse this request. Nonetheless he couldn't say no. Gordy had become a friend. He wanted to make one thing

140

clear, however. "I don't know anything about birthing."

"You just need to keep Gordy company outside till the baby's born," Sunny assured him.

"I said when Nan's time came, I'd go to town for him," Noah recalled.

"And then when you return with Mrs. Ashford, you can sit outside with him, keep him company. Will you?"

Noah nodded. "I can do that." Suddenly he wondered, *How would I feel if Sunny lost a baby? Our baby?* He forced down a sudden lack of breath. "I will."

Sunny exhaled. "Good. It will make it easier on Nan."

Dawn squirmed and Sunny let her down. The little girl crawled straight to Noah and pulled herself up at the end of the bench next to him, grinning.

"I'm almost jealous," Sunny teased. "She prefers your company to mine."

He grinned at the baby and ran his fingers through her red-gold curls. "Hey there, Dawnie."

The little girl crowed with delight.

Noah picked her up and swung her high above his head. Dawn's innocent happiness lifted him. He shouldn't scold Sunny about the bear. They lived in a forest and nothing had happened. He was glad he hadn't sparked another argument.

"Children are a joy," he said without meaning

to. His gaze connected with Sunny's and he couldn't look away. If only the war hadn't come and swept away the joy of living, he and Sunny wouldn't be separated by the past, his past. He set Dawn down on her feet again.

The baby flapped her palms against the bench, scolding him.

He touched her nose. "I've got to feed the cattle quick, little lady. We will meet again."

He left without meeting Sunny's eye. "I won't be long."

The next morning, Gordy, his curly blond hair wild from the wind, came running into the clearing. "Noah!"

Noah had been busy laying a rock foundation for the spring house, a place where they could keep food like milk cool. He intended to buy a cow before winter. Now he climbed out of the trench he'd dug around the spring. "What is it?" But even before the words left his mouth, Noah knew what had brought Gordy hurrying to their door.

"It's Nan's time. Will you—"

"I'll just wash my hands and be off to town," Noah replied. Hiding the jolt Gordy's words brought, he turned and called, "Sunny!"

"I heard, Noah." Sunny stood in the open door. "Just let me get a few things together, Gordy, and I'll come with you."

Noah washed his muddy hands in the basin by

the door. He could hear Sunny opening the chest inside. Gordy stood in the midst of their clearing, plainly jumpy with nerves.

Noah didn't bother to saddle his horse. He just threw a blanket over his mount and climbed on. He waved to Gordy and took off. "See you at the Osbournes!" he called to Sunny.

Careful to keep his mount on the faint wagon track, Noah let his horse go at a brisk run, which the animal appeared to enjoy. Soon he arrived at Ashford's store, hitched his horse and swung down. The bell jingled as he opened the door. "Mr. Ashford!"

After the bright sunlight Noah paused just inside the store door to let his eyes adjust to the fainter light inside.

"What can I do for you?" the storekeeper's familiar voice came from the shadows.

"I need Mrs. Ashford. Mrs. Osbourne's time has come and your wife said she'd help."

"I'll get her right away." Ashford turned and hurried up the steps to their living quarters over the store.

Then Noah noticed that a rough-looking stranger stood near the old preacher who was also in the store with his daughter-in-law, a tall, spare woman with silver in her hair. Belatedly removing his hat, Noah nodded politely, hoping the older man wouldn't start a conversation.

"You tell Mrs. Osbourne that I'll continue

praying she has a safe delivery," Old Saul said.

"I will, sir."

The stranger lounged against the counter, eyeing Noah. The man's expression made Noah uncomfortable. He hoped Ashford kept an eye on him. The storekeeper hurried down the stairs. "Mrs. Ashford says she'll come right after her bread is out of the oven."

Noah didn't welcome this delay. He propped his hands on his hips. "Does she know the way to the Osbournes?"

"Give me the directions," the storekeeper said, "and I'll explain them to her."

Noah told him and then stood there anyway, wanting to move the man's wife along quicker.

Ashford chuckled and winked. "Don't worry, young man. Babies aren't usually in a rush to be born. There's time."

The preacher's daughter-in-law spoke up. "I'll come, Mr. Whitmore. We haven't spoken, but I'm Lavina Caruthers. I've helped deliver babies, too."

Wanting to avoid more contact with the preacher, Noah hedged. "That's nice of you, ma'am, but I don't want to put you out."

"It's no problem. Old Saul can drive home by himself and I'll come with you. We brought our extra horse into town to be shod, so I'll ride over. Sometimes an extra pair of hands are good to have."

Noah said his thanks and walked outside. He

threw a leg over his horse and headed toward the Osbournes. He didn't like returning without help —what if Ashford was wrong? What if the baby came before the midwife?

When Noah arrived at the Osbournes, he found Gordy outside sitting hunched on a log. Since the day was fine, both Dawn and Guthrie played at his feet. The man glanced up, looking strained but hopeful.

With a tight throat Noah delivered the news. "Mrs. Ashford has to finish baking her bread before she comes."

Sunny was standing in the doorway. "Did Mrs. Ashford say how soon that would be?"

"Not long. The preacher's daughter-in-law was at the store and said she'll be coming soon, too." He tried to gauge how things were progressing with Nan but could read nothing but concern in his wife's stance. Sunny nodded and then went back inside.

Noah hobbled his horse to graze at the edge of the clearing and then went to sit on the log beside Gordy. He forced himself to ask, "How are things going?"

"Nan says not to worry. Everything's going as it should." Gordy's voice sounded on edge.

Noah had no idea what this meant but found he didn't want to know. What could they talk about to get their minds on something else? "You heard about the bear?"

Gordy chuckled and shook his head. "Takes a lot to ruffle my wife."

Noah couldn't think of anything to say to that, and the men sat in more silence. Noah knew he wasn't helping. "I'm thinking of clearing more land. I need to put in a garden and plant some corn," he finally said.

Gordy glanced around at his heavily wooded land. "Same here. We'll have to get busy with that soon."

Even more silence descended. Noah knew he was failing, and when he heard a horse approaching, he jumped up, grateful someone had come.

The preacher's daughter-in-law arrived, then Mrs. Ashford, a plump woman who had a determined cast to her face, drove up in a wagon. The women disappeared inside, and the long hours went on and on. In the shade, the two toddlers napped on a blanket. Noah could tell Gordy was worried and gave up trying to make him talk. Gordy's eyes strayed toward the cabin constantly. Noah suddenly couldn't stand the tension. He rose abruptly. "You know, why don't we split some wood for kindling?" A man could always use more wood.

Gordy stood also. "Sounds like a good idea."

The two men headed toward the stump and the stack of logs nearby. "I'll watch the kids first while you split."

Gordy nodded. The two worked hard as if they could help the birth by chopping wood. Noah watched Gordy's strained face, wondering how he would feel if their roles were reversed. Nan could die. The baby could, too. The thoughts made Noah's mouth go dry. He wished he had some comfort to give Gordy.

Through the open door Sunny heard the sound of the ax hitting wood. "Sounds like the men are keeping busy." The sound of their normal chore helped calm Sunny. And she needed to be calm for Nan's sake. The preacher's kin Lavina sat by the open window and sewed as if the day were just like any other.

Nan and Sunny were pacing slowly back and forth in the cabin, Nan leaning on Sunny's arm. Mrs. Ashford said walking would hurry the birth along. So they paced the dirt floor, packed down hard.

That floor bothered Sunny. Gordy hadn't taken the extra effort to make a half-log floor. This cabin wouldn't be as snug as hers and Noah's would be this winter. Was it because the Osbournes were from farther south and didn't know how the cold would come up from the frozen earth?

Mrs. Ashford stood over the fire. Comfrey leaves steeped in a pot of boiled water gave off a dreadful smell. "My grandma taught me how to brew this. We'll soak cloths in it and then, when your time is near, we'll poultice you and the baby will have an easier time making his appearance."

As a labor pain wrenched her, Nan paused, turning to grasp Sunny's elbows. Sunny braced herself to withstand Nan's fierce grip.

"They're getting closer together," Lavina commented, looking up from her sewing.

Slumping with evident relief after the contraction, Nan leaned her head on Sunny's shoulder, gasping for air. "That was a hard one."

Sunny felt helpless. She could do nothing to ease her friend's pain. But Lavina was right—the pains were much closer together now and seemed more powerful. That was good news, hard but good. *God, protect my friend Nan in this time. Please.*

"It's near past supper time. I'm going to make sandwiches and take them out to the men and children." Lavina rose and began preparations.

"Let's see how you're doing, Nan." Mrs. Ashford motioned toward a makeshift pallet near the fire, prepared for the birthing. Nan had refused to use her bed for the messy business of child-bearing.

Sunny helped her friend lie down and endure the intrusive examination. Averting her eyes, she wondered what Noah was thinking.

Noah had been so angry about her and Nan encountering the bear. Did that mean he cared? She remembered giving birth to Dawn. No man had waited like Gordy was. But Noah would care; he already had taken to Dawn, hadn't he?

Noah and Gordy had finished chopping enough kindling to last the family for a month or two. Now back on the log, the fathers each held a child. Staying calm for Gordy's sake, Noah swallowed the question that had plagued him repeatedly since he arrived: How are things going?

A pained moan—very loud, very long—came from inside.

Gordy jerked up as if to go inside, but remained in place.

Noah's heart thudded dully.

A long low bellow issued from the cabin, louder and filled with pain and hurt.

Goose bumps rose on Noah's arms.

Gordy moaned and then uttered a fervent prayer, "Oh, God, oh, God, take care of my Nan. What would I do without her?"

Noah felt the words as his own. *Oh, God, oh, God, what would I do without Sunny and Dawn?*

Almost two hours later, with the spent sun nearly setting, Sunny came outside, beaming. "Gordy, your daughter's been born. You can come in now."

The weight lifted in an instant. Noah rose up and clapped Gordy on the back. "A girl! You've got a daughter!"

Gordy looked punch-drunk. "How's my wife?"

"Very tired but well," Mrs. Ashford said as she came out, pulling on her shawl. "Mr. Whitmore, would you hitch up my team?"

Gordy wrung the woman's hand. "Thank you, ma'am. Thank you." Then he swung his son up into his arms. "Let's go see your baby sister!"

Mrs. Ashford smiled and bustled toward Noah who had hurried to do the hitching. After he waved the storekeeper's wife off, he turned to find Sunny, who waited outside for him.

When he came abreast of Sunny, he murmured, "Is everything all right?"

"Yes, not a bad delivery according to Mrs. Ashford. She is a very competent midwife. That's good to know."

Then his throat closed up. Sunny's words about the midwife repeated in his mind. The import of what she said hit him. She meant if she ever got pregnant, a competent midwife lived nearby. Would he ever feel able to give Sunny children?

"Here she is," Gordy said, coming to the door and holding up a tiny red-faced baby wrapped in a small white blanket.

Noah tried to look appreciative but he'd never seen a newborn. No doubt the baby would look better as she got older.

"Beautiful," Sunny said from his side.

Lavina joined the knot at the door. "Nan will be lying in for a few days. I'll stay to help tonight."

"I'll come tomorrow," Sunny said. "I can come some every day." She looked to Noah as if asking approval.

"Of course," he said, unable to look away.

Dawn tugged on his pant leg and he swung her up in his arms.

"Sunny!"

Much later that night the sound of her name woke Sunny from a deep, exhausted sleep. Had she imagined it?

"Sunny!" The cry split the silence.

She sat bolt upright on her bedding. Her eyes adjusted to the dim light from the banked fire. Up in the loft Noah began moaning. Another nightmare.

She looked to Dawn. Noah's distress had not woken her yet.

"Sunny, Sunny," he moaned as if beseeching her to save him.

Sunny couldn't bear it. Throwing back her quilt, she hurried to the ladder and climbed up into the loft.

Noah thrashed, fighting his blankets. "Noah," she said in a firm, loud voice. She reached over and shook his shoulder. "Noah, you're having a nightmare." She repeated this several times, still shaking his shoulder more and more insistently.

Then he jerked and sat up. "What . . . what?"

"Noah, you were having a nightmare," she

said in an even tone without any scold in it. "You were calling my name."

He stared at her.

Was he fully awake? "Noah?" she whispered.

"Sorry." His voice was rough and dry.

"No need to apologize. I was just concerned." She patted his arm. "I'll sit with you till you fall asleep again."

"No need," he replied gruffly. "Sorry I bothered you."

Men didn't show weakness, she reminded herself. Nevertheless she had to choke down the urge to offer comfort again. "Good night then." She went to the ladder and then climbed down.

On the main floor she checked on Dawn, sleeping peacefully in her hammock, and then slipped between her quilts again. Would the nightmares ever end? She'd asked him, thinking she could help Noah by talking them out. He'd shut her out. Everything within her yearned toward this man, her husband. Oh, to have the privilege of holding him and comforting him. But the truth chilled her. *He doesn't want me. And maybe I'm not what he needs.*

Chapter Eight

Sunny felt shy with Noah at breakfast. Perhaps because she'd never before gone up into the loft when he had been there. She'd never tried to help him in the midst of his nightmares. Had she done right or wrong?

Right, she told herself. *He is my husband.*

She dragged her mind back to the present. She and Noah sat on opposite benches at the new table, eating a silent breakfast of cinnamon buns and salt pork. Dawn had crawled down from her lap and was trying to climb up onto the bench beside Noah. Sunny put down her cup. "I'll get her."

"No." Noah set down his fork. He lifted the little girl to sit on his lap. Dawn cooed happily and patted the edge of the table with both her palms. "She's always so happy." Wonderment resonated in Noah's voice.

Sunny had a hard time swallowing. Dawn somehow was able to pierce Noah's shell in a way that she couldn't. "She is a blessing," Sunny murmured.

"I'm so glad that Nan and the baby came through well." Relief radiated from each of

Noah's words. He looked closely at her, as if watching for her reaction.

Impulsively, she reached over and barely touched his hand lying on the table. "Me, too." Why was he still looking at her like that? Like there was something he wanted to say?

Careful not to overstep this fragile link between them, she removed her hand and went back to eating the last of her breakfast. As they ate, Dawn's cooing and the birdsong from outside were the only sounds.

"Noah, I'm going to clean up after breakfast and do my morning chores. Then I'm going over to help with Nan and the baby. Is that all right?"

"Of course," Noah said as he helped Dawn stand up on his lap and then held her under her arms while she bobbed up and down. Dawn leaned against his chest, hugging him and talking baby talk to him.

She could tell Noah was taking pleasure in Dawn's innocent glee. And she was happy that Dawn could take him away from his cares, even if she couldn't.

"Sorry . . . about last night," Noah said as if he'd been struggling with what to say all morning.

"It was nothing, Noah," she assured him. "I'll leave your lunch keeping warm in the back of the hearth." In spite of his dark mood, Noah had eaten four of her cinnamon rolls, and that made her feel she wasn't completely a failure at being a good wife.

"Fine. I'm going to start clearing more land for our garden. Gordy and I are going to help each other get everything planted as soon as the frost danger is past, near the end of this month."

"I've never tended a garden," she admitted, rising to clear the table. No gardens behind saloons. For her whole life until she'd lived with the Gabriels, all her food had come from cafés. What did Noah think of a wife who'd never tended a garden?

"It's not hard to learn," Noah said, wiping his lips with his colorful pocket handkerchief. "I'll teach you what weeds look like and then it's just a matter of watering and weeding." He rose, still holding Dawn.

Something Old Saul had said in a recent sermon came into her mind, about their lives being like gardens and prayers being the key to weeding out the bad. *I need to pray for my husband more.*

Noah handed her Dawn, who complained loudly. He touched Dawn's nose and promised to play with her later.

Constance Gabriel had taught Sunny that she could pray anytime and anywhere and in any way. Sunny had always felt that she had no right to claim God's ear. *But this is for Noah, not me,* she thought.

Sunny felt an almost physical movement around

her heart and, with awe, wondered if this was what Constance had meant by the Inner Light.

"Anything wrong?" Noah asked, pausing just outside the door.

Sunny felt herself beaming as the prayer formed in her mind. "No, nothing."

Dear God, heal my Noah's heart.

Noah stood outside, the morning sun warming his head and shoulders. He watched Sunny, carrying Dawn on her hip, on their way to Nan's house. Though glad she was going to help, he found he wished she was staying home.

The wish caught him by surprise.

Sunny always lived up to her name, and Dawn did, too. He clamped down on the good feeling trying to rise in him. One brief recollection of the humiliation of Sunny climbing up into the loft because he'd wakened her again did the trick. His heart turned to brick.

But he had blessed work to do. He turned to tackle choosing the best place for the garden. He loved string beans and ruby-red beets and their tender greens with scarlet veins that tasted like sugar. His mouth watered just thinking of the produce he'd harvest this summer, God willing. He heard the last two words repeat in his mind, God willing. Why had he thought that now?

He gazed up at the green trees, singing with the breeze. But got no answer. He loved this forest.

However it did make finding a full-sun area difficult. And a garden needed water, too. He started
walking toward the creek, trying to block out
Sunny's concerned expression over breakfast.
*I've got her walking on eggs again and I don't
want her to feel that way.*

No matter how he tried to keep her out, Sunny
kept finding her way back into his thoughts.

The sound of cheery whistling announced that
Gordy had come as promised. "Mornin', Noah!"

Noah turned to greet the man, noticing how
different his neighbor looked today. The tension
of the birthing had melted away and now a
proud, happy father marched into the clearing.
Gordy carried his ax over his shoulder and a smile
covered his face.

"Morning. How's your wife and babe?"

"Fine. When he was a baby, Guthrie was some
colicky, but this one—we named her after my ma
and Nan's, Pearl Louise—just whimpers a little
when she's hungry."

Noah let the man's good humor and joy flow
over him. Gordy had a right to feel good. Noah
refused to let his mind drift back to Sunny.

"Well, where do you think you want your
garden?" Gordy asked.

"I'm thinking near the creek. More sun there
and water will be near if the rain is sparse."

"Good thinking. Let's see the lay of the land."
They walked together to the nearby creek.

Noah decided then that he'd try to work himself to exhaustion today and then perhaps he'd sleep so sound he wouldn't dream and disturb Sunny.

He hadn't made it more than five seconds without thinking of her again.

"Have you ever sent a letter?" Gordy asked out of the blue.

With a pang Noah recalled all the letters he'd written while encamped in the army, letters to his brothers who always wrote back. But never to his father. Those dark days gripped him momentarily. "Yes . . . yes."

"I've never done it. Never had to. But I need to write and tell my family and Nan's that we have a daughter and that we're doing well. I feel bad we haven't written home before now."

Noah heard in his mind his elder brother's words at his wedding about keeping in touch. "I haven't written my . . . brothers, either."

"Who do you think handles the post hereabouts?"

"Probably Ashford. Usually if there isn't a post office, the post comes to the general store. Sunny and I are going to town for seeds—we can pick up paper and ink, if you need it."

Gordy nodded and hefted his ax handle in his hand. "Let's get your garden plot cleared today. And we'll tackle mine tomorrow." He looked up at the cloudless sky. "If this weather holds. We'll almost be farmers then."

The two walked up and down the creek and chose a spot on an upper slope of one the gentle hills. The slight elevation would keep a heavy rain from flooding the garden. They chose the trees that needed to be thinned to let full sun fall on the plot for most of the daylight hours. Then the sound of their axes echoed in the clearing. For a brief time, Noah's mind quieted and he was able to work in peace.

Six days later Sunny let Noah help her up onto the bench of their wagon. Then he swung Dawn up to her arms. Soon he sat on her other side and slapped the reins. Sunny had pocketed a list of items for them and for the Osbournes.

The warmth of the sun eased her tension and she relaxed against the back of the bench. She was going to town with her husband and daughter to bring home supplies just like any other family. She glanced at Noah from the corner of her eye. They even looked like every family hereabout.

She'd taken extra care with her appearance and Dawn's, and planned to be very careful in town to look the part of a contented wife and do nothing to call attention to herself. Her concern over saying or doing something that would reveal her past was becoming a burden. Would it lift in time?

Dawn had learned to patty-cake and was showing off, trying to get Noah to pay attention to her. And it was working. The grim mood he'd awakened with appeared to be lightening.

Soon they pulled into town and halted in front of the general store. Sunny's easy happiness vanished in a blink.

Mr. Ashford was chasing a woman from his store and swatting her back with his broom, hard. A little boy was hitting Ashford's leg, yelling for him to stop.

Without thinking, Sunny jumped down, throwing herself between the storekeeper and woman. The broom came down upon her back with force, nearly knocking the wind from her. She cried out.

No second blow fell. Instead Mr. Ashford cried out in shock.

Sunny whirled around to see Noah jerk the broom from the storekeeper's hands. He threw the man backward against his store, pinning Ashford to the window with the broom across his neck. Murder blazed in his expression.

Everything had happened so fast, leaving Sunny shaken by her own behavior as much as anyone else's. "I'm all right, Noah," she said, hurrying to pick up Dawn where Noah had set her on the wooden sidewalk.

Mr. Ashford made a gurgling sound, his face turning red.

"Noah," Sunny implored, hurrying to him. "You can let Mr. Ashford go."

"I didn't mean to hit your wife," the storekeeper

croaked with difficulty. "Just that thieving woman."

Noah stepped back, releasing the man. He still held the broom like a sparring stick.

The storekeeper rubbed his neck and gasped. "She was stealing from me . . . behind my back . . . that Indian."

Indian? Sunny turned to see the woman racing north along the river with a little child by the hand.

A horrific scene from Sunny's childhood streaked through her and she started off, calling after the woman. She caught up, panting. "Please, please!" she called. "Stop!"

The woman ran on and Sunny pursued her.

Then Sunny got a hitch in her side and had to stop. She leaned over, gasping and rubbing her side.

"Are you all right?" a hesitant voice asked.

Sunny looked up into the woman's pinched face and, between gasps, asked the same question, "Are you all right?"

"I am sorry the storekeeper hit you."

Sunny nearly repeated the same words, but stopped herself. Instead she let the woman help her to stand upright again. "I just got a stitch in my side."

The woman was wearing clothes much like Sunny's, not the buckskin dress of Indian women out West. Sunny offered the woman her hand. "I'm Sunny Whitmore. This is my daughter, Dawn."

The woman looked surprised but shook Sunny's hand. "Then her name is like mine. I am Bid'a ban. It means It Begins to Dawn. This is my son, Miigwans, Little Feather."

Sunny listened but paid more attention to how shabby their clothing was and how thin they looked. The woman would have been pretty if her face hadn't been so drawn and her eyes so desperate. "You need help," Sunny said simply.

Bid'a ban pressed her lips together.

"I'm sorry. Sometimes I speak out of turn." But Sunny didn't leave. This woman obviously needed aid urgently. Sunny knew how the edge of desperation could cut deeply. The little boy looked to be about ten years old. He clung to his mother's hand as if ready to defend her yet uncertain if he could.

"I do need help," the woman admitted. "Since my man was killed in the war, I have . . . trouble."

"The war? You mean the War Between the States?"

"Yes, my man fought for the Union. Many Ojibwa, or white call us Chippewa and Winnebago, went to war," the woman continued.

"My husband did, too."

The two women gazed at each other, linked by this connection. Sunny couldn't ignore the need she saw. And there was more to the story than the woman would admit—Sunny could see it in her eyes.

She heard Noah coming up behind her. She cringed, wondering how he was taking this.

At first she couldn't make herself look into his face. Nonetheless she felt the waves of tension flowing from him. A stolen glance upward told her that he was clearly angry.

"Bid'a ban, where do you live?" she asked.

"Along the river, the Chippewa." The woman motioned northward. "About three miles north from town."

Sunny nodded. "I'll come visit you. Soon."

The woman took one look at Noah's face and then turned and began walking briskly away, her son in hand.

"We've got shopping to do," Noah said curtly.

Sunny merely nodded. Now wasn't the time to contradict him. She knew why he'd become upset with her. She'd made a scene, which was exactly what Noah wanted to avoid at all costs.

She hurried alongside him to the store. Inside, the atmosphere was strained, wrapping around her, nearly smothering her.

"I'm sorry, Mrs. Whitmore. I didn't mean to strike you," Mr. Ashford said stiffly.

"I know you didn't, Mr. Ashford. I just acted . . . without thinking. I put myself in the way of hurt." Sunny smiled though she felt like telling the man what she thought of his actions.

Noah fumed silently at her side.

"I'm very sorry," she apologized again,

though the words nearly stuck in her throat.

"No problem, ma'am. What can I do for you today?"

One glance told Sunny that Noah remained too upset to speak. "We need seed for our garden, writing materials and a few other items. We're also picking up things for the Osbournes." She removed the list from her pocket. She and the storekeeper went through the list with Noah a brooding presence.

Finally Noah carried out the newspaper-wrapped packages. Mr. Ashford hovered near Sunny at the door. "I'm really sorry. We don't have any law hereabouts and what's a man to do to protect his property?"

Sunny checked her own feelings, making sure she concealed them. "Mr. Ashford, I understand completely." Sunny didn't like prevarication, but she knew better than to say that she understood thievery couldn't be tolerated but that this was a case of unmistakable need. "Please give Mrs. Ashford my kind regards."

He smiled and nodded, finally looking relieved.

Noah helped Sunny up onto the wagon. Dawn was fussing, wanting to nurse. Sunny soothed her till they drove into the cover of the trees. Then she put the child to nurse and prayed for the right words.

"I'm sorry, Noah. I didn't mean to make a scene."

He did not reply.

Sunny held herself together. Noah might be angry but he wasn't going to strike her or leave her. He just needed time to cool off. Then she could discuss the widow's plight. Sunny silently rolled the unusual names around in her mouth, Bid'a ban and Miigwans. Sunny had never realized that Indians might have fought in the same war as Noah. Sunny knew what having no one to turn to felt like. She'd faced life alone—after her mother died. She recalled the day a man had attacked her mother and her, just like Bid'a ban. Would she be able to make Noah understand why she must do something to help this woman and child? Or would she have to do it against his disapproval?

At home Noah helped her down. Dawn slept in her arms so she went inside to lay the child in the hammock. Noah and she carried in the packages from the store, then he left the cabin without a word. She heard through the open door Noah unhitch the oxen and then put the cattle to graze among the trees. They had intended to stop at the Osbournes and leave their supplies, but obviously Noah was in no mood to visit neighbors.

Burdened with a heaviness, Sunny washed her hands outside, then refilled the pitcher with water. Inside she lifted off her bonnet and donned her apron. With a potholder she lifted the kettle she'd left simmering at the back away from the fire. The grouse stew with beans and wild mushrooms would be ready when Noah came in.

She bowed her head. Unbidden the parable of the Good Samaritan came to mind.

The Gabriels had explained the story to her. A man who had been beaten up by thieves and left for dead. Two holy people had walked by without helping him, till the Samaritan—a person considered to be unholy—had stopped and cared for the man. Everyone in Pepin—if they knew the truth about her—probably would class her as a Samaritan. So she'd do what the Good Samaritan had done. Somehow, someway, she'd help this woman. Whether Noah agreed or not.

"Noah! Come eat!" she called later, stepping outside. She waited.

He didn't come.

She picked up Dawn and listened, shushing the child's prattle. She heard Noah working on the spring house foundation. She took a deep breath and headed toward him. He'd had a couple of hours to calm down, but regardless, they needed to eat. "Noah, dinner's ready."

Noah stood hip deep in the shallow pit he'd dug around the natural spring that he'd found on their land. He paused in his work, leaning on his shovel.

"I know you're upset with me," she said conversationally but with determination. "But we need to talk about what's bothering you and then eat our dinner without upset stomachs."

Noah did not look up, which wasn't like him.

She'd spent hours pondering how to get him to talk about what had upset him, to get it out into the daylight. "I know you don't want us to stand out different than others. I didn't mean to make a scene in town. But I didn't do it on purpose. I couldn't help myself."

Noah still wouldn't look at her.

She jiggled Dawn, who was trying to get down to go to Noah. Sunny felt the same urge. Perhaps she should just tell him here and now.

"Noah, when I was a little girl, one preacher in a town we lived in for a short while would stand out in front of the saloon and shout at the women inside."

She had tried to forget this incident. "One day my mother and I were walking home from eating at the café and he came out of a store and started shouting at my mother, calling her a harlot and worse. Then he snatched up a walking stick and began hitting my mother. She picked me up and ran for the saloon."

A lonely mourning dove cooed in a nearby tree. Even Dawn had stilled. Sunny's voice had gotten away from her and had come out with stronger emotion than she wanted to show. The memory still had the power to make her tremble.

"No one helped us. They just watched him

beat her as we ran. When we got safely through the saloon doors, he stopped. But he kept shouting till the bartender brought out his shotgun and threatened the man." She looked at Noah for any sign of understanding.

"No one helped us," she repeated in a whisper. She refused to cry. All that had happened so long ago. She hugged Dawn to her, thanking God no one would ever do that to her little girl.

Finally Noah climbed out of the spring house foundation. He looked like he didn't know what to say. "You said dinner was ready?"

She nodded, looking away.

"Then let's go eat."

Sunny wanted more than this, knew Noah needed to talk this out to let it go. But evidently he wasn't ready. She pressed her lips together. She would wait and pray.

But she would also go tomorrow and find Bid'a ban and help her. And there was nothing anyone could do to stop her. Not even Noah Whitmore.

The next morning, Noah rubbed his gritty eyes. He hadn't had any nightmares last night because he hadn't slept. He kept seeing Ashford hitting his wife. Then he imagined Sunny as a little girl running from a preacher who was beating her mother.

Sunny poured his coffee and he wrapped his hands around its warmth. He had rarely given much thought about Sunny's life before they'd met. But now he knew she'd been born into the saloon. And that moved him.

Sunny sat down with her coffee across from him. Their plates of breakfast sitting untouched. Dawn sat on the floor, knocking over blocks and prattling. He sipped the steaming coffee in a strained silence at the table. He wanted to speak, to comfort Sunny, to make things right. But how?

She cleared her throat. "Noah, I want to take the horse north along the shore to the river and find that woman. If I can. She's hungry and it's not right to leave her and the boy that way."

Shocked at this unexpected request, Noah put down his cup. "You want to what?"

She repeated her intentions. What caught him was that she sounded like she expected him to argue with her. Was that what she thought of him? "I would never let any woman go hungry," he said fiercely.

Sunny rested her hand beside his. "I know you wouldn't but after yesterday, I didn't know if you'd want me to go after her. People don't think much of Indians—"

He cut her off with a sweep of his hand. "That doesn't weigh with me." The words he'd held back rolled forth. "Yesterday upset me because Ashford struck you. I'm supposed to protect you."

Silence. Then Sunny wrapped a hand over his. "Thank you, Noah, you did protect me. And today I don't think anybody will bother me, but I have to help this woman. She doesn't have anyone else to turn to."

He recalled the times when he'd tried to help others. "Some people don't like taking charity. I haven't met many Indians, but they're proud people."

"Maybe she doesn't need charity," Sunny replied. "She told me her husband served in the Union Army and was killed. Shouldn't she be getting a widow's pension?"

"Her husband was a soldier?" He sat up straighter. Indignation burned in his stomach.

"I want to find her, help her get what's coming to her," Sunny said.

"She should be getting her husband's pension," Noah stated firmly. "The government promised that." He turned the problem over in his mind. "She may not have told you the truth about where she's living. I've heard the government is trying to move all the Indians hereabout out of Wisconsin."

Sunny frowned. "I don't think she lied to me. She said her place was north on the Chippewa River."

"The Chippewa does run north of town. It flows into the Mississippi." He began to calculate how to get there, how long it would take.

"Would you let me take the horse? And some food?" Sunny sounded determined but uncertain. "I don't want to leave her in need."

"No."

Her face fell.

"I'll take you myself. I can't let you go alone. Why would you think I'd let you do this alone?"

"Noah, I'm sorry." She reached for his hand, smiling tremulously. "I didn't understand. You didn't tell me."

He offered her a shrug in apology and then picked up his fork. His stomach burned and he had no appetite, but he needed strength to do this. "We better eat and then get ready to go."

"Yes, Noah." She looked at him as if he'd just done something special. That kind of hurt. *I should be kinder to my wife. I'm not doing a very good job of being a good husband.*

Chapter Nine

Noah stood beside the table, figuring out how to do this thing, how to go to help this widow in need. They couldn't take the wagon since there probably wasn't a road or even a trail where they would be going.

As usual, Dawn had gravitated to his side. Her constant preference for him managed to lighten his heavy heart. As he looked down into Dawn's eager face, he had an idea. "Sunny, I need a large dishcloth or a baby blanket."

Sunny looked surprised.

"I need to make something so we can carry Dawn with us on horseback."

Sunny nodded, though obviously mystified, and got him one of Dawn's smaller blankets.

"While I get this rigged up, you gather some food and necessities for the woman and her boy." While he sounded as if this were an everyday occurrence, he carried this new responsibility as a palpable burden.

Sunny gathered some essentials, such as food and pans, and stowed them in a couple of flour sacks while Noah folded the blanket corner to corner and tied it over one shoulder. As he did so, he considered the possibility that he was planning, once again, to go against the community he lived within. The thought didn't please him.

"Oh, you're making a little hammock for her," Sunny said.

He nodded. "I saw women working in the fields in the South carry their babies like this. See? My hands are free."

"I'll put a fresh diaper on her and two extra soakers."

He smiled at her thoughtfulness. And her kind nature. Of course Sunny wouldn't let this widow and fatherless child suffer.

Soon they were outside. Dawn didn't mind Noah settling her against him. In fact, she looked happy to be so close to him. He tried not to let this hearten him and failed. Dawn had captured him all right.

He climbed on the saddle and then helped Sunny up behind him. The sacks of provisions and necessities had been hung on the saddle or tucked into the saddlebags. Through the towering trees Noah set off westward toward the river. He wondered what she'd do if they couldn't find the woman and her boy.

Even worse, they would have to ride through town. He hadn't wanted to go there again so soon. He'd wanted to give people a chance to exhaust all the gossip about Sunny and Ashford. But it couldn't be avoided. A soldier's widow needed help. And they had to go where he could follow the river.

When they rode through town, Noah tried to keep his mind blank. The emotions and images from the day before kept trying to rise up and bring back the anger he'd burned with when he saw Ashford hit Sunny. The magnitude of his rage had scared him—still scared him. For those few moments he'd lost control, consumed by fury. Finally Sunny's voice, her gentle voice, urgent but soothing, had penetrated his fiery haze. That had saved him. *She* had saved him.

"Sunny," he said, "I was upset at Ashford for striking you. But if we stood out as different than everybody else, it was my anger, not your . . . charity."

Sunny pressed against his back and tightened her arms linked around him under Dawn's sling. "Maybe we can't help being a bit different," she said in a hesitant voice for his ears only. "I mean, you and me have lived different lives than most around here . . ." Her voice trailed off.

He pressed a hand over hers for a moment to show he understood. His tongue tied again, he couldn't speak more. They rode unflinchingly through town, mostly deserted today. As if nothing was wrong, he doffed his hat at a woman coming out of the store and Sunny called out a friendly greeting.

When they put town behind them, Noah breathed easier but the thought of trying to find the Indian woman tightened his nerves—for many reasons.

They covered the remaining miles northward along the Mississippi till they reached the mouth of the Chippewa, flowing into the wide blue. Then they turned their backs to the big river and started eastward. Noah thought of the hungry woman. He'd never known hunger till serving in the army. It gnawed and weakened a person, sharpening every bad feeling.

Much to Noah's relief they'd only ridden a few miles upriver when he saw a thin trail of smoke above the trees. "See," he said to Sunny, pointing to it. "That might be her fire." He urged his mount through the trees toward the smoke,

174

hoping their quest had come to an end. They came out of the forest to a tiny rough clearing with the ruin of an old cabin, only half its roof intact.

The little boy stood in the gap where there should have been a door. Upon sight of them he ducked farther inside.

"Don't be afraid!" Sunny called out. "I'm the lady who helped you in town yesterday. My husband and I have come like I promised. Where's your mother?"

The little boy stepped outside. "Please. Come. She has a fever."

Noah slid down and helped Sunny dismount. "Go on."

Sunny hurried inside with Noah bringing up the rear. A low fire burned in the old fireplace and Bid'a ban lay by it, wrapped in a tattered blanket. "I've . . . we've come to help," Sunny said simply, and knelt down by the woman.

With a soft exclamation Bid'a ban turned to her, looking starved and wan.

Sunny felt her forehead and then looked up at Noah. "She is feverish. I'll need to make her some willow tea and something to eat." She patted the woman's arm. "Don't worry now. I'll do my best for you."

Bid'a ban gripped her hand weakly and tried to speak but couldn't.

Hurriedly, Noah brought in the saddlebags and lay them on the hard earth floor by his wife.

The woman's sickly pallor drained his relief at finding her. "I'm going to keep Dawn away from the contagion."

"Good." Sunny didn't even glance at him. "But please. I need water."

"I'll get some," the little boy said. He grabbed a water skin hanging by the fire and hurried outside.

Noah followed and watched the boy fill the skin with river water. Dawn had fallen snugly asleep against him. The dilapidated wreck of a cabin, probably built by a fur trapper years and years ago, depressed him. He brooded about Bid'a ban's husband, no doubt buried somewhere far from home.

The boy's father hadn't wanted this for his wife and son. Resolve hardened inside Noah. He couldn't help the thousands of war widows and orphans, but he could help this family—or what remained of it.

The boy hurried past Noah.

"After you take that inside, we're going to gather wood and then fish," Noah said.

"You got a hook and line?" The boy glanced up at him then, his eyes shadowed with fear.

"Always." He remembered to smile as he followed toward the door. "Don't you worry. My wife is good at nursing people to health." He didn't know where this assurance had come from, but Sunny had shown herself to be wise in many ways.

The boy came outside. Noah offered his hand. "I'm Noah Whitmore."

"I'm Miigwans." He put out his small hand, trusting Noah's larger one.

Noah gripped it, letting the boy feel his support. Standing just outside the doorway, Noah watched Sunny quickly fill the trivet pot they'd brought. She set it in the fire to heat.

The woman seemed even weaker than yesterday. She barely made a sound or said a word. Sunny bathed her face with water.

Noah hoped the woman wasn't as close to death as she appeared from her sunken eyes. But he could do nothing for her just standing here.

He forced himself to speak without betraying worry. "Miigwans, let's find us a willow branch for a fishing pole." The two headed for the riverbank, thick with black willow trees. "Your mother is in good hands."

The boy reluctantly walked beside Noah, looking back at the cabin. Noah gripped the boy's shoulder, encouraging him. "We're here. Don't worry." He knew he was saying it as much for himself as the boy.

The long chilly night had ended. Sunny's knees ached from kneeling on the cold hard earth beside Bid'a ban. Had her help come soon enough for this woman? Would she recover fully from this fever?

In the thin light of morning falling on them from the open roof, Sunny gazed at Noah. Sound asleep, he rested back against the wall, his long legs stretched out in front of him. Dawn slept on his chest in the sling that he still wore. And opposite Dawn, Miigwans rested his head on Noah's belly, one arm thrown over him.

This sight told her everything about her husband. Once again she suppressed the physical pull toward him. *Lord, You gave me a good man.*

"Sunny?" Bid'a ban said, her voice a thread.

Sunny glanced down. "Good morning." With an encouraging smile, she rested her wrist on the woman's forehead. "Your fever broke early this morning."

"I feel so weak."

Sunny forced the worry from her voice. "That's the fever's work. But we'll get you back to health soon." Sunny knew that fevers that might not kill could still weaken a heart, a life. She prayed that wouldn't be the case with this brave woman.

"Her fever broke?" Noah asked softly.

Sunny had a hard time holding in her gratitude toward him. Pressing down the words she wanted to say, she merely nodded.

"Let's have some of that oatmeal then and head home."

Oh, no, she couldn't leave yet. "Noah, I can't—"

"We'll *all* go home. We can't leave them here like this." Noah addressed Bid'a ban. "Ma'am,

178

you and your boy will come home with us. You need to get your strength back and we need to write the government about your widow's pension."

Bid'a ban began to weep.

Sunny understood. They were tears of relief. She patted the woman's shoulder. "Don't worry any more. My Noah will see that you get what's coming to you."

"I will," Noah promised.

Suddenly Sunny realized a plain, simple, lovely truth: she had fallen in love with her husband.

If only he loved her back.

Dread pooled in Sunny's middle. Just ahead lay town. And they must ride through it. The dense forest away from the flats of the Mississippi shore made travel too difficult. She and Bid'a ban rode on the horse. Noah had strapped the weak woman to Sunny so she wouldn't fall off. Miigwans walked beside Noah, who still carried Dawn in the sling. Her sweet daughter prattled happily, occasionally playing patty-cake to make Noah smile.

Sleeping nearly outside and not being able to shake out their clothing or even comb their hair—what a sight they would be. And with Bid'a ban and her son with them. Sunny knew the deep prejudice that most whites felt toward Indians.

She braced herself and lifted her chin higher.

They entered town. And only then did Sunny

remember that it was Sunday. Her stomach sank to her knees. Nearly the whole community had gathered in front of Ashford's store. And nearly the whole community turned to gawk at them. Sunny refused to bow her head. Stolidly she gazed at the faces turned toward her as if she weren't doing anything unusual.

"Morning, Mr. and Mrs. Whitmore!" Old Saul called out from Ashford's porch.

Noah doffed his hat but kept moving. Sunny nodded, acknowledging the older man's greeting. But they didn't pause. No one else said a word. Not even Gordy, there without Nan who was still lying in. That cut deep.

Well, they'd done it now. Nothing could have made them stand out more than what they'd just done. But Sunny couldn't feel any dismay. And Noah looked determined in spite of it all. They might be outcasts from now on, but she couldn't have stayed home and done nothing.

She—*they*—had done the right thing.

The next afternoon Noah heard the sound of a wagon coming close. Miigwans was helping him finish the spring house. After their parade through town during Sunday meeting, Noah couldn't guess who was coming or what to expect. Then he saw Old Saul driving into the clearing.

"That old man was in town yesterday," Miigwans said.

Who had Miigwans thought was coming? "Yes, he's the preacher hereabouts. Come on." Noah's strained voice grated his throat. "We need to wash our hands and be polite."

The two of them cleaned up and then Noah grimly strode to the wagon, dreading this visit. *I don't care what he says or what people think.*

Noah took a deep breath and rested a hand on Miigwans's shoulder. "Good day, Preacher."

"Call me Old Saul," the old man said.

After a polite nod, Noah helped him down as he had the last visit.

"Who is this young fellow?"

Noah introduced Miigwans, who was too shy to speak.

"I'm stiff," Old Saul said. "It would be good for me to walk a bit. Show me how you're doing on that spring house."

"Miigwans has been helping me," Noah replied, letting the man lean on his arm. Surely the preacher had heard about the ruckus in town between him and Ashford and he must have come to put his two cents in. Irritation bit and chewed on Noah's mood.

The older man stood by the spring house, nodding with approval. "You've done well. I think I could use a cup of that good spring water of yours. I hear from Lavina you finished that table I saw you making on my last visit."

After fetching the water, Noah led Saul to the

house. The moment had come to introduce him to Bid'a ban. "Sunny, the preacher's here."

"I heard," she replied. "Come in. I have the kettle on and am making fresh coffee."

"Noah's got spring water for me, but after that, a cup of coffee would be welcome, ma'am. And who is this?" he asked, after he crossed the threshold.

Standing beside Bid'a ban, who was lying in bedding near the fire, Sunny performed the introductions. Bid'a ban looked fearful and Noah wondered if she feared white people in general or some in particular.

Old Saul surprised Noah by kneeling beside the woman and taking her hand. "I'm so glad you found the help you needed, ma'am." Then the old preacher said a prayer over her. "Miigwans," he said. "I can get down by myself but I need a hand up."

The little boy hurried to help him to his feet. Noah came, too, in case he was needed. He wanted to thank the old preacher for his prayer and kindness, but words couldn't fit through Noah's tight throat.

Old Saul patted the boy's shoulder. "Thank you, son. Noah, I'll take that cold water now."

Miigwans stayed beside his mother while Noah and Old Saul sat at the table. The older man ran his hand over the tabletop appreciatively. "I heard all about Ashford hitting your wife and then saw you ride through town with Bid'a ban and I figured out what had happened. I came to see if I could help."

This struck Noah completely speechless.

Sunny spoke up. "Noah is going to write to Washington, D.C., for Bid'a ban so she can get her widow's pension. Her husband served with the Union Army."

Old Saul shook his head with evident sorrow. "We lost so many good men. War brings such suffering that words fail me."

Then a familiar voice from outside hailed them, "Hello, the house!"

"It's Martin!" Sunny exclaimed and got up, hurrying toward the door.

Noah and Old Saul trailed after her. Noah glanced at Martin's round, honest face and grinned in spite of himself. The man sat beside a pretty woman and looked about to burst with pride. "Who is this lady with you, Martin?" Noah teased.

"This is my bride, Ophelia Steward. We won't get down. I just wanted Ophelia to see where our closest neighbors live." Then Martin carried out the introductions.

Ophelia was a pretty little thing with curly brown hair and big brown eyes. But if she had aged a day over seventeen Noah would eat his old hat.

Martin waved toward the back of his wagon

where a cow was tied and a noisy crate of chickens sat. "I brought extra chickens to give you and the Osbournes so you'll have eggs. And now we'll have a milk cow, too."

Noah congratulated him and thanked him for his generosity.

"I'll come over and visit as soon as I can," Sunny was saying. "We're so glad you are here. Martin has worked so hard to make a home for you."

Old Saul stepped forward. "We hope to see you this Sunday, weather permitting."

"Yes, sir," Ophelia said, "we'll be there."

"You'll find you have another new neighbor," Noah said.

Martin glanced at him. "Somebody else staked a homestead claim?"

"No, Nan and Gordy have a little girl now."

"Well, that's fine," Martin said, beaming. "We'll go now and meet our newest neighbor." Then the young man's face changed. "Who's that standing in the door?"

Noah braced himself, hoping Martin wouldn't turn against them as Gordy seemed to have done. "Miigwans, come here and meet our neighbors."

The little boy reluctantly came to stand beside Noah.

"He and his mother are staying with us till she feels better." Noah read the shock on both

Martin's and Ophelia's faces as they took in that Miigwans wasn't white.

The newlyweds left soon after this realization. Noah stiffened inside.

"They're young," Old Saul said. "They haven't lived among strangers like you have, Noah."

Noah looked into the wrinkled face. How did this old man sense things, sense Noah's feelings? Then he noticed Saul's fatigue. "Why don't we go inside so you can finish your coffee?"

Old Saul took Noah's arm and the two walked slowly into the cabin. Noah settled him into the rocker and brought his coffee to him.

Sunny looked worried and quickly sliced some corn bread and sprinkled it with sugar for Saul and then gave some to everyone.

"I thank you for that," Old Saul said. "I was feeling down." After he'd finished the snack, he looked at Noah. "Will you help me to my wagon?"

Noah moved to help Saul up, walked him out to the wagon and then boosted him up onto the bench.

Old Saul thanked him. "I can remember being a young sprout like that boy inside. I couldn't sit still and now I'm as creaky as a rusted gate." He shook his head ruefully. "You and Sunny have done right to help this woman and child."

"Most won't like it."

"God loves everyone regardless of their color. Don't let what others think keep you away on Sunday."

Noah didn't think highly of this suggestion. "I'll talk to Sunny."

"Then I know I'll see you on Sunday. You married a strong woman. Pretty, too." He grinned and slapped the reins and soon the old wagon rocked away down the uneven track.

Sunny met Noah outside. "Don't take it so hard. Martin and his bride will come around. And the Osbournes, too. They're good people."

Noah shrugged. "It doesn't matter. We did right. Did what we needed to do."

Sunny leaned forward and rested her head on his chest. "That's right." Then she turned and hurried inside.

Awash in a flow of emotion and sensation, Noah watched her go and watched Miigwans come to him.

"Are we going to work some more?" the boy asked.

Noah ruffled his dark chocolate-colored hair. "Yes. Come on." As he walked toward the spring house, he recalled what Sunny had said to him before about their being different because their lives had been so different. They had that in common, all right. And he went over what Saul had said. He had married a strong woman. And that was right and made him proud.

Noah knew too well how it felt to be rejected for being out of the ordinary. If his neighbors didn't like them taking in these two—so be it.

Sunday morning had come and Noah climbed down the ladder from the loft, hearing the preacher's words repeat in his mind. His nerves churned. But he knew that they had to go to worship.

Sunny had dressed earlier and was fixing breakfast. Now strong enough to sit at the table, Bid'a ban still looked much too thin and frail. Miigwans had become Noah's shadow, trailing him outside where both of them washed their hands and faces.

Back inside Noah sat down. Dawn crawled to him and pulled herself up beside him, baby talking all the while. He tousled her golden curls, marveling at their softness. Then he announced what he'd decided. "Sunny, we'll be going to Sunday meeting today."

Sunny nearly dropped the ladle of oatmeal she held over Bid'a ban's bowl. "We're going?" Her voice quavered.

"Yes, we are. Old Saul asked us specifically to come." Noah didn't know where his forceful spirit had returned from but he was ready and willing to take on the whole town today.

Sunny sat down and gazed at him intently. Then she nodded. "I'm with you."

Bid'a ban looked back and forth between them as if trying to read the veiled tension. She opened her mouth to say something to Sunny, but seemed to change her mind. Again Noah thought she looked afraid.

"What's the Sunday meeting?" Miigwans asked.

"You remember that older man with the white hair that came to visit?"

Miigwans nodded.

"He is a preacher and on Sundays he tells us about God and how we should live."

"Oh," Miigwans said. "Can I go?"

Sunny was trying to hide her worry, but Noah read it clearly. "I think you should stay home and take care of your mother today."

"I will." But the boy had caught the unspoken worry and it showed on his face.

Noah patted his arm. "Everything will be fine." He hoped that would be true.

As they left for the meeting, Noah drove over the uneven track and thought about the unfriendly reception they were likely to receive.

On Thursday he'd walked over to Gordy's to give him his seed and such, and had immediately felt an unusual coolness. Maybe not coolness, but more a wariness. He'd helped Gordy log out his garden but he hadn't been invited inside. And Gordy had said that they would be driving into town on Sunday with Martin and his bride, offering no invitation to join them. Even though he'd expected rejection when he'd decided to keep Bid'a ban, he hadn't expected it from Gordy. He drew in a sharp breath. The memory of the ride through town last Sunday rippled through him. But he'd stood up to his own meeting all those years ago. He couldn't back down now.

Finally they drove out of the trees to the flats at the river and joined the gathering in front of Ashford's store. A few people waved to them but most just stared.

Maybe he shouldn't put Sunny through this.

"Do you want to go home?" he whispered to her.

She looked at him and her eyes blazed, reminding him of how she'd looked when she'd put herself between Ashford and Bid'a ban. "No, we have done nothing wrong. We need to face this head on."

Proud of her, he climbed off the bench and went around to help her down. When he lowered her, he took her by the hand and led her to the out-skirts of the gathering. Sunny looked at him in surprise, then squeezed his hand. No one welcomed them, though Gordy looked worried and shuffled closer to them. Was he coming to back them or cross them?

Old Saul's son drove up and helped the older man down and to the porch. Lavina waved to Sunny and Sunny returned the gesture. Soon the hymn singing had started. Sunny didn't sing as usual and Noah felt a surge of protectiveness for his obviously uncomfortable yet brave wife. Nobody better say anything rude to her.

Old Saul rose, opened the worn Bible and read, " 'Pure religion and undefiled before God and the Father is this, To visit the fatherless and widows in their affliction, and to keep himself unspotted from the world.' St. James tells us this in the first chapter of his book. Last Sunday we witnessed a living example of this when the Whitmores passed through town."

The older man's words seemed to galvanize his hearers. They all stiffened, yet no one turned to look at Noah and Sunny. Dawn's baby talk was the only sound for a few seconds. Noah increased his grip on Sunny's hand. He had a hard time drawing a full breath. Out of the corner of his eye, he noticed someone familiar. It took him a moment to place the man: the stranger who had been lurking at the general store. He stood far back from the crowd, uneasy and edgy. Noah turned his attention back to Saul.

"I visited the Whitmores on Monday and met the Ojibwa widow and her son. The woman is a widow because her husband served in the Union Army and gave his last full measure of devotion for our country. Noah and many of you also served and witnessed the terrible loss of husbands, fathers, brothers and sons."

A few of the men shifted on their feet and then turned and nodded at Noah who returned the same to them. The tight band around his lungs loosened a notch.

"Mr. Whitmore," Old Saul continued, "is going to write to the government—"

"I have already written to the War Department," Noah declared. He drew the letter from his pocket. "Need to leave this with Mr. Ashford to go out on the next mail boat. The widow and her boy should be getting a pension. They will be staying with us till we get papers from Washington, D.C. Then she wants to go to her people in the lakes area farther north and east." *Let anybody try to fight me about this.*

"We'd appreciate prayer," Sunny requested then. "We'd like her to be able to go north before winter and you know how slow government is about matters."

Rueful laughter agreed to this. Leave it to Sunny to sweeten up people. He smiled down at her in appreciation.

Old Saul grinned, too. "Now I hope you will all pray for the Ojibwa woman and her son and for all the widows and orphans left by the war. Lavina, I need to sit down. Will you start the next hymn?"

At the end of worship some people came to Noah and Sunny, but many kept their distance. Men who'd also served in the army gathered around the Whitmores, offering their help. Noah forced himself to accept their hands and words, but the looks they'd sent to him and Sunny last week still rankled.

Prejudice against Indians was not going away anytime soon.

Finally Martin and Ophelia came to them with Gordy. "We'll help, too," Gordy said. "We just didn't know what you were doing."

"Well, now you know." Noah tried to keep the twist of hurt from his voice, but failed.

Gordy flushed red and looked down.

"Misunderstandings can happen," Ophelia said tactfully. "I'd like to invite you and Nan over for a sewing circle this week, Sunny. Nan's lying in will be over then. From what I've seen of the little boy, he could use some new clothes."

"Thank you," Sunny said. "That would be a help."

As Sunny and Noah made their way to their wagon, Noah remembered the stranger, and took a look over his shoulder. The man stood apart, watching Noah and Sunny carefully. Noah's instincts told him the man was up to no good. After he helped Sunny into the wagon, he looked back again. But the man was nowhere to be seen.

Noah kept his observations to himself.

On Monday in midafternoon Sunny walked toward Martin's house. She carried Dawn on her right hip and her sewing basket on her left elbow. Today would be the first day she'd faced people without Noah beside her since the scene in town.

Once again Noah had shown everyone his regard for her and he'd stood up to everyone. She let pride in him flow through her.

The month of May had proved to be changeable just like the people in Wisconsin. Today was overcast and a cool wind blew in from the west. Sunny wondered when summer would arrive and what a Wisconsin summer would be like—more like Idaho or Pennsylvania?

Ahead through the trees Sunny glimpsed the smoke from Martin's cabin. Would Ophelia prove to be a friend? Sunny had grown up with real friends. To the women who lived their lives above a saloon, friendship meant a lot. They depended on each other because they had no one else. Did friendship mean as much to women who had husbands and families?

Before she'd reached the cabin, she heard Nan call her name. Sunny paused, letting Nan catch up, her heart beating fast.

"Gordy and I are right sorry he didn't come straight over and see what was going on at your place," Nan said. "In town he heard *such talk—* about Noah beating up Mr. Ashford and Indians coming back hereabouts. We should have known Noah and you would only do what's right."

Sunny didn't know how to respond to this.

"Didn't you bring the Indian woman with you today?" Nan asked in her unabashed way.

"She is still too weak to walk far and is very

shy," Sunny said while beginning to walk toward the door.

Nan grasped her arm, stopping her. "Please say you forgive us, Sunny. And I'll never doubt you and yours again. I promise."

Sunny gazed up into Nan's plump, honest face. From the Sunday before last, the humiliation of the ride through town—unkempt and with Bid'a ban tied to her—snared her. What it would have meant to her that first Sunday if Gordy had stepped out from the crowd and asked if they needed anything.

Nan bowed her head, her little one in her arms whimpering.

Who am I to stand in judgment of anyone? "Of course, Nan. Forgiven. Forgotten."

"You were so good to me when Pearl Louise was coming," Nan said with a sad smile.

Sunny put one arm around her friend. "I'm glad to see you're up and around. Now we best get to the door. If Ophelia is peeking out the window, she'll think we're gossiping about her."

Nan nodded, but momentarily pressed a cheek against Sunny's. Then the two walked toward the cabin.

"Hello, the house!" Nan called out in her normally cheery voice.

Ophelia opened the door and burst into tears.

Sunny and Nan exchanged glances and hurried forward.

Chapter Ten

Several minutes passed before Sunny and Nan could calm Ophelia enough to make sense of what she was saying in the midst of her sobs. Nan laid her baby girl on the bed in the corner to nap and they set the two toddlers on the floor to play. Finally they all sat on a bench at the table—Sunny on one side of the bride and Nan on the other. Then they were able to staunch the tears.

"Now you can tell me and Sunny anythin'," Nan said. "We don't gossip and we want the best for you and Martin."

"Yes, that's right," Sunny agreed, patting Ophelia's arm.

"I just didn't know . . ." Ophelia inhaled deeply and wiped her eyes with a frilly hankie. "I didn't know I'd miss my family so much."

"Ah, homesickness," Nan said knowingly. "It is hard leaving home for the first time."

Ophelia nodded forlornly.

"But it will pass," Nan said. "Won't it, Sunny?"

The question rattled Sunny. She could not remember ever being homesick. One had to have a home in the first place and she'd never had one. Until now. But homesickness might be something like the mourning she'd felt after her mother had died. Maybe someone homesick missed the people, not the home. "Everything in this life passes," Sunny said truthfully.

Over the bride's head Nan lifted an eyebrow at her, but went on soothing the girl. "Now the secret to getting through homesickness is keeping busy. How about we start sewing?"

Ophelia nodded glumly. The women opened their sewing baskets.

"I brought fabric," Sunny said. "Miigwans needs a new pair of pants. His are about worn through. I chalked a rough pattern from his old pair onto this cloth." She rose and smoothed the heavy brown broadcloth out on the tabletop. "Does this look right, Nan? Ophelia? I've never made boy's pants before."

"I have two little brothers." And then the bride burst into tears again.

Sunny and Nan exchanged looks. Not much sewing would be accomplished today, it seemed.

"I'm sorry," Ophelia sniffled.

"Why don't you tell us about it?" Sunny asked, sitting down again. Perhaps the girl just needed to talk it out.

"It's just that everything is so different here." Ophelia waved her hands. "I've never lived out of town before."

"You're a town girl?" Nan commented, sounding intrigued.

"Yes, I lived in Galena. It's much smaller now that the mining has gone down, but I'm not used to being where there are no streetlamps at night or paved streets."

"I've never lived in a big town," Sunny said, and then stopped herself before revealing more. The old fear of exposure tugged at her as she noted how much more stylish Ophelia's dress was than either hers or Nan's.

"Me, neither," Nan said.

"Will this awful emptiness really go away?" the bride asked.

The girl's forlorn tone prompted Sunny to press her hand over hers. "Yes, you will find that Martin becomes your home. I mean, if he's with you then you are home."

The truth of this flooded Sunny. Wherever Noah and Dawn were, that meant home for her. "I felt a bit lonely here at first till I met Caroline and Nan. But now I don't feel so lonely." Sunny decided she better stop talking. Her sympathy might lead her to indiscreet words.

"Mama warned me that it would be hard to live on the frontier," Nan said.

"I know I should be stronger, but . . ." Ophelia looked lost.

"You're young," Sunny said.

"But you'll get older!" Nan added in her usual sassy way.

This forced a trace of a smile from Ophelia. "I

said I wanted to help make clothes for that little Indian boy. So let's do that. Now, I have sewn clothing for my brothers, and we should make a really deep hem because they grow so fast."

Sunny silently sighed with relief. "That makes good sense." Sunny drew out her white tailor chalk and drew the pant legs several inches longer.

"Is it funny having an Indian living with you?" Nan asked. "I mean, how do you understand her?"

Sunny stiffened. "Bid'a ban speaks English and so does her son."

"Really? And she doesn't wear deerskin like I thought Indians wore." Nan folded the fabric in two.

"I haven't asked her about that." That had struck Sunny as unusual, too. Western tribes wore buckskin. She began cutting the fabric along the chalk lines. "Maybe it's because the French lived around here almost two hundred years ago."

Nan looked surprised. "Two hundred years ago?"

"Yes, Noah told me." Sunny felt a touch of pride in Noah's knowledge.

After the pant pieces were cut, the women arranged them together.

"I'll sew one pant leg and you can sit across and sew the other," Ophelia offered.

Finally the time to go home arrived. With Ophelia's help, Sunny nearly had the pants sewn. She'd just need to do some finishing work to them. Nan and the bride had been helpful and Sunny felt almost natural with them again.

"I need a favor," Ophelia said, her eyes downcast.

Caution jabbed Sunny.

"What do you need? We'll help," Nan offered genially as she changed the baby's diaper on the bench.

"I learned to cook and clean, but my mother never let me help with the laundry. She always sent it out to be done." The bride lifted both hands. "But I can't do that here."

Sunny and Nan both stared at the girl momentarily.

"Where did your ma send the laundry to be done?" Nan said as if she didn't quite believe this had happened.

"An Irish woman in town took in laundry," Ophelia replied.

Sunny had sent her laundry to the Chinese in Idaho, but most everyone in town had. "Ophelia," Sunny said, "I'm doing laundry toward the end of the week. You can bring your laundry over and we'll do it together."

Nan and Sunny left with waves and pleasantries. As they were about to part ways, Nan paused. "I'm glad we're not brides. We've learned about being married and know our husbands and are settled."

Pinched by this thought, Sunny tried to look as

if she agreed. She knew now that she'd come to love Noah, but did she know him? Were they settled? Not really.

As Sunny walked home, an idea occurred to her, a wild idea that frightened her almost immediately.

What if I told him? What would Noah Whitmore do if I told him I loved him?

Laundry day dawned bright and balmy. Sunny usually enjoyed the act of cleaning their clothing, making everything fresh and sweet smelling. Would Martin's bride show up? Or decide she didn't really want to come to a house where Indians lived?

Just then Ophelia appeared, trudging up the trail through the trees. Sunny mustered a welcoming smile. The girl must be desperate to learn. *Or perhaps I'm judging her. And wrongly.* "Good morning!"

Ophelia waved. She was half carrying, half dragging a full cloth sack.

Sunny sensed Bid'a ban standing in the doorway. She turned. "Come out, Bid'a ban. Sunshine will be good for you."

The thin woman slipped outside and came near Sunny. "You have a friend come?"

"Yes, she needs to learn how to do laundry."

Bid'a ban looked surprised at this. "I'll go inside."

"No, stay," Sunny murmured. She wasn't going to let her guest be ignored.

Ophelia came close and then halted shyly.

"Ophelia, this is Bid'a ban." She introduced the two as if it were a normal meeting. "Now, Ophelia, have you separated your laundry?"

"What does that mean?" Ophelia asked.

"Spill out your sack and we'll make two piles— one for colored clothing and one for whites. If we mix the two, you will no longer have any whites," Sunny teased.

Ophelia grinned and proceeded to dump the contents of her bag onto the dewy grass. Sunny helped her divide the clothing while Bid'a ban observed. Ophelia kept stealing glances at Bid'a ban as if uncertain of her.

Overlooking this, Sunny showed Ophelia how to shave soap into the deep pot set up outside over a fire. Soon the whites were simmering and Sunny set Ophelia to stir the clothing with a broom handle. The acrid odor of lye hung in the air.

"This is how white women do laundry?" Bid'a ban asked curiously.

"How do Indian women do laundry?" Ophelia asked, sounding interested in spite of herself.

"We take our clothing to the river and lay it on broad river rock and beat it with a stick."

Sunny recalled that she had seen men doing this in a mining camp.

"Why do you heat the water?" Bid'a ban asked, peering into the simmering pot.

"I think it gets the dirt out better. We don't beat it but we do rub places where the dirt is ground in on this." She lifted the washboard that had been leaning against the cabin.

Bid'a ban stroked the rough washboard. "I see." Ophelia glanced over and looked intrigued, too.

Sunny had become used to doing the laundry. The curiosity of the two other women made her reconsider this weekly chore. "Keeping clean is important. It's healthier."

"Mother always said, 'Cleanliness is next to godliness,' " Ophelia added piously.

Bid'a ban stroked the washboard once more with a dubious expression.

Just then Noah came into the clearing from the creek with Dawn in his arms and Miigwans beside him. "We're going to take the oxen over to Gordy's to pull out stumps today."

"Noah says I can go with him, Mother," Miigwans said.

Bid'a ban sent a look of concern toward Noah.

Noah gripped the boy's shoulder. "He'll be fine, Bid'a ban. I want him to learn how to handle a team."

"Please, Mother," Miigwans begged.

Bid'a ban nodded. Noah deposited the sleeping Dawn in her hammock inside and then he hitched the oxen and they were off down the track.

"You have a good man," Bid'a ban murmured.

Sunny nodded, touched by Noah's kindness to the fatherless child. She thought of her idea yesterday, her idea to tell Noah that she loved him. She wasn't sure she was supposed to—was the man supposed to say such things? What if he said he didn't feel that way—what then? Would he leave her?

The sound of a horse coming broke into Sunny's thoughts. A stranger appeared through the trees, riding slowly up the trail to their house. Strangers were such a rarity, a shot of fear jolted through Sunny. "Ophelia, Bid'a ban—come stand behind me. Now." Sunny's voice sharpened. Better safe than sorry.

The two women looked startled. Ophelia scurried to stand behind Sunny, who positioned herself in front of the doorway. Bid'a ban seemed frozen in place for a moment, then she moved behind Sunny as well, hidden from view.

"They told me there was an Indian here," the man said. "Indians aren't allowed here anymore. The government moved them all away to Nebraska." The man's tone was menacing.

Sunny edged backward, nudging the other two women through the door. Her heart thudded, but this was her fight. She must take charge. She studied the man's face so she could identify him. He had dirty blond hair that hung around his shoulders. He sported a mustache, flecked with gray, and his eyes were hooded. He'd tied what looked like a woman's scarf around his neck.

When the other women had taken shelter in the cabin, she reached inside the door. She drew out the loaded rifle that Noah always left there for protection. "You are on my husband's property," Sunny said evenly, quelling her spiking fear. "I think you'd better leave."

The man spit sideways. "I lost my family in Minnesota to Indians in '62."

"You had better leave," Sunny repeated and raised her rifle so it would be easy to take aim and fire. She forced her arms not to show how she shook inside.

"Can you shoot that, woman?" the man sneered.

"Yes." She raised the rifle higher and took aim. Her heart leaped against her breastbone.

Ophelia squealed and ducked lower behind Sunny.

The man stared hard at her. "This isn't over." He spat again as if in contempt.

"Come back when my husband is here," Sunny said, "and it will be over."

"Your husband a tough man?" The stranger turned his horse as if the rifle in her hand didn't bother him.

"He's a Union Army veteran and has the scars to prove it," Sunny said, careful not to let her voice reveal how close to panic she'd come.

"This isn't over," he repeated and then rode away at an insolently slow pace.

Once he disappeared from sight, Sunny backed inside and shut and barred the door. Then she sank onto the rocking chair, trembling all over.

Ophelia sat hunched on the bench by the table as white as paper. "You were so brave."

Sunny could barely nod; she was still shaking.

On the floor, Bid'a ban wept silently, leaning against the wall. "I bring trouble on you."

"No," Sunny said. "He's a man looking for trouble. There are men like him all over." She'd seen his ilk before. Men who rode into a town, aching for a fistfight or gunfight. "They don't need a reason. They just want to shed blood."

"Do you think he'll come back?" Ophelia asked.

"Yes," Sunny said with certainty. She pressed a hand over her heart as if that could calm it. "But my Noah will settle matters with him." And she was positive of that. Noah knew how to fight. He'd survived four years of a bloody war. This stranger didn't know who he'd come up against.

At Gordy's, Noah had set Miigwans on the neck and shoulders of one of the oxen for his safety. The big creatures were docile but their very size caused them to be a danger to a small child. The men had roped the team to a stump and Noah was encouraging them to wrest the stump from the sandy soil.

As soon as Gordy and Martin had seen he'd brought the boy, they'd gotten quiet. Yet they had greeted Miigwans politely. For his part, Miigwans had also become silent and watchful. But Noah had decided since Miigwans had no father, it was best for the boy to be with the men and learn men's work. And Noah thought if these were his friends, they would take the boy in stride—*if* they were his friends.

The stump creaked and groaned as the roots fought to stay in the earth. Then came a cracking sound as when ropes in a high wind snapped. With a groan, the stump sprang free. "Ho!" Noah halted the team.

"Well, that's one down and a many more to go," Gordy said wryly.

"But it has to be done," Martin commented. "I look forward to the day when we'll all have our fields cleared."

Gordy agreed, releasing the ropes from the stump. "We might have to work logging or something to make ends meet."

"I think logging might be a poor choice," Noah said, his arm tingling with remembered pain. "Old Saul said I could work as a stonemason building hearths for people."

"You also know how to make furniture," Martin said, helping Gordy tie the ropes around the next stump. "You're a knowing man. I spent a lot of time reading law."

"You're an edjicated man?" Gordy asked.

Martin nodded, flushing with embarrassment. "Ophelia comes from a prosperous family. Her father is a judge. They didn't like her marrying me and coming to the frontier. But that's what her father did when he was young. Went West and established himself."

From the corner of his eye Noah suddenly caught the sign of movement. He stilled. The likelihood of any wild animal attacking in daylight was scant. He focused and realized it was a dog, crawling on its belly toward them.

"A dog," Miigwans piped up.

The animal crooned pitifully and halted. It had long brown ears, a sleek head of the same brown and a white and speckled body. It looked starved.

"Everyone be quiet. Here, boy," Noah called and held out his hand. "It's okay. We like dogs."

The animal very plainly looked at him, assessing, and then it crawled forward. The clearing had gone absolutely quiet except for the dog's whining and the huffing of the winded oxen. A flash of memory carried Noah back to a battlefield after the cannon had fallen silent— wounded men crawling and begging for help. He stopped his mind there, shaken.

The dog stopped a few feet from Noah, who then knelt on one knee. "Come here, boy." He patted his leg and offered a hand, keeping the past at bay.

The dog crawled slowly, slowly toward the men, still whining piteously, till it reached Noah. It put one paw on Noah's knee. The bloody paw had something embedded in it.

"What happened, boy? Did you run into a porcupine?"

"Be careful, Noah," Gordy cautioned. "He doesn't know you."

"But he is asking for my help." Noah petted the dog's head warily and spoke soothing words to him. When the dog relaxed, Noah drew out his knife. "I'm going to get that out of you now."

With the dog watching his every move, Noah stripped from the quill the barbs that had prevented the dog from working the quill out himself. Then Noah pulled out his handkerchief and grasped the end. "This is going to hurt, boy," he said to the dog.

Gordy took a sharp breath.

The dog stared into Noah's eyes and Noah read the trust and appeal there. He tightened his grip and yanked. The quill came out as the dog yowled with pain and snapped just over Noah's hand. Then the dog immediately began licking the wound.

"You helped him," Miigwans said, rich with feeling. "He's a good dog, isn't he? He didn't bite you."

Noah stroked the dog's head and long ears, his own nerves easing. "Yes, he's a smart dog, too. He knew he needed help. He must have lost his family. Are you lonely, boy?"

Gordy and Martin approached quietly, slowly. "Looks like a hunting dog. They can be worth their weight in gold to a man."

The dog rested its head on Noah's knee for a few seconds as if in thanks.

"Well, he's adopted you, Noah," Martin said. "You're his new master."

Noah knew it was foolish, but a rush of warmth coursed through him. "He'll be a fine dog after I get him cleaned up a bit. Martin, bring me my sack. I'll give him my lunch. He looks starved."

Soon Noah was feeding the dog. It stood and Noah ran his hands over him. "Well, I guess I should be calling you 'girl.' " He felt her bulging abdomen. "And you're full of pups."

"Whoa, that's good. Put me down for one," Gordy said. "Please."

The last word sounded uncertain as if Gordy didn't know if he could ask this of Noah. This told Noah more than anything else could that Gordy felt their estrangement maybe as much as Noah did. "Sure. How about you, Martin?"

"Excellent. I've always had a dog," the younger man replied, sounding touched.

"Can I have one?" Miigwans asked.

"We'll ask your mother. And we don't know how many she'll have or if they'll all be healthy." Noah watched both Gordy and Martin lean forward to pet the stray. Then Miigwans ventured to touch the dog's head. The dog licked the boy's hand.

"She likes me." Miigwans smiled.

"Means she's a good judge of character, son," Gordy said.

Noah's heart warmed toward this man—his friend.

"Ninga wegimind! My mother!" Miigwans shouted as he ran ahead of the oxen into Noah's clearing where the clotheslines sagged with clothing. "We have a dog!"

Noah and Martin walked beside the oxen and exchanged grins at the boy's exuberance.

Sunny raced out of the cabin and straight to Noah. She flung her arms around his chest. "Oh, I'm so glad you're home." Her voice vibrated with fear.

Noah dropped the oxen leads and wrapped his arms around her as she shivered against him. "What's happened?" he said, his voice sharp.

"A man came and threatened us," Ophelia said, running to Martin. "I've been so frightened. I couldn't walk home without an escort. Oh, Martin, he threatened us and Sunny aimed a rifle at him."

Shock shot through Noah in barbed waves, followed by hot rage. "A man? Threatened you?"

Sunny drew in a deep breath and looked up at

him. "I'm glad you always leave a loaded rifle inside the door. I think that's the only reason he backed off."

"But why did he threaten you?" Noah asked, gripping Sunny's elbows. Anger leaped inside him like flames.

"Because of me," Bid'a ban said from the doorway. "He came to get me."

"Why?" Martin asked.

Bid'a ban's eyes filled with tears and she seemed unable to answer.

"He said that Indians aren't supposed to be here," Ophelia said, then lowered her eyes and voice. "He said that he'd lost his family in the trouble in '62."

"What trouble?" Noah asked, trying to control his white-hot anger. He'd been too busy in 1862 just trying to stay alive to catch much news.

"The Dakota tried to push the whites out of Minnesota. Many whites and Dakota died," Bid'a ban said. "I'm not Dakota. My people have lived in peace with the whites for a long time. I should have stayed in Lac du Flambeau with my people, not come south. All I have gotten is trouble here."

Noah tried to absorb all this information. But the main point was that a stranger had come and threatened his wife. He held Sunny close, feeling her softness against him, feeling her fear. "Describe him to me." *I will find him and teach him to leave my family alone.*

As Sunny told Noah what the man looked like, Noah immediately thought of the stranger he'd seen lingering in town, staring at them.

He looked at Bid'a ban, who would not meet anyone's eyes.

There was something more to this story than he and Sunny knew.

Chapter Eleven

Distracted with worry, Sunny somehow got herself busy preparing supper. Since Martin had taken Ophelia home, Bid'a ban had remained silent, sitting against the wall near the hearth, looking crushed. Sunny tried not to look at the rifle, propped again by the door. Perversely her eyes insisted on drifting toward it, prompting her heart to race—just as it had when she'd confronted the stranger. What would happen now? Would the stranger return?

Noah sat in the rocking chair, brooding. The dog he'd brought home lay in front of the door, tracking Noah with its soulful brown eyes. Sunny had bathed the dog's paw with salt water to help it heal and then fed her some leftover corn bread. Even Dawn appeared to have absorbed everyone's pensive mood. As usual, she'd pulled herself up at Noah's knee. But instead of filling the cabin with her baby talk, she merely gazed up at him.

Sunny wished she could break the heavy silence. But she could think of nothing to say that wouldn't make Noah feel worse—no doubt he was upset that he'd been away when trouble came to their door. But as soon as Noah had come home, she'd felt instantly safe. Should she tell him that?

Stopping herself from adding salt to the pot a second time, she sighed. "Let's eat, even if we don't have much of an appetite." The four of them gathered at the table. Noah said grace and they began eating, still in melancholy silence.

Finally Noah looked across the table to Bid'a ban. "What did bring you so far south from home?"

Sunny wondered at his question.

The woman looked distressed. "My husband was Ho-Chunk. The whites call them Winnebago. His people lived near here. He came north to work logging. We married. After he died, I thought I should visit his mother. But I arrived at the wrong time." She put an arm around her son. "The soldiers came and made the Ho-Chunk leave, go to Nebraska."

"Nebraska?" Sunny echoed. "Why so far?"

"When the Western tribes cause trouble, we all suffer." Bid'a ban looked down. "I could not persuade the soldiers I was Ojibwa and should go north, go home. When we went south through

Iowa, my husband's mother died. I buried her. Then we slipped away. You see I dress like a white woman. With my bonnet, no one could see I wasn't white. I put a hat on Miigwans and we slipped away."

Sunny read between the lines—the injustice, the outrage, the helplessness of being swept up in something like this, something like an avalanche she had witnessed in Idaho. Sunny knew how being overpowered by life felt. She reached across and patted Bid'a ban's hand.

"Have you ever seen that stranger before, Bid'a ban?" Noah asked.

At first Bid'a ban didn't answer Noah, and Sunny was upset with him for asking such a question. But the silence was heavy as they waited to hear what she'd say, and Sunny began to wonder if Noah was right to ask her such a thing. Finally Bid'a ban looked Noah in the eye and said, "I know him."

Sunny was stunned. "How, Bid'a ban?"

"When I reached Wisconsin, my bonnet did not fool him. He knew what I was. He knew I couldn't ask others for help. I had to . . . live with him."

Sunny felt sick to her stomach. She understood exactly what Bid'a ban wasn't saying. They were more alike than Bid'a ban would ever know.

"Was he lying when he said his family had been killed by Indians?" Noah asked.

"All I can say is that he is a man who hates

Indians. All Indians," Bid'a ban said, her voice barely more than a whisper.

Sunny read more than the words. The man had abused Bid'a ban and terrified her. This woman had fled just as Sunny had when she went to the Gabriels. Sunny swallowed down her own memories. "You will stay here with us, Bid'a ban. You will stay here until we know you and Miigwans are safe."

Noah looked sharply at Sunny, causing her face to burn. Had she said something wrong? Surely Noah agreed with her—didn't he?

Bid'a ban glanced at Noah, looking both afraid and resentful.

Sunny didn't blame her. She fought the fear that whispered up her spine. *I'm not alone and neither are you, Bid'a ban.*

After supper Bid'a ban sat by the fire, sewing the final details on Miigwans's new pants. Sunny tried to do some mending but her needle kept poking her. Noah and the boy led the dog to the creek to take a bath with them. When the three returned, the dog hesitated at the door. Noah beckoned her in by the fire.

Noah's adopting the stray didn't surprise Sunny. She watched him stroke the dog and speak to it softly. She felt her love for him rise up inside her again.

"We should name her," Miigwans said.

Bid'a ban scolded him in their language.

"I mean *you* should name her," the chastened boy amended.

Noah ruffled Miigwans's hair. "What do you think we should name her?"

"She's awful pretty," the boy said, petting the dog.

"It is time to sleep," Bid'a ban said abruptly. "Can the dog get a name tomorrow?"

"Fine," Noah assented and led the dog to lie in front of the door. "I think it would be best if we all remained dressed tonight."

Sunny paused in putting Dawn in her hammock, anxiety bringing up gooseflesh on her arms. Noah meant trouble might come in the night. She looked at Noah. But he was busy barring the door and securing the shutters from inside.

Bid'a ban came close to her and whispered, "I am better now. You should go back to your man." She motioned toward the loft. "You belong there."

The suggestion hit Sunny, completely unexpected. She couldn't think of a word to say, a word she *could* say. She looked to Noah, knowing that if she hesitated to do what Bid'a ban suggested, Noah would be cast in a strange light.

"Thank you, Bid'a ban," Noah said. Then he motioned for Sunny to precede him up the ladder while he received her blankets from Bid'a ban.

Sunny felt as if she were on stage and a host of onlookers ogled her as she climbed the ladder to the loft, the loft where she had only ventured once before when Noah was in the cabin. Being up here alone with Noah would only sharpen her shame over his rejection of her. She swallowed hard, keeping her emotions in check.

Noah came up the ladder and offered her the blankets.

She busied herself arranging them several feet from his bedding. "I'm sorry," she whispered lamely.

"Sunny," Noah said in a low voice, "Bid'a ban cannot stay here long."

"But, Noah—"

"That is final. We will help her as best we can, but she cannot stay here indefinitely."

"But she needs our help, Noah!" She spoke in a heated whisper.

"It is not safe for you, or for Dawn or for the other women and children who live nearby. We don't know what he might do to force us to give her up."

"You don't understand what Bid'a ban's been through. You cannot put her out. She's in danger. He'll find her and hurt her."

Noah gazed into her eyes. "I know that."

Sunny waited for him to go on. In vain.

"Good night, Sunny." Noah wrapped himself in his blankets and turned his back to her.

Tears moistened her eyes as she loosened her clothing and settled herself in her bedding. The soft wool blanket muffled her weeping. She hadn't felt this lonely since the night her mother had died.

The next morning Noah had planned to meet up with the other men at Gordy's, but he didn't think he should leave the women and children alone. He lifted his coffee cup and gazed at Sunny. He noticed that she was looking everywhere but at him. Was she upset by their conversation last night? Or by having to sleep in the loft with him?

He'd awakened several times as if aware—even in sleep—of her presence. He'd found listening to her breathing a soothing sound. But having her so close merely sharpened to a razor-edge his failure to perform as a husband. Well, there was one way in which he could not fail her: keeping her safe from harm.

But how could he do that if Bid'a ban still lived with them?

He considered how many weeks a letter could take to arrive in Washington, D.C. He concluded if they were lucky, the War Department would reply by snowfall. Conceivably, Bid'a ban and her son might need somewhere to stay till next spring. Two more mouths to feed and a long winter ahead. "Bid'a ban," he began.

Sunny lifted her eyes to Noah as if suspicious of anything he said to Bid'a ban.

Before he could go on, the dog by the door interrupted, barking.

"Hello, the house!" Gordy's voice rang out.

"Quiet, girl. It's a friend." Maybe Gordy had come to help. Noah rose quickly and opened the door. Growling low, the dog came to his side as if ready to defend against the intruder.

"I thought I was supposed to come to your place today," Noah said.

Stepping inside, Gordy looked pained. And for the first time he carried a rifle to their door. "Martin brought his wife over early this morning and told me what happened here yesterday. We think the women should all come with you to our place today. Shouldn't be left alone."

Noah faced Gordy. The younger man looked uncharacteristically stern. Noah felt his own face harden into harsh lines. "I think that makes good sense."

"Any man who will threaten decent women on their own land is trouble. Can't be trusted to act normal."

Noah frowned at Gordy and gave the tiniest shake of his head. He didn't want Gordy frightening the women any further.

Gordy nodded a fraction, letting Noah know he understood.

"Sunny," Noah said, "I'll do the outside chores while you and Bid'a ban get ready to spend the day at the Osbournes'." This solved the problem of how to protect the women today, but this crisis demanded a permanent solution. Just how *permanent* a solution this stranger would make necessary remained to be seen.

Sunny came close to Noah. He walked outside and waited for her. Gordy politely remained inside. Beside Noah, Sunny stood on tiptoe. "Thank you for not putting Bid'a ban out today."

Noah looked shocked. "I never meant to. How could you think that?"

Sunny felt helpless to explain. "You wouldn't answer me last night. What are we going to do?"

"I don't know. But something will occur to us. I can't believe you thought I'd knowingly let any man take advantage of a woman."

She recalled how he'd confronted that awful man on the main street that day he returned to Pennsylvania. She tried to form words to let him know how much his helping Bid'a ban meant to her. But she merely touched his cheek and then hurried back inside to prepare for the day away from home.

A little over an hour later, Noah, Gordy and Martin stood in a tight circle, contemplating Gordy's garden of stumps. Noah had set Miigwans to stay in front of Gordy's cabin with the dog to sound the alarm if the stranger came back. The little boy had looked determined to protect his mother.

Now Noah's real intent was to discuss privately with his two neighbors what he planned to do.

And the last of his doubts as to whether they were friends or not had vanished with one look at their faces when he'd explained exactly what had happened, and who the man was. Their expressions had said clearly that the threat to Noah and his family was deemed a threat to them all.

"So what's the plan?" Gordy asked, his rifle on a strap slung over his back.

"I'm going into town to see if I can find the stranger. Sunny described him in detail to me. I'm going to *persuade* him to leave us alone," Noah said.

"How're you going to do that?" Martin asked, gripping his rifle with white knuckles.

"I'll start with words," Noah replied, his lungs constricting. He breathed deeply, trying to loosen the tension.

Gordy nodded. "I'm comin' with you."

"Me, too," Martin said. A heron squawked from the creek over the hill.

"No." Noah stepped back from them. "I don't want to leave the women alone."

"I see," Gordy said, folding his arms. "Well, then one of us should stay here with the women and the other two should go into town and see if the stranger has cleared out. Or not."

Noah held up a forestalling hand. "I can handle this—"

"No," Martin said, edging forward. "You're not doing this alone."

Noah stared at them and realized they were dead serious. "All right. Martin, will you stay behind and guard the women and children?"

"I will." Martin looked determined.

"So we'll just ride to town to mail a few letters Nan and me wrote to family," Gordy said with false nonchalance, the tacit understanding in his stance that this is what they'd tell the women so as not to worry them.

Like a bow string at the ready, anxiety tautened within Noah. He'd been called to arms again.

Noah and Gordy rode through the forest, approaching town. He couldn't get out of his mind the look on Sunny's face as they'd left. He'd seen fear in her eyes. But something else was there, too. Admiration. Gratitude. It warmed him. She'd merely whispered in his ear, "Be safe." But he would do what it took to protect his family.

Would that mean adding another killing to his soul? A weight settled over his heart.

"I been in something like this before," Gordy spoke up from behind Noah.

"Oh?"

"A gang of thieves set up in our county. We didn't have no law nearby, either. Finally they . . . hurt a woman . . . bad."

Noah understood the implication and his own resolve to settle this intensified.

"So the decent men got together and one night

ambushed them. I was just sixteen and scared stiff."

"Did you get the job done?" Two crows landed in a tree overhead, complaining stridently about something.

"Yes."

Lord, help me run the man out of town, nothing more.

When they rode into town, the dirt street along the river appeared as usual, nearly empty.

"Where do you think we can find him?" Gordy asked.

"We'll ask Ashford. He doesn't miss much."

"Doesn't miss anything," Gordy added with a hint of amusement.

The two dismounted, hitched their horses and entered the store. Ashford looked up warily. "Hello, what can I do for you gents?"

"We're looking for a stranger," Noah said, focused, intent. "He's got longish dark blond hair, a mustache and wears a woman's scarf around his neck."

"I've seen him all right." The storekeeper's tone announced his low opinion of the stranger loud and clear. "He rode into town a few days ago and spends most of his time at the saloon. Came in here once to buy tobacco. Didn't have much to say about himself." Ashford paused. "But he asked me about that Indian woman you have at your place. He'd heard about her, I guess."

Noah stilled. He refused to ask Ashford what he'd told the man.

"That stranger came out to Noah's place and threatened his wife," Gordy said.

Ashford's face expanded with shock. "That's not called for. A man threatening a decent woman? We can't have that."

"That's why we're here," Gordy said.

Noah turned, heading for the door. "Thanks, Ashford. We'll see if he's at the saloon." As he and Gordy marched down the street, he heard Ashford's door slam again. Behind them Ashford had taken off running to another store.

Noah's gut constricted as it always did before a fight. But he wouldn't stop till he'd settled this threat. Sunny wasn't going to live in fear. He couldn't do everything a husband should do for a wife, but he would protect her and Dawn.

Noah pushed through the doors into the nearly empty saloon. He spotted the man sitting alone at a table in the back, shuffling cards. Sunny's description fit him perfectly. "Let me handle this," Noah muttered to Gordy who nodded but stayed by his side.

The two of them went straight to the man. "You trespassed on my land yesterday," Noah said, staring hard into the man's eyes. "I've come to tell you not to come near my place or mine again."

The man's face sneered. "I came for the Indian—"

So much for words. Noah upended the table toward the man with a crash.

The bartender shouted. The stranger leaped up, face fiery red. He reached for a gun on his side.

Striking his hand away, Noah grabbed the man's collar and yanked him around the table. He flung him back against the bar, grabbed the man's gun and tossed it to the barkeep, who caught it.

As Noah fended off the man's every attempt to get past his guard, he said, punctuating each movement with a word, "You-are-going-to-leave-town. Now."

"I'm going to get my Indian!" the man roared.

"No, you're not." A voice from the door startled Noah but he didn't need to look around. It was Ashford. The stranger's face drained of color. Now Noah stepped back and glanced over his shoulder.

Ashford and a few other men he recognized stood in the doorway. Each one carried a rifle or a club.

"We don't want your kind in our town," Ashford ordered, slapping his club in one palm. "Not a man who threatens a decent woman on her husband's land. Now clear out. All of us know what you look like and we can describe you to the county sheriff. Clear out."

The man looked cowed. He reached for his gun only to remember he didn't have it. The barkeep emptied the chambers and then handed it to him. The man let loose some choice words and bumped into Noah on purpose but kept on moving. All the men followed him outside and watched him get on his horse and ride north, away from town.

Noah tried to take in what had just happened. He couldn't find his voice. He'd put himself in the line of fire again and hadn't flinched. Sudden relief loosed through him.

"Well, thanks a lot," Gordy said to the men. "I think Noah was quite able to run the trouble-maker out—"

"I got the other men in town to come, too," Ashford spoke up. "We wanted to make it clear that it wasn't just you and Whitmore that wanted him gone. We got a peaceable town here and we don't need his sort."

Noah nodded. A powerful reaction he couldn't describe flowed through him. "Thanks" was all he could say.

That night Sunny settled Dawn in her hammock and looked up into the loft, her stomach tying and retying itself into knots.

"Good night," Bid'a ban said, tucking Miigwans in beside her on the floor.

Sunny returned the same wish. Her relief over the stranger leaving town had been tempered by the worry that he might not have gone for good. That question just wouldn't leave her alone.

The still-nameless dog lay against the barred door. Sunny walked over and stroked the dog's head. She appreciated having her. If anybody approached by stealth in the night, she would sound the alarm.

Noah had preceded Sunny up into the loft. When she climbed up near him, she found him lying on his side. He didn't look away.

She must voice her concern even though he might not like it. Kneeling beside him and bending close, she whispered, "Do you think that stranger really left for good?"

Noah leaned up on one elbow. "I don't know. But the fact that more than just Gordy and me came against him might make him realize it's not worth the trouble. Starting a fight with one man is different than taking on a whole town."

"None of them would have stood up for Bid'a ban if you hadn't first," she said, her voice low yet strong.

"I'm no hero, Sunny. You've heard me. I have nightmares like a scared kid."

His tone so filled with anger at himself hurt her and made her brave. "You dream about the war, don't you?"

He didn't answer.

She wouldn't give up this time. "It's the war, isn't it?"

"Yes." The one word sounded dragged from deep inside him.

Longing to touch him, show him comfort, strangled her. "I don't know how you did it, how you faced death over and over." *Noah, please talk to me, let it out.*

"I couldn't talk about it—when I came home. I was just supposed to forget it. But some things a man can't forget."

Sunny inched closer to him, encouraging him to trust her.

"The first battle, I just froze. I should have died, but an older man shoved me behind a tree and told me to get myself under control."

"I'm glad you didn't die," she said simply.

And then something wonderful happened.

Noah opened his arms and drew her close. "Don't worry about that stranger," he whispered close to her ear. "I won't ever let anyone hurt you or Dawn. You know that, right?" He rubbed her back tentatively.

She nodded against his chest, nearly afraid to inhale, not wanting to break this connection as delicate as a breath. For several moments he held her and then he kissed her forehead. "Now go to sleep. You're safe."

She moved away from him with reluctance. As she lay on her back, looking at the darkness, she savored the fact that Noah had held her for the first time, and kissed her and spoken of his nightmares. She could find hope for their future based on these small acts. Maybe there would come a day when they truly would be as normal as their friends believed them to be.

●●●

The next day was even warmer than the day before. With Miigwans and the dog at his side Noah stood at the edge of his clearing, looking things over, dismissing yesterday's drama from his mind. Still his rifle rested against the nearest tree, close at hand.

His cabin and spring house stood against the clear sky and leafy trees, well built to last. But he needed a barn before winter. When he'd visited this area in March, the snow had been deep and the wind bitter. His oxen and his horse would need more shelter—the lean-to just kept the rain off them. And he wanted to get more chickens and a cow of his own, or a goat. Dawn would need milk when she stopped nursing.

"I've been thinking of names for your dog," Miigwans said.

"What have you come up with?"

Noah considered whether he'd have to clear more trees before building a barn. He'd want a big sturdy one, so it would do them for years.

"We could call her friend. In our language, that's *Neechee.*"

Noah looked down at the boy and tried to read his expression. This wasn't just about a dog.

"If we named the dog a word from my language, when you say her name, you would remember me." The boy looked down.

Touched, Noah stooped to be at eye level with

him. "*Neechee?* That will be a good name for her. And, Miigwans, I will remember you. I am your *Neechee.*"

Miigwans looked up and grinned shyly.

The dog barked an alert, looking behind them toward the track. Noah petted the dog and silenced her. He reached for his rifle.

The jingle of a harness and the creaking of a wagon sounded amid the birdsong. He guessed who was coming and wasn't disappointed when he finally glimpsed the old preacher through the trees. He couldn't figure out what kept bringing Old Saul here. What did he want from them— from Noah?

Nonetheless, soon he was helping the older man down from the wagon. Breathing quickly, Old Saul stopped and looked around. "You've a fine start here. But you need a barn before winter."

Noah chuckled. It sounded rusty, but felt good, too. "I was just thinking the same thing. What can we do for you, sir?"

The older man sent him a reproving look.

"I mean, what can we do for you, *Old Saul*?"

The preacher rested a hand on Miigwans's shoulder. "Is that your dog, son?"

"No, it belongs to Noah. Her name is Neechee. That means friend."

The older man nodded several times. "A good name. Is your mother inside?"

"Yes, *Nimishómiss*, my Grandfather."

"Take me to her." Beaming at the compliment, Old Saul took Miigwans's hand.

The three of them walked to the cabin. Inside, Sunny was kneading dough on the table and Bid'a ban was sewing a shirt for her son.

"Good day, ladies." The old preacher removed his hat and Noah hung it on a peg by the door.

Sunny curtsied but nodded toward her hands, deep in the bread dough. "I have to keep at this, sir."

"Please do. I came because I needed to discuss something with your guest."

"With me?" Bid'a ban looked startled and a little afraid. Her glance darted to Noah and Sunny, and back to the preacher.

"Yes." Old Saul accepted Noah's polite gesture and sat in the rocking chair while Miigwans sat near the door with Neechee.

Noah stood, his back against the wall, curious in spite of himself.

"I heard all about that stranger." The older man looked strained as he spoke to Bid'a ban. "And even though he has evidently left the area, I think it wise that we take further action to protect this woman and her child."

When Bid'a ban could not respond, Noah stepped in.

"What do you propose?" Noah asked.

"At fifteen, my grandson is old enough to offer adequate protection for a woman. I propose that he take our horse and accompany this woman and her child north to her people."

Bid'a ban looked startled. "Take me home?" she managed to say.

"We haven't heard back from Washington yet," Noah pointed out, straightening up.

"That's so. But when you do, my grandson will ride up there and give the letter to Bid'a ban. If I'm right, there will be an Indian agent up north, I think in Bayfield on Lake Superior. Her pension might be conveyed through him."

"There's something you're not telling me," Noah said, the worry from yesterday perched on top of his midsection.

Old Saul nodded. "I've been thinking on this. That stranger can still cause trouble for this woman and child. The Indians in this part of Wisconsin have been sent to Nebraska. If he tells someone in the army that she's here, they could come and take her away. And he wouldn't have to go too far. Fort Snelling in Minnesota is about sixty miles away across the Mississippi."

Bid'a ban gasped.

Noah felt the same lurch inside.

And Miigwans protectively hurried to her side. "No."

"I didn't think of that." Noah chewed his lower lip. "What do you say, Bid'a ban? Would you go north with Old Saul's grandson?"

"Yes! I want to be with my family again." Bid'a

ban stood and bowed with gratitude to Old Saul. "Would your grandson do this?"

"He's old enough to test his wings," Old Saul said. "His parents are some worried about him going so far alone, but he's got to start being a man sometime, no longer a boy. It will do you good and him good. In a few years he might have a wife and child to care for like you, Noah. Better start practicing. People nowadays coddle their young." Old Saul shook his head, frowning.

"*Migwetch.*" Bid'a ban wrung Old Saul's hand. "Thank you." She repeated the words several times, bowing.

"I'm glad you will be reunited with your family." Old Saul patted her shoulder. "Tomorrow my grandson will come to get you."

"We'll have food ready for him to take along," Sunny said.

Noah's gut loosened some. This was for the best. This woman and her son would be much safer among her own people than here.

Old Saul rose with some effort. "I'll be going home then and getting the young man ready for the journey."

With the boy and dog trailing behind, Noah walked Old Saul outside and helped him back onto the wagon. When the older man sat on the bench again, Noah looked up at him. "I hadn't thought about that stranger stirring up more trouble. I'm glad you did."

"I'm glad you helped her." The old man lifted his reins. "She could have died and left that boy an orphan. You're a fine man, Noah Whitmore."

Noah reacted with a sound of derision. "I just want to live my life in peace."

"Peace. Yes, we old soldiers all crave that." Old Saul started his team turning around to go home. "War leaves a mark on a man."

"You mean like Cain?" Noah said, charged with sudden anger at himself, at what he had done. "Marked for killing his brother? I saw that happen—brothers coming face-to-face, one in gray, one in blue." He couldn't go on. The anger left him as quickly as it had come.

The older man paused and stared at him for several moments. "Someday we'll talk about that. But not today. I've got to go home and soothe my daughter-in-law's worries about her 'baby boy' going all the way to Lake Superior on his own."

Still digesting the comment about old soldiers, Noah just raised his hand in farewell. The wagon rocked and creaked its way down the track to the rough road.

Beside him, Miigwans's head hung low.

"Don't you want to go home?" Noah asked.

The boy looked up. "I won't get to see the pups born. I wanted to see Neechee's babies."

Noah pulled the boy into a one-armed hug. "Don't worry. If the pups are strong and there are at least three, I'll send one to you—a girl if I can, so she can have pups, too. Then you can have dogs that remind you of Neechee and me."

Noah let the boy lean into him for a moment. His father had always pushed him away. He vowed he would never do that to a child.

From the doorway Dawn called to Noah in her baby talk, cheering him up as always. He scooped up Miigwans and tossed him into the air and caught him. The boy squealed with laughter. And a grin won over Noah's face. Then Noah ran to Dawn, set down Miigwans and lifted her with both hands, jiggling her and making her laugh, too.

Sunny watched him from just inside. The tenderness in her gaze was directed to him, not Dawn. A frisson of awareness vibrated between them, wonderful yet terrifying.

Chapter Twelve

"I don't know why that old man is showing us kindness," Bid'a ban murmured to Sunny that evening. They were washing the dishes from supper alone in front of the cabin.

Sunny had wondered why Bid'a ban had remained so silent ever since Old Saul had left. "He's a good man."

Bid'a ban nodded, drying a bowl and then setting it on a shelf that Noah had crafted and hung. "Why? What makes one man bad, and another, like your husband, so kind?"

Sunny thought over what she'd learned when her life changed, when she'd gone to live with the Gabriels. She'd asked them why they were willing to help her in spite of the stigma attached to her. They had quoted the Bible, saying they were showing her God's love. How would an Ojibwa woman take that for an answer?

"I think it has to do with God," Sunny ventured.

"You mean *Gitchie Manitou*, the Great Spirit?"

"Do you know about God, Bid'a ban?" Sunny paused in scrubbing the stew pot.

"Who can know Him? His name also means the Great Mystery and he is to us, his children."

God remained a great mystery to her, too. "I don't know much about God. But I have learned that those who love Him, *truly* love Him, show that love to others. That's why Old Saul can be kind."

Sunny recalled that awful day so long ago when the other preacher had chased and beaten her mother. Why hadn't he shown any of God's love that day? Being a preacher evidently didn't prove one knew much of God.

Bid'a ban nodded, looking thoughtful. "At my home a *Zhaagnaash*, a white man, comes to speak to us about the white man's God."

"Does he show love?" Sunny asked.

"Yes, he is kind and helps us."

Sunny's tension eased. "Then listen to him." They finished washing and drying and went inside to put away the clean pot and dishes.

"I will listen to that *Zhaagnaash*," Bid'a ban said.

Sunny wanted to say more, but couldn't find the words. Instead she pressed her cheek to Bid'a ban's and the woman returned the gesture. Sunny realized that she felt differently with Bid'a ban than with her other friends. She didn't have to guard every word from this woman. This woman understood how life could be cruel in the same way that Sunny herself did.

Noah, Miigwans and Dawn came inside and the moment with Bid'a ban ended. Noah sat down on the bench. Neechee lay down across the threshold. Miigwans sat beside her, petting the dog.

Sunny praised God for this sturdy cabin, and for the man who'd built it and who now held her daughter on his knee, playing pony. Bid'a ban sat by the fire and began finishing Miigwans's new shirt. And Sunny began packing food for Bid'a ban's trip, trying not to think of their parting.

The next morning found them outside the cabin early, while dew still wet the grass. Caught between laughter and sorrow, Sunny picked up Dawn and hid behind her daughter. How could she bear to bid her friend goodbye?

Standing opposite her by the wagon, Old Saul, his son and daughter-in-law Lavina waited with Saul's gawky grandsons. The one named Isaiah, who was going with Bid'a ban, held the reins of the packhorse. Noah was securing two sacks of provisions onto the horse's back along with those Isaiah had already packed on.

Finished, Noah crossed to Miigwans who stood with a hand on Neechee's head. When Noah reached Miigwans, the boy swung an arm around Noah's waist. Nearby, his mother hesitated beside Sunny.

Bid'a ban appeared to be experiencing the same crosscurrents of emotions as Sunny. Nevertheless, she held out a hand toward Noah. "I can never thank you enough for what you did for me, *Nin awema*, my brother."

"We were glad to help," Noah said, squeezing and releasing her hand, a trace of a smile flickering on his somber face.

Sunny couldn't stop herself. With Dawn on one hip, she wrapped one arm around Bid'a ban. "I'll miss you," she murmured.

"I will miss you, *Nimissè*, my sister." Bid'a ban pressed her lips together as if holding back tears and stroked Dawn's curls lovingly.

Sunny rubbed the woman's arm. "I know you will be safe with Isaiah." The young man barely sported peach fuzz on his chin but he looked sturdy and sensible. She recalled Ophelia's homesickness. No doubt he'd feel the same distress. But he looked like the kind who would stick to this journey and see it through.

"I think we should be going," Isaiah said, blushing when his voice cracked. "I want to put as many miles behind us as we can before sundown." They would follow the Chippewa River northeast to the Flambeau River, which would lead them onto the Ojibwa land. About a week or so and they would reach Bid'a ban's family.

Bid'a ban motioned, wordlessly prompting Miigwans to come away with her.

The boy buried his face into Noah's shirt.

Sunny ached for the boy who'd found a father for a short time—and was now leaving him.

With an arm around the boy's shoulders, Noah pressed the child close. "You'll be fine. And Isaiah will bring you news of us and maybe a pup sometime before snow. I will miss you, Miigwans." Noah's voice halted, as if he, too, were choking back the sadness of parting.

Sunny moved closer to Noah and hugged Miigwans, who then bent to hug Neechee around the neck. The dog barked once and licked Miigwans's face. The boy rose and went to his mother. Waving a pudgy little hand, Dawn babbled baby talk as if also saying farewell.

"We'll pray once more." Old Saul removed his hat and bowed his head. "God, we know that we are in Your hands. Keep our Isaiah and this lady and her son safe as they travel north. Bring help if they need it and good weather. We thank You, Lord. Amen."

"I will say *Gigawabamin Menawah*. That means we will meet again," Bid'a ban said, lifting her hand in farewell. Miigwans echoed her greeting, hanging his head.

Sunny sucked in air, not wanting to cry.

As Isaiah's mother wiped away tears, the threesome—Isaiah leading the packhorse, Bid'a ban with Miigwans nearby—turned and walked down the trail.

"I'm sure they'll be fine," Sunny murmured to Lavina.

The older woman sighed long. "He's in God's hands, as he always has been. We'll see you Sunday then?"

"We'll be there," Noah replied. Sunny went and took her place beside him as the other family settled themselves on the wagon and headed down the track for home. Noah laid his arm upon her shoulder and she drew closer to him.

Noah and Sunny didn't move until the wagon disappeared around the bend thick with trees, until they were alone again.

Dawn began squirming and holding out both hands toward Noah and he lifted her from Sunny's arms. "I'll play with her for a moment. Then I have to go to Martin's to work on pulling out stumps."

Missing his touch, Sunny didn't relish being left

alone. "Do you think the stranger is gone for good then?"

"I should have said *we'll* be going to Martin's."

Sunny nodded. The heaviness of fear had lifted some but she agreed with Noah. They couldn't let down their guard. "You don't think he'll be able to find out that Isaiah has taken Bid'a ban north and go after them, do you?"

Noah considered this as he swung Dawn up and down like a swing. "No, but I think he might tell the military at Fort Snelling. Though that won't make any trouble for us. And if they come for her, she'll already be far away. Are you ready to leave?" he asked.

"I'll get my sewing basket." Sunny wondered how long she'd have to spend every day with one of her neighbors. Inside, she checked on the slowly simmering pot of salt pork and beans that she had hung over the banked fire. She inhaled deeply, pushing away the grave sorrow of parting. And then gathered what she needed for her day's visit with Ophelia.

Within an hour she and Noah arrived at the young couple's cabin. Martin met them at the door, looking strained. "I'm glad you've come, Mrs. Whitmore." Before she could respond, he began talking to Noah.

Noah was carrying Dawn on his shoulders and he lifted her down to give her to Sunny. The baby squawked and struggled to stay with Noah.

"She sure loves her papa," Martin said, grinning.

The comment stung some hidden place deep inside Sunny. Of course no one here would ever know that Noah was not Dawn's father. So she smiled as expected. Noah headed toward the nearly cleared garden with Neechee and Martin.

With difficulty, Sunny carried the squirming and complaining child into the cabin.

Where she found Ophelia bent over the chamber pot, retching.

"Oh, dear!" Setting down Dawn, Sunny dropped to her knees. "Are you ill?"

Ophelia, pale and clammy looking, gazed at her in obvious misery. "I don't have a fever, but I was sick like this the last two mornings and now again today. Yet I'm fine by lunchtime. What's wrong with me, Sunny?"

At this unexpected news, Sunny sighed and hurried to dampen a cloth to wipe the young woman's face. After several more minutes bent over the chamber pot, Ophelia found the strength to rise and sit on a chair at the table.

Suddenly Sunny noticed that Dawn was not making a sound. She looked around the neat cabin, dropped to her knees to look under the bed—no Dawn. And then she realized the door stood ajar. She rushed outside and cast frantic glances around, looking for the child and calling, "Dawn? Dawn!"

Then just as she recalled Dawn's insistence on wanting to go with Noah, she heard Neechee's frantic barking. She raced toward the sound. "Noah!" she shrieked. "Dawn's outside! Watch for her!" Sunny ran the short distance toward the garden by the spring.

In one dreadful moment she spotted Dawn crawling fast only a yard or so from the men. Neechee was barking the alarm, and Noah—at the head of the team of oxen—turned.

His face blanched. "Ho!" he ordered the team to stop and swooped down to intercept the baby nearly concealed by the high grass.

"What were you thinking?" he thundered at Sunny.

She couldn't speak. The image of her baby under the feet of the huge oxen left her feeling light-headed.

"She could have been crushed!" Noah roared, holding Dawn close.

His loud voice frightened the baby and she began wailing.

Still light-headed and with her heart throbbing painfully, Sunny walked toward him slowly, as if walking through thick mud.

"Why did you let her get away from you?" Noah asked.

"Ophelia isn't feeling well and I was distracted. I'm sorry. Dawn has never before tried to go outside without me." Sunny heard her voice as if from a distance. She realized she was about to faint. She dropped onto the nearest broad stump and lowered her head.

"Are you all right?" Noah asked, his voice now soft with concern.

"I feel faint, that's all," she said, her voice still sounding as if it were coming from somewhere else.

Noah hovered over her, comforting Dawn and speaking gently to Sunny. "I didn't mean to yell at you. I was just so scared for her."

Sunny nodded, the earth beneath her still swaying.

"Sunny?" Ophelia came to her side. "Mr. Whitmore, let me have the baby. I'll walk your wife back to the cabin and give her a stiff cup of coffee."

Noah helped Sunny up. "I'll come, too."

Sunny held up a hand. "No, I'll be fine. You go on with your work."

Ophelia carried Dawn and walked Sunny back to her cabin. There, Ophelia settled them in a chair at the table and poured Sunny coffee. "This will buck you up."

Sunny didn't want coffee, but lifted the cup anyway.

A sudden fit of dry heaves came over Ophelia. The young woman bent away from Sunny. Finally she regained command of herself. "I apologize. I just don't know what's happening to me."

Sunny did.

"How long have you and Martin been married now?"

"Almost six weeks." Ophelia looked at her.

Sunny sighed. "Have you ever heard of morning sickness?"

Ophelia shook her head no.

"Not all women get it but some do. It means you may be expecting a child."

Ophelia's mouth dropped open and stayed open.

"Didn't your mother explain the signs of pregnancy to you?"

Ophelia again shook her head.

This disgusted Sunny. Not teaching Ophelia how to do laundry was one thing. But how could a mother send her daughter away without sharing these very necessary facts with her? So Sunny explained to the young bride how it felt to some women to be pregnant. And how a woman knew she was with child.

Though Ophelia appeared dumbfounded and slightly afraid, she asked, "Is there anything I should be doing? I mean for the baby, so it will be healthy?"

"Just eat well and loosen your stays. We'll need to sew you a Mother Hubbard dress for when your regular dresses don't fit—though with the first baby women don't show as early as with the following pregnancies."

Ophelia nodded solemnly.

Then they heard Nan's voice call from outside and she opened the door. One look at them prompted her to ask, "What's wrong?"

"I'm expecting," Ophelia said, and promptly burst into tears.

"Well, that happened fast." Grinning, Nan shut the door firmly and settled Guthrie to play with Dawn on the floor. Sunny then lifted Pearl Louise from her mother's arms and cuddled her.

Smiling her thanks, Nan soothed Ophelia and went about brewing her a cup of chamomile tea. "Now, you'll be just fine. It's common to be emotional—I mean extra emotional—all the way through and even after the baby's born. But this morning sickness usually only lasts for a few months. Then you'll be fine, right, Sunny?"

Sunny didn't reveal that since she'd worked every night in the saloon, she'd experienced her morning sickness in the afternoon. She merely nodded in agreement.

"Let's see," Nan said, looking thoughtful. "You'll be having a baby about the end of winter then. Late February, maybe March."

"I didn't plan on having a baby so soon."

Nan laughed heartily at this. "Babies have a way of coming when they will."

Sunny was not about to reveal that she knew how to prevent pregnancy but she'd gotten pregnant anyway. Nan was right—babies did come.

"I'm so glad I have the two of you nearby." Impulsively, Ophelia claimed one hand from each of them and held on. "There's so much about being a married woman I don't know."

Sunny echoed the same thought silently. Neither of these women lived the complex, hidden life she did. But this large, good-natured blonde and this innocent, pretty brunette had become her friends. She smiled and squeezed Ophelia's hand, encouraging her. And kissed little Pearl Louise's forehead.

Sunny paused a moment to recall her daughter demanding to be in Noah's arms. That they had been a family for only near to two months was hard to believe. Dawn certainly didn't remember a time when Noah wasn't there to play with her.

The fact that Sunny had not yet become this good man's wife completely twinged sharply within. *I must be grateful for what I have. Dawn will have a good life and I have a sheltered one.* The memory of Noah's light kiss and brief embrace eased the twinge. *I must be grateful for what I have,* she repeated to herself. But she couldn't help but wonder now that Bid'a ban had gone, would she return to sleeping by the fire tonight?

Over a week later in the early balmy afternoon, Sunny drove into town with Nan and Ophelia, who rode behind in the wagon bed with the children. At the end of Sunday's gathering Mrs. Ashford had issued an invitation to come to town to join a quilting circle.

Noah, along with the other two husbands, had decided that the threat from the stranger had ended and the three women could go to town without any male escort. So Sunny had of course accepted along with Nan and Ophelia. But Sunny didn't really relish visiting Mrs. Ashford, a woman who seemed to take herself very seriously.

Now each of them got down and carried a child and a sewing basket, Ophelia carrying Nan's Guthrie. Mrs. Ashford, with gray threads in her dark hair and wearing a crisp dress of navy blue bombazine, stood outside her husband's store. She was chatting with Lavina. Both women waved in welcome.

Then for the first time, Sunny followed Mrs. Ashford through the store past a beaming Mr. Ashford and up the stairs into the beautiful living quarters above. Why had Mrs. Ashford—who behaved as if she were the leader of Pepin "society"—invited them?

Surely Sunny and Noah had branded themselves as renegades?

"I'm so glad that you were able to come," Mrs. Ashford said, motioning them to take seats around a long dining table near the large lace-curtained windows that overlooked the street.

"You have a lovely view of the Mississippi,"

Ophelia commented. Across the street sunlight glinted on the wide blue river, dazzling.

"I do enjoy it. I don't like living in a forest. I can't see what's coming."

"I find the forest cozy," Sunny said, surprising herself. "The trees are like arms around me."

All the women looked at her.

"Sometimes I have funny thoughts," she apologized, her cheeks warm.

"That was kind of like poetry," Nan said.

Sunny looked at Nan. Poetry from her?

Mrs. Ashford lifted one eyebrow.

"Well, I like both, forest and town," Ophelia said. "I saw that three more families have staked homesteads hereabouts. Have you met them, Mrs. Ashford?"

"Yes, but only one brought a family with him." Mrs. Ashford's tone disapproved of the two bachelors. "I think having a family steadies a man."

Lavina nodded. They all sat around the table, which looked to be polished walnut with very ornately carved legs. Mrs. Ashford's parlor and dining room combined was larger than Nan's whole cabin. The room contrasted with Sunny's simple cabin. To her, this room felt crowded with too much furniture and bric-a-brac. Sunny found herself unimpressed by the finery. She began to relax.

Mrs. Ashford's youngest daughter, a thin

thirteen-year-old, volunteered to take the children out back to play. But neither toddler would leave their mother. So the girl, holding Nan's baby, lured the children to the sitting area by the cold fireplace and spread out blocks and two rag dolls on the floor. Dawn began chewing a block and Guthrie flapped one of the rag dolls on the floor like a hammer.

"I've started a quilt," Mrs. Ashford said, standing at the head of the table and unrolling a partially sewn quilt top. "And I thought it would be nice to have a community quilting circle. We probably won't meet very often during the summer months—we'll have gardens to tend and preserving and canning to do. But the long winter will be much easier on us if we have a monthly circle to look forward to. Don't you think?"

Even though Sunny's nerves had at first been tightened into little hard knots, the plan for a regular social get-together did appeal to her. So no more at ease, she smiled with the other ladies and murmured something polite.

The fact that she had never quilted before in her life set her teeth on edge. But she listened and watched. From a bag, Mrs. Ashford plucked out colorful scraps of cloth and distributed some to each woman to create a quilt square. Sunny watched Nan play with the scraps she had been given and was intrigued when Nan began to set them into a pattern.

Sunny mimicked Nan and began to enjoy herself. Soon she was sewing the pieces together and listening to the women discuss babies and husbands.

"I hear your father is a judge in Illinois?" Mrs. Ashford quizzed Ophelia.

"Yes, he is a circuit court judge. My Martin has read law, too."

"How interesting." Mrs. Ashford turned to Sunny. "Your husband is certainly becoming a leader in our community."

Sunny's needle poked her finger and she slipped it in her mouth so she didn't bleed on the fabric. "Noah?"

"Yes, indeed," Lavina agreed.

"Gordy really respects Noah," Nan added.

"And Martin does, too," Ophelia said, nodding decidedly. "He says Noah can do so many things, knows so much."

"And isn't afraid to take a stand and see it through." Lavina stopped sewing. "Maybe people didn't like that Indian woman and her boy coming here, but they respect that Noah stood up for them."

"And was able to put that stranger in his place without violence," Mrs. Ashford said. "And everybody can tell Noah Whitmore's educated. And a Union Army veteran, too. Your husband has a future in this community."

Dawn suddenly demanded loudly to be nursed,

which set off Nan's baby, too. This saved Sunny from having to reply. Sunny and Nan went to sit in comfortable rockers near the cold hearth. Sunny hummed to Dawn as she nursed, pondering all the storekeeper's wife had just said. Sunny was proud of Noah but hadn't realized others noticed how special he was.

The other women continued quilting and discussing the latest fashion. Skirts were becoming more and more narrow and the hoop had definitely gone out. Sunny could barely listen—all she could think about was what the women had said about her husband.

Noah was the kind of man who garnered respect. She just hoped nobody would say this to him—after all, only a month and a half ago they'd had their first argument over whether or not to even associate with their neighbors. But it turned out Noah wasn't the kind of man who ignored the needs of others. Which was exactly why she had fallen in love with him. When would she have the courage to tell him that?

The image of Dawn in her spotless white pinafore standing in the schoolyard came to mind. And Sunny knew for certain that in the future Dawn would be proud of her father.

Sunny's face felt hot as she thought about the night after Bid'a ban left, when Noah had not suggested by word or look that Sunny should leave the loft to him alone at night. They still slept far apart but they were at least on the same level now.

"What are you smilin' about?" Nan asked in an undertone.

Sunny blushed. "Noah."

Nan chuckled and murmured for her ears only, "Yes, we both got handsome husbands."

Sunny smiled but didn't reply.

"Katharine!" Mr. Ashford called up the stairs.

Mrs. Ashford hurried to the open rear door. "Yes, Ned?"

"Tell Mrs. Whitmore that a mail boat just came in and I have a letter for her husband from Pennsylvania. That's quick all right. Only took about two weeks. The new railroads are making mail faster all right."

A letter for Noah? Sunny wondered if it brought good news or bad news. Remembering Noah's conflict with his disapproving father, she hoped Noah's brother had written instead.

Noah and Neechee met Sunny at the head of their track. "I heard you ladies coming."

From the wagon bed Sunny smiled at him. The quilting circle had been fun, but mainly because of her two friends and Lavina. Mrs. Ashford obviously was forming her "social" circle with the women she thought prominent.

From subtle clues Sunny had realized that Nan would not have been included except for her obvious friendship with both Sunny and Ophelia. Katharine Ashford did not deceive Sunny. Her friendship was paper-thin while Nan's ran to the bone. And Ophelia's affection shone as honest, too.

Even after such a short separation Sunny experienced a rush of affection for Noah. But of course she couldn't show it. It wouldn't be appropriate in front of the other women.

Soon Nan drove away toward Ophelia's. Dawn insisted that Noah hold her, so Sunny only carried her sewing basket as they walked toward their cabin. Neechee barked playfully at Dawn. Now that they were alone, Sunny reached into her pocket. "Noah, I have something for you."

He looked up.

She held out the letter that she'd tucked into her pocket with care.

Noah stared at it as if he didn't know what it was.

She extended her hand farther, insisting he receive it. Why did he hesitate?

"It looks like it's from your brothers. Or your father."

He finally took the letter and stared at it as though he could read it through the envelope.

She waited till Dawn's struggling to get Noah's attention became impossible to ignore. She retrieved the child and set her down. Determined, Dawn crawled straight back to Noah and pulled herself up, using his pant leg. Noah ignored Dawn, an unusual occurrence. Neechee barked once as if trying to shake Noah's preoccupation.

Maybe it's me. "I'll let you read your letter in privacy." She moved toward the cabin.

"No." He slipped the letter into his breast pocket. "I've got some work to do." He picked Dawn up and then handed the child back to Sunny. He walked away, Neechee trailing after him.

Sunny was dumbfounded. There was something in that letter that Noah did not want to face. What was Noah hiding from her?

That evening the letter sat on the mantel unopened. Noah watched as Sunny got ready to serve supper. On the floor Dawn crawled after a ball of leather he'd fashioned for her. Neechee lay across the threshold as usual, but her gaze fixed on her master. Noah sat on the bench by the table and stared at the letter. He knew he must open it. He wouldn't sleep, knowing it sat there. Noah had just sent a note about arriving safely. He struggled with the fact that he feared reading it. His brother wouldn't have responded so quickly unless he had important news. To him that boded ill.

Delay in opening the letter had ruined the afternoon, making it more miserable than any in recent memory. Though Sunny had not asked why he didn't just open the letter, she acted as if she were stepping on eggs again. She kept glancing up at the letter and then away.

He hated upsetting her. He must read it now.

He stood. Retrieved the letter. And sat down. Sunny paused and then went back to stirring the pot. Dawn crawled over and watched him slit open the letter with his pocket knife.

He spread it out on the table, smoothing the creases. He read the brief, poignant letter and tried to decide what he was feeling. He couldn't.

Still Sunny didn't ask. She kept her back to him.

He took a deep breath, trying to shift the solid block of grief within. "Nathan, my eldest brother, wrote to tell me that my father has had a stroke and is now bedridden."

Sunny turned quickly. "I'm so sorry to hear that."

"He also tells me that our father can't speak."

"That is bad." She looked to him as if asking what he meant to do about this.

"My brother says they have hired a nurse to care for him. So I'm not to worry."

"These things happen," she replied, pouring stew into bowls on the table.

These things happen. Noah realized that he was once again frozen inside. He folded the letter and returned it to the envelope.

Sunny sat across from him with Dawn on her lap. "Your father didn't seem to approve of you going to war."

Her timid words touched a sore spot. He snorted. "It wasn't just that. Nothing I ever did pleased my father. We could never understand why everything I did irritated him."

"I'm sorry."

He shrugged.

"Will you say grace, Noah?"

He nodded and bowed his head. A few words and they began to eat.

Why was it that no matter how far he went, ties of blood still held? Why did a father love some sons and not others?

Dawn babbled. Then quite clearly she said, "No-No." He glanced over at her. "No-No."

Sunny looked thunderstruck.

"No-No," Dawn repeated, patting the table and staring at Noah. "No-No."

"I think she's trying to say *Noah,*" Sunny said with wonder in her voice.

Strong emotion brought tears just behind Noah's eyes. Reaching across the table, he gripped one of Dawn's plump little hands. "Hey, Dawn."

"No-No!" she squealed triumphantly.

He rose and lifted the baby into his arms, his spirit rising. "I'm Papa, Dawn. I'm your papa."

"No-No." Dawn flung herself against Noah's chest, giving him one of her unabashed hugs.

He smiled, his joy overflowing. "Okay, for now you can call me No-No. Sunny, you'll have to start calling me her pa. We'll scandalize the neighborhood if we let her call me Noah."

Sunny rose and came to stand beside him. She leaned her cheek against his arm as she spoke to their daughter. "This is your papa. Pa-pa."

Yes, Dawn, you're my little girl. And then one tear slipped down his cheek. His father lay ill far away, but he'd always been far away from Noah. His daughter was here, now.

What had he ever done to deserve this little girl and her mother?

Chapter Thirteen

Near his garden, Noah, Gordy and Martin stood, exhausted but satisfied. Fleetingly, the image of Miigwans's face came to mind. Neechee lay in the shade nearby, another reminder of the little boy. Was he safe now?

Turning from these thoughts, Noah leaned against one of his oxen and stroked the animal's back. "Couldn't have done it without you," he murmured to the animal.

"You were smart to invest in oxen, Noah," Martin said. "They can outwork our draft horses."

Noah patted his ox's rump once more. "My father always used oxen. We had horses for driving, but oxen for the heavy work." He thought of his stiff-necked father now reduced only in his fifties to an invalid and at such a young age. Life took many strange twists and turns.

Matters here hadn't turned out just the way Noah had imagined. He'd married Sunny in part so he wouldn't be totally alone here. But events had caused him to make friends, real friends. These men had stood with him against that stranger. And they seemed to now look to him as the one who knew what had to be done. He'd never quite thought of himself as a leader before, but it wasn't necessarily a bad thing.

"We all need barns before winter," he suddenly announced.

The other two men looked at him in dismay.

"Noah Whitmore, you beat all," Gordy said, shoving back his hat to wipe the sweat on his forehead with his sleeve. "We just got the final garden cleared and still need to plow and plant. And you're talkin' about winter."

Martin groaned and moved as if his back were aching. "This starting from scratch is more work than I anticipated."

Noah looked at the younger man. "You thinking of going back to Illinois?"

"No," Martin said firmly. "I've read law but I was raised on a farm and I can do the work. It's just that my dad did the hard work of settling and getting a farm started. He warned me how it'd be."

"Well, I could have stayed home and worked with my pa and brothers," Gordy offered. "But I wanted better, more for my Nan and kids, a place of our own."

"Then we better talk about raising our barns before snow flies," Noah said laconically. "The preacher said something to me about holding barn raisings this summer. Maybe we should ask who else needs a barn. If everybody works at logging out what they need, we could gather and get a barn up in a day or two. Maybe do one a month. How's that sound?"

"Sounds like you have that all figured out right well," Gordy said. Then he paused. "I hate to ask but my cabin was not tight and warm for winter last year. Nan and me nearly froze to death. I see, Noah, how you built a foundation for your cabin and a log floor . . ." Gordy's voice trailed off.

Noah folded his arms and nodded. "I'll help you add on a larger room and you can use the old cabin as a cold room this winter. I might ask to store some provisions there, too."

"You'd be welcome to." Gordy looked and sounded relieved.

"I'll help, too," Martin volunteered.

"And if I run short of money, I'll let it be known that I can work in stone," Noah continued.

"I figure I can cut more firewood than I'll need," Gordy said, "and sell some for hard cash or barter at the store."

"I'm thinking of holding school a couple of days a week come fall. But until then we'll be raising barns and another cabin. Whew," Martin breathed out. "We're all going to be trim and with muscles like rock."

This hit Noah funny. He broke out into a laugh.

"Well," Gordy said, smiling broadly, "I guess Noah Whitmore can laugh."

Noah hadn't realized they'd notice his lack of humor. This made him think of how Dawn was the one who'd brought back his laughter. Noah thought of Dawn's latest feat. "A few days ago Dawn said her first word—my name. She called me No-No." Noah had never understood the expression puffed-up before but he felt it now.

"Wow," Gordy said, looking impressed. "That's early to be talking. And now that you got one child up a bit—" Gordy winked "—I guess you'll be the next family expectin' another young-un."

Noah's good mood evaporated.

Oblivious, Gordy settled his hat back on his head. "I'll head home now. I think there'll be enough light I can get my plowing started today."

Martin made his farewell also. The two younger men headed off together. Noah didn't turn to watch them go. Gordy's words lay heavy, souring his stomach. If matters went on the way they had, Dawn would be his only child.

He hadn't realized that he would like being a father. Noah leaned against the ox. He recalled every time Sunny had touched him. How pretty she was and he glimpsed then that he desired her. But that was all. He didn't seem to be able to move forward. What would it take to make him whole again?

Sunday turned out gloomy. Sunny tried not to let it further dull her mood. She had begun to worry about Isaiah and Bid'a ban and Miigwans. Since they'd left, three Sundays had come and gone; the gardens had all been planted. Had the three-some reached Lac du Flambeau?

Sunday meetings in town had become a looked-for event. People smiled and waved at them as they arrived in Gordy's wagon. It was a far cry from the chilly reception they'd once received.

Martin had an arm around Ophelia who was struggling still with morning sickness. The tender care that Martin showed his bride had increased and it nipped Sunny in a tender spot. The young couple's love for each other gleamed so apparent. How must it feel to be loved like that?

Very pale, Ophelia had her handkerchief pressed to her mouth and Sunny hoped she wouldn't be sick in town—every gossip would know that she was expecting. Both Sunny and Nan had counseled her to wait till the crucial third month had passed before letting the news be known. Better to wait till the worry of early miscarriage passed.

Gordy parked the wagon under a spreading oak. Noah helped Sunny down and swung Dawn to sit up on his shoulders. The little girl squealed with delight.

Old Saul and his family already waited on Ashford's porch. Sunny moved forward, greeting people who greeted her back and smiling generally, always mindful that these were the people Dawn would grow up amongst.

When closer, Sunny noticed that Lavina looked strained. So Isaiah had not yet returned. Sunny hoped sincerely that no harm had come to him. And she hoped Bid'a ban and Miigwans were even now safe in the arms of their family.

Sunny determined to say a few encouraging phrases to Lavina. Surely God was protecting the young man who had volunteered to help a widow and orphan. Isn't that the kind of thing God did?

Lavina and her husband started the service with hymn singing. Sunny hummed along and smiled, watching Dawn on her high perch listen intently to the music. After a few rousing hymns, Old Saul stood from his chair and raised both hands. "Another Lord's Day, what a blessing to see you all and know that he is here with us."

He opened his Bible but did not look down as he recited, " 'My little children, these things write I unto you, that ye sin not. And if any man sin, we have an advocate with the Father, Jesus

Christ, the righteous: And he is the propitiation for our sins: and not for ours only, but also for the sins of the whole world.' "

Suddenly Sunny noticed that everyone was glancing behind to the west and she heard the sound of a boat's horn. A riverboat must be docking.

Old Saul chuckled. "Let's sing some more. I know everybody wants to see if anybody or anything's getting off the boat."

Lavina stepped forward and began a hymn. People sang along but, in truth, the boat docking had distracted everyone. Sunny felt the pull of curiosity, too. So little happened outside the daily routine of chores. The boat would bring newspapers from downriver and maybe mail.

Then Sunny heard Ophelia gasp. The bride turned completely toward the river. Sunny swung around to face the same way.

From the boat ramp, an older, very expensively dressed lady with a younger woman was advancing toward the Sunday gathering. The hymn trailed off.

The older woman waved a lace handkerchief and hurried forward. "Ophelia!" she exclaimed.

"Mother?" Ophelia said, her eyes wide.

"Yes, Ophelia, I'm here." The woman said the words as if Ophelia lay on her death bed.

Just before Ophelia's mother reached her, the bride pressed the handkerchief over her mouth and wailed softly, wordlessly.

Quickly, Sunny moved to Ophelia's side. "Are you indisposed?"

"Yes." The young woman looked about to faint. Sunny took charge. "Mrs. Ashford! Mrs. Steward is indisposed! May we take her upstairs to your quarters, please?"

Mrs. Ashford swooped down and helped Sunny assist Ophelia inside. Martin hurried behind them and Ophelia's mother began calling out instructions in rapid fire from the rear.

Soon the five of them arrived in the Ashfords' parlor. Martin had carried Ophelia up the steps at Sunny's suggestion. He lay his wife on the sofa and stood beside her. "Do you need anything?"

Sunny noted that Ophelia was trying to swallow down nausea. "Mrs. Ashford, a basin please."

"Is my child ill?" the newcomer demanded in a voice that went up Sunny's spine like a coarse brush.

Mrs. Ashford handed Sunny the basin just in time. Ophelia lost the scant breakfast she must have eaten.

"Is there a doctor in town?" Ophelia's mother demanded.

Sunny wished the woman would show some sensitivity. She offered her free hand. "No, we don't have a doctor yet. I'm Mrs. Noah Whitmore, ma'am, Ophelia's neighbor."

"I'm Mrs. Buford Cantrell, Ophelia's mother." With lifted nose, the woman shook hands as if she were the lady and they were the lowly and then turned to her daughter. "I can see I didn't come a moment too soon." She began chafing Ophelia's wrist trying to increase circulation.

Martin retreated, but stayed near his wife.

"Mother, please," Ophelia begged faintly, "don't fuss. I'm fine."

Mrs. Cantrell managed to snort in a very refined way. "I told you that you were too delicate to venture onto the frontier. I had this terrible premonition that something awful—"

"I don't think expecting her first child is something awful." Nan's matter-of-fact voice startled all of them. They glanced toward the top of the stairs where Nan stood near Martin. Nan came forward, smiling with outstretched hand. "I'm Nan Osbourne, another friend of Ophelia's."

Mrs. Cantrell's mouth gathered up like a drawstring purse and instead of taking Nan's hand, she nodded curtly. "Mrs. Buford Cantrell. Charmed, I'm sure."

Sunny bristled.

"Oh, a baby—this is good news," Mrs. Ashford said, obviously trying to help keep everything polite. "I'm so happy for you, Mrs. Steward."

Mrs. Cantrell ignored this and went on. "I had a premonition that my Ophelia needed me. I can see she must come home where I can care for her."

"Mother!" Ophelia protested. "I'm not going home with anybody but Martin."

"But there's no doctor here," Mrs. Cantrell protested. "And anyone can see you're in need of one."

Sunny wanted to shake the melodramatic woman.

"She's having a baby, that's all," Nan said. "She'll be fine. Mrs. Ashford helped birth my little Pearl Louise not too long ago."

Mrs. Cantrell looked as if she wanted to say more—much more—but evidently realized that she couldn't disparage Mrs. Ashford in her own home. So she turned on Nan. "You obviously are the kind of hefty woman who has no trouble with childbearing, but my Ophelia is so delicate."

Sunny caught the insult and gasped.

Ophelia sat up on the sofa. "Mother! Why have you come?"

"Because I thought by now you'd realize that you don't belong here."

"I belong wherever my husband is."

Sunny realized why Ophelia had married so young and had been willing to leave for the frontier. Mrs. Cantrell struck her as a bad dream.

Finally, when Ophelia burst into tears over her mother's unkind words, the younger woman who had arrived with Mrs. Cantrell stepped into the room and cleared her throat. "I think, Auntie, it would be best if we returned to the riverboat now. Your daughter needs peace and some rest. And our noon meal will be served soon."

This precise and very cool speech caught Mrs. Cantrell in midstream. She blinked.

The young woman, who was also dressed stylishly, looked to Martin. "Martin, why don't you convey Ophelia home and then return to town and take us out to see your place? I know I'm eager to meet your friends and see how much you've accomplished. That's why we came." The young woman emphasized ever so slightly the last sentence.

Sunny waited for a backlash—in vain. Mrs. Cantrell swallowed several times and then pinned a painfully artificial smile on her face. "An excellent idea, Ellen. I'm afraid finding Ophelia in such straits discomposed me."

Her head resting on the back of the sofa, Ophelia spoke up. "Everyone, this is my cousin, Miss Ellen Thurston. I'm happy to see you, Ellen."

Ellen inclined her head to all politely and gestured for the older woman to precede her down the stairs. Ellen then turned to Mrs. Ashford. "Thank you so much for opening your charming home to strangers like us. So kind."

Beaming at the compliment, Mrs. Ashford accepted the younger woman's thanks and showed the ladies down the staircase. Ophelia looked to Martin and burst into fresh tears of frustration as soon as her mother was gone.

Nan sat down and put her arms around her. "There, there," she murmured, "this is just commotion, that's all. We'll all smile about it in the future."

Sunny thought that would be much, much further in the future. Maybe when they were grandmothers.

Martin looked chagrined, but said gently, "Are you able to go downstairs?"

Ophelia held out both her hands. "Oh, Martin, I'm so sorry. I hate the way she talks to you."

He took her hands and helped her up. "Now, Mrs. Osbourne is exactly right. This is all sound and fury, nothing to concern you. Your mother is just being herself—I'm only grateful I'm married to you, not her." He shepherded his wife to the stairs and over her protests, carried her down.

"What next?" Nan asked, shaking her head. "I got an aunt just like Ophelia's mother—loves an audience. Shoulda gone on the stage."

Sunny laughed out loud and then put her hand over her mouth. And the two of them followed the young couple downstairs and outside. What next indeed?

Sunny recalled her mother's pretty face and sweet smile. Warmed, she knew her mother would have loved Noah, loved seeing Sunny and Dawn with him. *I still haven't been able to tell him I love him.* A sad thought, one that prodded her.

Later that day Noah remained dressed in his Sunday best, as did Sunny. They sat on a bench just outside their door, enjoying the spring day. The gloomy layer of clouds had blown away and now the sun shone down and a breeze fluttered the leaves overhead. Sunny was beside him, Dawn asleep on his lap, Neechee lying at his feet. He recognized it as a moment of contentment, something he'd not felt for a long time.

Martin had made a plan for the afternoon with the Osbournes, and with Noah and Sunny. He would drive his mother-in-law and Ellen Thurston to his homestead and then on their way back to the river, stop to visit Noah and Sunny. Gordy had been invited to come also. Strength in numbers, Noah thought.

Martin had muttered to Noah and Gordy that his mother-in-law was the main reason he had headed for Wisconsin. The woman considered herself among the leading lights in Galena society and deemed Ophelia to have married beneath her. Martin had Noah's sincere sympathy.

Neechee stood up and barked once. "Well, Neechee's right. I hear a wagon coming."

Nodding, Noah stroked Dawn's fine hair. The little one had fallen asleep in his lap after lunch. She didn't stir now.

Sunny smiled at the babe. Noah's fingers brushed Sunny's cheek. He tried to ignore the urge to lean forward and follow the touch with a kiss. These feelings startled him.

"I feel sorry for Martin," Noah muttered.

Sunny had stayed very still after he brushed her soft cheek. Now she sighed as if releasing some pent-up emotion. Looking as if she agreed.

Then they heard an unexpected sound—horse hooves, not a wagon creaking. Up the track rode Isaiah.

Elated, Noah rose, lifting Dawn to his shoulder. "Isaiah!"

Sunny bounced up, too. "Oh, you're home. I'm so glad!"

The lanky teen slipped off his horse. "Got home in time for Sunday dinner. But wanted to bring you news and gifts from Bid'a ban right away."

Sunny pressed her hands together as if trying to contain her obvious happiness. "They're well then?"

"The trip north took a bit longer than I'd guessed. But we got there and her family celebrated her homecoming for three days." Isaiah beamed at them. "Relatives from her clan came from miles around. They thought they had lost her for sure."

Neechee barked again. Noah looked past Isaiah, expecting to see Martin. But instead Old Saul and his family were arriving.

"I'm glad I baked a double layer cake yesterday," Sunny whispered to Noah. They went forward to welcome their guests. Then Noah and Isaiah carried out the table and the other bench for their company.

"What a beautiful day," Lavina said, looking happier than she had in many weeks.

Noah brought out the rocker for Old Saul and the older man lowered himself into it. Before he got settled, Martin's wagon drove into the yard with Ophelia and her family on the bench and the Osbourne family riding in the back.

For a moment Noah was taken aback by the prospect of entertaining so many—and all at once.

"This should prove interesting," Sunny murmured and then went forward in welcome.

For a few minutes Sunny bustled around, making coffee and bringing out the cake. Mrs. Buford Cantrell sat in stony silence at the table. On the other hand Miss Ellen Thurston spoke cordially to everyone as if she were accustomed to sitting outside a cabin in the woods.

As soon as everyone was settled and began eating cake and sipping strong coffee, Old Saul nodded to Isaiah. "Our guests don't know that my grandson just returned from a trip north to Chippewa land. Why don't you tell us all about it, son?"

"Why would he go to Indian land?" Mrs. Cantrell snapped.

Complete silence.

"Mother, you don't have much time before your boat leaves in the morning," Ophelia said. "Maybe we should just finish our cake and take you back to town."

Mrs. Cantrell sniffed.

"We're very happy to have your daughter and her husband in our town," Old Saul said.

"This is not the life I wanted for my daughter." The older woman seemed to have reached her limit. She sounded like an over-tired child who wasn't getting her way. "And now my first grandchild will be born in a cabin," she complained.

Again, silence.

Sunny almost felt sorry for the woman. She must be very used to getting her way.

Lavina cleared her throat. "I understand how you feel, ma'am, but our children only belong to us till they grow up and leave home. Still, it's hard not to want to continue protecting them, guiding them. I'm afraid in spite of my praying for Isaiah, I worried every day till he returned home. I know I should have more trust in God to take care of him, but he's my baby."

"Mother," Isaiah objected.

"But of course he's a young man now," Lavina said with an apologetic smile. "And this trip has helped him see his path forward."

"Yes, I learned so much and saw so much," Isaiah put in eagerly. "There is such need there, especially for teaching."

His enthusiasm impressed Sunny.

"I don't know what any of this is about," Mrs. Cantrell said. "Or why my daughter would want to live here in the wilderness." She stood abruptly.

"Martin, it doesn't seem as if I can make my daughter see sense. Take us back to the riverboat."

Ophelia looked mortified but Martin looked relieved. "If that's what you wish, Mother Cantrell."

The woman marched to the wagon and Martin hurried after her. Miss Thurston wiped her lips and rose. "Mrs. Whitmore, the cake was delicious. Thank you so much for the refreshments. The setting of your home is lovely and I know from my cousin Ophelia how supportive her neighbors have been. I must, however, bid you farewell. For now."

Everyone bid the nice young woman a warm goodbye and Martin drove off. Ophelia rode in the back, looking forlorn.

A moment of strained silence followed their departure.

"Ophelia's mother told me that Miss Thurston's uncle is a state senator in the Illinois legislature," Nan informed them, "and she comes from a wealthy family, too." Nan's tone informed them that Mrs. Cantrell had sought and failed to impress Nan.

"Well, she's a much happier woman than Ophelia's mother," Old Saul said mildly. "Meddling is a sin, too."

"And I think all she has accomplished is that she's alienated her daughter," Lavina said.

Sunny agreed silently. And determined never to behave so foolishly with Dawn.

"So, Isaiah, how's Miigwans?" Noah asked.

Isaiah grinned. "He is fine. Missing you, but fine. He is hoping for a pup real bad."

Noah shook his head, smiling. "Scamp."

"Isaiah, what was it like up that way?" Sunny asked.

"Beautiful. Lakes everywhere. I mean, everywhere. So blue and crystal clear water." His face darkened. "But such poverty. It nearly broke my heart. There's a lay preacher there and an old priest. They do their best to help bridge the gap between the Ojibwa and the whites. But it's hard to see some of their men who ought to provide for their families drunk on our liquor."

"Well, that could be said of any town in our country," Old Saul commented.

"The lay preacher is named Sam White. I plan on going back this fall to work with him through the winter."

Lavina and her husband looked shocked. Old Saul nodded, unperturbed.

Isaiah plunged ahead. "Sam says he needs someone to help him. He's over seventy and is suffering with arthritis bad. He holds classes for people who want to learn how to read and write English and he teaches a Bible Study weekly. He supports himself as a trapper and will teach me that, too."

Sunny watched Lavina absorb this. She glanced at Dawn, lying drowsily on Noah's shoulder, and wondered what it would be like when her daughter brought a young man in and said she was marrying and leaving home. An icy needle pierced Sunny's heart. Slight understanding of Ophelia's mother flickered.

"Oh!" Isaiah stood and lifted down one of his saddlebags. "Bid'a ban sent gifts from her family to you and Mrs. Osbourne." He pulled out four small pairs of moccasins, each beaded with skill and lined with rabbit fur. "For the children." He handed two pairs to Nan—and two to Sunny. "To keep their feet warm this winter."

Noah took one of the small moccasins, smiling at Dawn. Sunny put her hand on his arm, sharing the moment, their little girl's first pair of shoes. Bid'a ban had made them.

"Oh, how sweet," Nan cooed.

At first, Sunny was confused. Then she blushed, thinking of Bid'a ban telling Sunny that she was better, and Sunny should return to the loft to be with Noah. She stroked the soft deerskin leather and silken fur lining. "How thoughtful. Thank you for bringing them." She looked at Noah, who had a strange smile on his face as he took in the two pairs of tiny shoes. That smile made her heart skip a beat.

As their guests prepared to leave a bit later, Noah helped Old Saul back onto the wagon.

"Well, we'll be seeing you for the first barn raising then. Two weeks from last Friday," the older man said.

"Are you sure you want to build mine first?" Noah asked.

"Yes, because you'll show everyone how a stone foundation should be done. Most don't know how and a good foundation is important. For barns as well as people."

The preacher's family rode away as Nan helped carry dishes to the outside basin. "This has been quite a day," Nan said with a sigh as she dried the final dish. "I'm ready to go home." Gordy took her hand and the couple and their children waved goodbye.

Sunny watched them leave. "Well, company is fine, but that's enough for a while," Sunny said.

Noah put an arm around her shoulder. "You did us proud with that cake."

At his unexpected praise and touch, Sunny had to swallow sudden tears. "My pleasure."

"But I like it when it's quiet here. Just the three of us." Neechee barked as if agreeing or arguing with Noah. "I mean the four of us."

Sunny bent to pet the faithful dog. As she stood back up, Noah shocked her.

He pulled her around and into his arms.

Chapter Fourteen

Drawing Sunny into his arms had felt as natural as a sunrise to Noah. The top of her head brushed the underside of his chin. Her hair smelled of the lavender water that she combed through it each morning. He liked her feminine ways, how she always looked trim and neat.

He savored the softness of her within his arms. *Sunny, I'm glad you're my wife.* He wished he could say the words to her—she deserved to hear them. But he couldn't make his throat and mouth work. Sunny had captured him and made him mute.

Then with an irresistible sigh she rested against him, trusting him to hold her.

He buried his face into her pale golden hair and tightened his arms around her. For once he didn't think of his life before Sunny. Like honey poured on a cut, her presence soothed and healed. He hoped she was as content as she always seemed. But he vowed to make her happy —truly happy—or die trying.

He would figure out how to be her husband—he owed her that.

He felt the familiar sensation of Dawn grabbing

his pant leg and pulling herself up to stand. He chuckled deep in his chest. His little Dawn.

"No-No," the baby said, patting his knee. "No-No."

Sunny stepped back. "Dawn wants her *pa-pa,*" Sunny said, emphasizing the two syllables. "Pa-pa," she repeated.

Dawn crowed, arching her back and squealing.

Noah swung her up into his arms. He kissed her cheek, and then bent and kissed Sunny's cheek for good measure.

"Maybe I'll invite Mrs. Buford Cantrell to stop by again sometime." Sunny's smile sparkled as she teased. "She seems to have had quite an effect on you."

The three of them sat again in a row on the bench outside their cabin. Dawn clamored to get down and roll in the grass with Neechee. Squirrels scampered from tree to tree, shaking branches and chasing each other, chirruping. Noah relaxed as the golden sun lowered behind the trees. He let his arm go around her waist and rest on the bench behind her. For the first time in recent memory contentment flowed through him, something he would never have again thought possible. And for now, he let himself enjoy it.

Sunny had rarely been this keyed up in her whole life. Eight families, including the old preacher's, were coming for the first barn raising at their place. She had put a haunch of pork wrapped with wild onions to slow roast in the large oven Noah had expertly crafted in their stone hearth. The scent tantalized her as she finished her grooming.

She ran her hands down over her crisp white apron. *Oh, Lord, please keep everyone safe today.* She remembered the day the tree had bounced into Noah and could have killed him. So many men working together could invite disaster.

Noah stepped into the doorway, their little girl hugging his neck. "Mmm. That pork sure makes my mouth water."

She managed a tight smile.

"Wonder what the other women will bring?" He offered her Dawn. "You'll have to keep her. They'll be arriving soon—"

Neechee's barking interrupted him. Sunny accepted the baby who complained loudly at being separated from Noah.

"Make sure the women keep watch over the children," Noah warned. "I don't want any children near us as we work with the stone."

Sunny nodded. "I'll make sure."

Then the families began arriving. Most left their wagons on the trail and walked up the track to the Whitmore clearing. Every face was smiling. The men shouldered spades, axes and shovels. The women, all in fresh white aprons, carried covered dishes and sewing or knitting baskets.

The Osbournes arrived, bringing more benches for the women to sit on while they sewed in front of the cabin. And the Stewards brought chairs. The weather couldn't have been better for a day of working outside. The sun shone bright and the breeze was warm without heat.

Soon the men were at the far side of the clearing. Noah had piled a hill of stone from plowing the garden and stacks of logs he, Gordy and Martin had felled in the past two weeks. With shovels in hand, the men began digging the foundation trench.

Sunny supervised the donated food. Some had been stowed in the spring house to keep cool and some set on the hearth to keep warm. When the breeze was just right, delectable fragrances wafted over the women.

After the initial greetings the ladies began telling about their families back home and how they'd come to settle in Pepin. Frantically, Sunny tried to remember what she'd told Caroline when they'd first met.

"Well, that's how Gordy and I picked Pepin—it was as far as our fare on the riverboat took us." Nan laughed at this. "We took it as God's providence and so it has been." Nan sent Sunny and Ophelia a special smile.

Sunny tried to hold on to that, but she had to concentrate on her words. Because it was her turn now. "I lived out West. After my mother died, a friend sent me back East to her family." That was true.

"Where was your pa?" one woman whom Sunny barely knew asked.

Sunny's mind spun. "We'd lost him years before."

"Losing both parents young is hard," Ophelia said solemnly. Murmurs of sympathy caused Sunny to writhe inwardly.

"How did you meet Noah?" Nan asked.

Sunny drew a deep breath. "He attended the same church as the family I lived with."

The women made cheery, knowing sounds, and Nan nudged her. "Flirting at church, hmm?"

Sunny knew she must smile and she curved her mouth, hiding how her lips threatened to tremble.

"How did you and Noah choose Pepin?" Lavina asked, looking up from the shirt she was mending. She cast a concerned glance toward the men. Her father-in-law, Old Saul, was insisting on helping with the stone foundation, obviously worrying her.

"Noah decided he wanted to homestead and early this year, he traveled to Illinois, Iowa, Minnesota and then Wisconsin. He liked Pepin best. He came home in April."

She caught herself just before she said "and we married." Horror over almost saying these indiscreet words nearly made her gasp. Instead she finished with, "We came here." *Please don't ask me any more. Please.*

"Now, Ophelia, you're the new bride," Nan said with a teasing voice. "How did you fall in love with your Martin?"

Ophelia began speaking about meeting Martin at a political rally for President Grant when he visited his home in Galena. The bride blushed sweetly.

Sunny sighed silently. She had made it through. She began to relax. The caution was all on her part; these women saw her as one of them, something she had doubted possible once.

The men had worked till early afternoon before stopping to eat lunch. After eating and then resting for a while, the men rose to troop back to the barn site.

Lavina walked beside Old Saul, trying to persuade him to lie down inside for a while. "You've been on your feet or sitting on a log for most of the day. You need to rest now."

Old Saul waved away her caution. "The sun is doing me good. I'll just sit and watch, Lavina. No harm in that."

Sunny watched the woman shake her head, obviously concerned.

Noah must have heard because he requested that the lady in the rocking chair give up her seat, and he carried it to a shady spot where Old Saul could watch the work in comfort.

"Your husband is such a thoughtful man,"

Lavina said softly to Sunny as Old Saul lowered himself into the chair.

Sunny nodded. "He is." She gazed at the barn, which was amazingly taking shape in one day. The stone foundation was almost done and men were notching the logs to fit together at the corners.

Then she heard Noah's shout. She swung her gaze to him. He was kneeling beside Old Saul who had slumped onto his shoulder.

Lavina ran toward their wagon. She retrieved a small bag and raced toward her father-in-law.

All work stopped. Everyone rushed forward to help.

Noah called out, "Everyone, please keep back! He needs air!"

Lavina knelt beside Noah and drew out a packet of pills. "Here's your digitalis." She slipped one into her father-in-law's mouth and called for water.

Sunny ran to get the pitcher of spring water and dipper. Noah accepted it from her and poured the dipper full. She stepped back, leaving Lavina and her husband to care for the older man.

His face etched with pain, Old Saul gasped for breath and pressed a hand over his heart.

Noah carefully held the dipper to his mouth and trickled water in.

Nan and Ophelia came and put their arms around Sunny. "Oh, I hope he'll be all right," Ophelia whispered.

Sunny echoed this silently. She was wringing her hands and realized then that this older man had become dear to her. He had shown love to Bid'a ban and Miigwans. Even Neechee voiced a long worried moan in the troubled silence in the clearing.

Oh, God, please help Old Saul.

The next day Noah sat on the bench at his table with his coffee cup, staring into space. In his mind's eye he saw the old preacher clutching his chest. Old Saul's face had gone sheet-white. Fear thrummed through Noah. He didn't want to lose the old preacher. He realized how much he'd come to like the older man's unexpected visits, and how helpful he'd been in so very many ways.

"No-No," Dawn called to him from the floor.

"Say pa-pa," Sunny corrected. "Noah is your pa-pa."

"No-No!" Dawn insisted.

Noah set down his cold coffee and lifted the child into his arms. How could he have known what a comfort holding this little child could be?

"No-No," she said, patting him happily. Oh, to be innocent of grief and pain like this little one.

He recalled how Old Saul had said a few words about being a soldier. It wasn't much, but it said everything. Maybe that was another reason he felt connected to Old Saul. They'd both faced war.

Sunny came up behind him and rested a hand on his shoulder. "I've been praying for Old Saul," she murmured.

He lifted a hand and pressed hers, nodding. Neechee growled and got to her feet.

"Hello, the house!" a familiar voice soon called out.

Noah rose and carried Dawn to the door. He looked out. "Isaiah?" His heart sank.

"My grandfather's alive!" the young man called out and slid from his horse. "He sent me to get you, Noah. He says he wants to talk to you."

Noah blanched. Not a deathbed visit—he'd done too many of those, kneeling beside comrades, watching the light flicker from their eyes. No.

"Don't worry," Isaiah said. "He says he's much better. He just wants to talk over some things with you. Says he's been meaning to talk to you for some time but keeps getting interrupted. Will you come?"

What could he say? This young man had taken Miigwans home. And Old Saul had proved himself a true friend to them. "Of course I'll come." He turned to Sunny. "Did you want to come along?"

Sunny looked to Isaiah. "Yes, I'll come, too. I'd like to visit Lavina today."

The preacher's family lived a couple of miles northeast of town along another creek that flowed into the Chippewa. As they traveled, Noah barely spoke a word to Isaiah. He felt wooden inside.

When they arrived, Lavina came out and greeted them in a subdued tone. "Saul will be glad to see you." She looked to Sunny.

"Shall we sit outside? It's such a nice day."

Lavina nodded and then said to Noah, "Go in."

Noah dismounted, handed Isaiah his reins and helped Sunny and Dawn down. Then he doffed his hat to enter the shadowy cabin. The dam inside him began to break up, unruly currents swirling. Noah tightened his self-control.

Old Saul lay on a narrow rope bed on the far side of the fireplace. "Noah." He lifted a hand momentarily and then, as if tired by the effort, let it fall.

Reluctantly Noah went and sat in a chair beside the bed. "Good morning, sir."

The older man shook a finger at him.

The reminder prodded Noah into a half chuckle. "I mean, Old Saul."

"I'm not planning on dying just yet," the preacher said in a gravelly voice. "But I've been wanting to talk to you about war."

Noah wanted to get up and leave, but he owed this man. Irritation ground inside him. "I don't like to talk about it."

"Then just listen to me as I talk." Old Saul inhaled a rattling breath and closed his eyes. "I was barely fourteen when war broke out with

England a second time. I had been raised on stories of the Revolution and was afraid I'd miss this war, my generation's war." The old man paused as if drawing up strength.

These words stirred up memories in Noah, wretched ones. Those awful weeks when he'd planned on enlisting and wondered how to tell his family, his fiancée. He fidgeted in the chair.

"I hear you were raised Quaker. I know they don't believe in going to war. I bet that made it harder for you to enlist."

Noah barked one unpleasant dry laugh. "I was put out of meeting. They had worked in the Underground Railroad, helping escaped slaves. When abolition helped trigger a war, they wanted none of it. But I couldn't turn a blind eye to the war that could bring freedom to so many."

Old Saul nodded. "My family was proud of me, but they were as ignorant as I was. At fourteen, I marched off with the other young men from my Kentucky town to fight under Andrew Jackson."

He fell silent, but his hands on top of the blanket moved restlessly. "I don't have to tell you what a shock the first battle was. I'd never killed a man before. I didn't know how that would tear at me afterward."

Noah tried to block images from his mind, but he was bombarded. Startled, agonized faces amid the black powder cloud—He bent his head into his hands. "Please, no more."

"I nearly died of a wound, and it weakened my heart," Old Saul continued. "But after my body healed, the worst was the nightmares. And the sudden fear that someone was aiming a gun at me. Or about to run me through."

Noah lifted his head and his gaze connected with the old man's. *So I'm not the only one.*

"I see the dark circles under your eyes. And the way you hold back from people. You must be suffering nightmares."

Finally the question that had plagued Noah could be asked. "Did you get over it? Get back to normal?"

"Yes, God healed me finally. I was wild after the war, wild to drink and carouse and incurred more damage to my body. It took nearly getting killed one night in a fracas to get my attention. I sobered up. Somehow I found a sweet wife who prayed for me and gifted me with children. Their love worked on me."

Noah felt Dawn's phantom touch, her little chubby hand patting his cheek.

The older man looked as if he were peering into the past. "I took long walks in the solitary woods talking to God. I was never the same—I was better. Any trial stretches a man, a person. I think that was the beginning of my wanting to preach."

Noah sat bent with his elbows on his knees, his hands clasped together. "I have a sweet wife. And a child."

"I know. I see a true, a humble, heart in Sunny. But she carries some burden, too. I just wanted you to know you can be restored. You need to let God in more and let his Holy Spirit do the healing."

Noah tried not to reject these words outright— Old Saul had earned a hearing. Yet healing just didn't seem possible. How could one wipe away all the blood he'd shed?

"I'm tired now, son."

Noah accepted the dismissal and rose. "Yes, rest. We still have more barns to raise this summer."

A smile tugged at the older man's mouth. "God be with you, Noah Whitmore."

"And with you," Noah said automatically.

Soon he mounted his horse with Sunny and Dawn, bid everyone farewell and headed home, turning over in his mind all that had been said. As usual, Sunny didn't speak when she realized he didn't want to. So he could just think.

He wanted to believe the old man but did his experience really match Noah's? Noah didn't know about opening himself to God. It sounded dangerous.

He'd worked so hard to keep everything in— could he let go without flying apart?

Two weeks later on Sunday, Sunny was surprised and pleased to see Old Saul had returned to meeting. He wasn't sitting on the porch as usual, but in his wagon bed in a rocking chair tied down tight. Would Old Saul's presence be good for Noah or not?

Noah had come home from Old Saul's and had been quiet for days. This had disturbed her but she merely tried to behave as if she didn't notice.

She would pray this morning silently for her husband during Old Saul's prayer when he asked for special requests. Surely if the old preacher asked God to bless Noah, he would.

On the porch Lavina and her husband lifted their hands and began the first hymn. Then Lavina's husband spoke the opening prayer. Sunny began to worry that Old Saul had come merely to observe, not to preach. But then, in the wagon, Old Saul lifted his hands in his usual signal that he was going to speak. Appreciation whispered through the gathering.

He cleared his throat. "Even if you didn't attend the first barn raising at the Whitmores, you must know by now that my heart let me know that it's older than my seventy-one years. I'm afraid I've put my heart through a lot."

Sunny thought that the older man looked straight at Noah then.

"It's had to beat longer, many more times than any of yours. I have a medicine that helps but it's just a matter of time till my heart will give out and I will no longer be among you."

A sad silence greeted this. Nothing but a seagull

squawking over the Mississippi sounded nearby, and gentle waves slapping a boat moored at the wharf. Sunny edged closer to Noah.

"I don't say this lightly, but for a purpose. Preachers are hard to come by on the frontier. After I pass, it might be some time before a new one will come to town. And not all preachers know God, know his love and forgiveness. Some preach so they will get the prime seats and free apple pies."

A few chuckled at this.

"There is a Bible passage that tells how the apostles chose someone to replace Judas Iscariot, the one who betrayed Christ with a kiss. They chose two worthy men and then cast lots to let God tell them who should be chosen."

A feeling of uncertainty slithered up Sunny's spine.

"Yesterday I asked my son to write down the name of every man who attends our meeting on a piece of paper. I want God to choose the right man to lead you when I'm gone."

Old Saul fell silent, gazing out to them, in turn catching the eye of each one.

Sunny didn't like where this was going. She edged closer still to Noah.

"What if you choose my name," Gordy spoke loud enough to be heard, "and I don't know enough about the Bible to do a good job?"

Old Saul nodded approvingly. "I'm doing this

now while I still have time and energy to instruct the one chosen. I must tell you that the Lord laid this on my heart. Over and over He has directed me to study over the choosing of prophets and kings and apostles. I feel certain that He has someone here in mind."

Everyone looked solemn and the men watchful. Only the children prattled and the gulls on a nearby sandbar fought over carrion. Sunny wanted to touch Noah's arm but didn't want to make any move that would call attention to them. She wondered if this was why Old Saul had summoned Noah.

Oh, Lord, not Noah. He didn't even want to attend meeting here.

" 'And a little child shall lead them,' " Old Saul quoted Isaiah. "Gordy, bring your boy up. He can choose."

Gordy carried the boy up and set him in the wagon.

Old Saul spoke quietly to the child and then asked him to pull out a paper from a cloth bag he opened.

Guthrie looked to Gordy who nodded and urged him to do as asked. The little boy stuck his hand in and drew out several slips.

"Choose just one," Saul said, holding up his index finger.

Guthrie looked at the slips in one hand and pulled one free. Old Saul received it with thanks.

Gordy lifted Guthrie and carried him back to Nan.

Everyone gazed at the slip of paper in Old Saul's hand. The older man opened it and then seemed to pray. Then he looked up. "God's choice is Noah Whitmore."

Sunny sucked in breath so fast she nearly choked.

Noah let out a gasp.

Still reeling, Sunny couldn't put everything together. People crowded around, saying words, smiling, patting her on the back. But nothing penetrated. She tried to smile and nod but could not quell her shock.

No, this can't be happening.

The ride home had been quiet, solemn and had stretched on like an endless journey. Sunny had barely been able to respond to the few comments their friends had made as they made their way in the wagon. Noah had been stone-cold silent. What would happen now?

Gordy drove into their clearing. Neechee barked in welcome and frolicked forward.

Noah helped Sunny down from the wagon bed. Sunny tried to smile for her friends but her mouth had frozen.

Gordy cleared his throat. "I know this has been a shock, Noah."

"A shock," Martin repeated.

"But an honor, too, Noah," Gordy said.

"We're behind you," Martin added. "We know it won't be easy to take on."

"If you need anything, you just ask, okay?" Gordy said with an earnestness that touched Sunny.

"We'll be prayin' for you," Nan said.

Ophelia whispered, "Yes, we'll all pray."

Noah nodded and raised a hand, bidding their friends a silent farewell. He and Sunny stood together, watching the wagon drive away. Somehow their friends' understanding of how hard this was proved once more their friendship.

Inside she had to remember to take off her bonnet. Then she stood in her kitchen, trying to think what she'd planned to have for dinner. A pot hung toward the back of the hearth. She went about the preparations but wondered if she'd be able to eat.

Noah came in, still holding Dawn. He sat down at the table and Dawn squirmed and prattled, letting him know she wanted to get down. Finally he set the child on the floor. Then he looked at Sunny. "I can't do it."

She sank on the same bench. What if Noah refused?

The image of Dawn in the schoolyard shifted, and now her friends didn't welcome her, they stood apart and whispered about her. Dawn looked miserable.

Sunny burst into tears.

"I can't do it," Noah said, his voice becoming stronger. "I can't teach people about God. Or lead them. I killed men. I'm a murderer."

And I was a prostitute, Sunny added silently, unable to say the words aloud. Tears rolled down her cheeks.

"I can't do it," he repeated.

"What will happen if you refuse?" she murmured.

"I don't care." Noah shot up from the bench and burst out the door.

Dawn shrieked his name, expressing Sunny's own feelings, but he didn't turn back.

How could this have happened? How could God have let this happen?

Chapter Fifteen

Sunny watched as a downhearted Neechee returned, whimpering in distress. Noah must have ordered the dog back. Sunny could do nothing but stand still, staring at the open door. Where had Noah gone? What would happen now?

The past bombarded Sunny with days and nights she longed to scrub from her memory. The repulsive sensation of being manhandled by a stranger swept through her as sharp edged as if it were happening today. She gagged and hurried outside to retch. She fell to her knees, enduring the spasms.

What am I going to do, God?

With her head bent, she wept bitter tears. Everything had been going so well. Hope, flaming within, had been blown out like a candle in the wind. All the horrible names she'd ever been called, all the scathing glances she'd ever endured slammed into her once again.

The tall trees stood high above her, their tops gently moving with the breeze as hot tears flowed down her face onto the grass.

Noah didn't come back.

Sunny dragged herself up. She went inside and changed Dawn's diaper and settled her into the hammock for a nap. Then Sunny stood in the middle of the empty cabin—bereft, alone.

I can't just let this happen. Just let that little slip of paper destroy everything.

Minutes passed. She kept listening, hoping to hear Noah returning. Neechee lay across the threshold, whimpering on and off, giving sound to Sunny's own longing and fear. What if Noah didn't come back? What if he just left her here?

Old Saul's lined, drawn face came to mind. He had started this—and she must go to him for help. But how could she? How could she explain why Noah wouldn't be a preacher and she—of all women—couldn't be a preacher's wife?

She shoved these questions to the back of her mind. Old Saul was the only one with the power to change this thing that had come upon them.

After saddling the horse, Sunny retrieved Dawn from her hammock and settled her into the sling that Noah always used. She managed to mount from a stump. She'd never ridden the horse alone here, but she knew how to ride and she knew where the preacher lived. She headed up the track.

Fortunately the town was deserted on Sunday afternoon. When she left it behind, she breathed easier, riding north along the Mississippi to the preacher's house.

Within an hour she walked the horse into the clearing of Old Saul's son's house. Lavina sat outside in a curved chair with her sewing basket open at her feet. The woman rose in greeting. "Sunny, what brings you here?"

"I need to talk to Old Saul." Sunny tasted her own sour breath as she spoke for the first time in many hours. She slid from the horse's back, now feeling presumptuous.

Lavina hurried forward. "You look distressed."

"I am," Sunny admitted. Why lie? "Can I see him?"

Lavina lifted a waking Dawn from the sling. "Of course. He's lying down, but he'll see you."

Sunny followed Lavina to the door.

"Saul, Sunny Whitmore has come to see you," the woman announced. Lavina waved Sunny inside. "I'll play with the baby and leave you two alone." She shut the door.

Sunny stood in the midst of the neat cabin, smelling the remnants of the noon meal, feeling very out of place.

On the other side of the hearth Old Saul lay on the bed, gazing at her steadily. He gestured toward a chair by his bed. "Come and tell me what's troubling you, Mrs. Whitmore."

Sunny perched on the chair. How could she make this man see what the casting of lots had triggered? She fingered her skirt, trying to think what words to say.

You must tell him everything.

Sunny did not know where the thought had come from and she most certainly did not want to do what it said. But would anything less work? This was not a time for half measures. She must make this man understand and help her to work matters out so she wouldn't lose Noah or this place that had become their home.

How could she again face strife as she had when they'd helped Bid'a ban? Turning down Old Saul would garner even more censure.

I love Noah. This has wounded him. And I can't let him suffer without doing everything to keep him, make him whole.

"You wish to speak to me in confidence?" Old Saul suggested.

She nodded woodenly. Her heart thumped,

making her feel sick again. If she told him the truth about herself, there would be no going back. She would be exposed and in this man's power.

Saul reached out and grasped her hand. "Trust me."

"I was a prostitute." The four simple words burst through her, shaking her so that she shuddered. She gasped for air.

Saul patted her hand. "Why are you telling me this?"

"So you'll see why I can't be a preacher's wife. It isn't fitting." The shaking continued. She clung to him, expecting him to shove her away, but Saul kept her hand in his, gripping it firmly.

"I find it hard to believe that you were in that trade. You don't have a hard look about you."

Sunny understood what he meant. The hard veneer of many of the women she had worked with had hidden deep wells of sorrow. But she'd had a mother who'd loved and protected her as much as she could. Maybe that had made the difference, kept her from becoming hard.

The guilt she'd carried for years overwhelmed her, wanting at last to be spoken. "My mother was a prostitute, too."

Each word cost her. "I've always felt guilty about that. You see, when she realized she was pregnant with me, she told the father . . ."

"And he abandoned her."

Sunny nodded, sick at heart. "And her own father shut her out of the family."

Old Saul exhaled long and slow. "I'm so sorry." He paused. "So you were born into that life?"

Holding back tears required all her strength. "Yes. My mother died when I was fourteen and I had no other way."

"Just a child." Saul kept her hand and patted it with his other. "You poor child."

His sympathetic tone helped her breathe, helped her go on. "So you see, I can't be a preacher's wife. Not after what I've done." She forced herself to look him in the eye. Would he keep her confidence? Or was her new life now ruined?

"No one will ever hear this from me," he said solemnly as if reading her thoughts.

She drew in a ragged breath, still shaking. "Thank you," she whispered.

"Does Noah know this?" he asked.

"Yes."

"But he wanted you for his wife?"

"Yes." *And I don't know why.*

Old Saul nodded. "Have you ever heard the story of David and Bathsheba?"

His abrupt change of topic caught her off guard. "No, I've never heard of them. Are they in the Bible?"

Old Saul squeezed her hand and shifted his position in bed. "Yes. And a sad story it is. David was a young shepherd boy who grew to be a

301

man of God and God set him as king over all of
Israel. David was handsome and he took many
wives." Old Saul looked at her. "That was when
a man could have as many wives as he could
afford. And David had become rich."

Sunny tried to keep her focus on what the man
was saying, but so far it didn't mean anything to her.

The old man paused, sighing. "To give you the
main part of the sad story, David forgot God and
took another man's wife in secret. That was
Bathsheba. Then she found herself pregnant
while her rightful husband was off to war and
unable to father the child. So David had her
husband killed in battle."

"This is in the Bible?" Sunny had a hard time
believing this. "A man like that?"

Old Saul looked directly into her eyes. "Yes, a
man like that. God called David 'a man after
his own heart.' And he was an ancestor of Christ.
But even though David knew God, he committed
both adultery and murder."

"What did God do to him?" She couldn't have
guessed that there were sinners in the Bible.

"God confronted David with his sin. And the
child conceived in adultery died."

Sunny sucked in a sharp breath and glanced
toward the door, cold with fear. *Would God take
Dawn?*

"Do you know what God did then?" Old Saul
prompted.

Sunny was afraid to even shake her head no.

"After David confessed his sin, God forgave David and Bathsheba, and blessed them with another son, who became a king known as Solomon, the wisest man who ever lived."

Sunny tried to absorb this but couldn't. "I don't understand."

"Psalm 103 tells us, 'as far as the east is from the west, so far hath He removed our transgressions from us.' Have you confessed your sins to God?"

"He knows them." Sunny felt defeated. None of this made sense.

"Ah, you speak wisely. God knows our sins. Did you repent of your sins—not just adultery but everything else?"

Sunny gave this some thought. "I did."

"Then He forgave you and wiped your sins away."

Trusting this man who had not been shocked by her past, she asked the question that had plagued her since meeting the Gabriel family. "I don't understand. How can He just wipe them away?"

"God can do things we can't. Let me show you a bit of how He thinks of us. Dawn is your child. Is there anything she could do that would cause you to stop loving her? Would you put her out of your house?"

"No. Never." Had her grandfather loved her

mother at all? He couldn't have, not if he sent her into a life of prostitution.

"God is our father. Your mother's father may have put his daughter out but God never did."

"Then why didn't God help her stay out of the saloon?" *Why did I end up there?*

"I don't know. We are told that God always provides a way of escape. Maybe your mother didn't know to look for that other way. I don't know her heart. But I do know your heart, Sunny Whitmore."

This confused her more. She tilted her head as if questioning him.

"You have a loving, willing, humble heart. And you want to please God."

"Yes," she whispered. "But I never know how I'm supposed to feel. How does it *feel* when we are forgiven?"

He gripped her hand again. "It isn't about how you feel. It's about God being the one who can and does forgive. Sometimes a person will feel something when they come to God with a repentant heart, but not always. Yet that doesn't mean the person isn't forgiven."

Sunny held the older man's large hand in hers. She turned over all he had said in her mind. "I just have to believe I'm forgiven? Like having faith in God?"

"Exactly."

"Noah doesn't know that," she said haltingly.

"He thinks he's guilty of murder because he fought in the war."

"Your husband is a man capable of deep feelings and unwavering conviction. He sacrificed much to fight for the end of slavery, was willing to give his life to accomplish that. Nevertheless, it's time he put that war to rest."

"How?" She listened intently, hoping.

"He must do what you have done. Have faith in God. Have faith in God's power to forgive and to heal."

Sunny had heard some of this from the Gabriels but not how it worked, how it demanded faith. "It sounds too simple."

"It is. The world likes to make God and faith hard but what's real, what matters, is very simple."

She shook her head. "But having faith is hard to do."

"Yes, it's giving up control. Letting God do it for us goes against our nature. We want to have to do some made-up penance. We humans are strange beings."

The two sat, their hands still clasped. And Sunny did feel something, a lightening of her spirit. *I am forgiven,* she repeated, trying to believe it, etch it into her heart.

"I don't know what Noah is going to do. He just up and left. He said he couldn't be the preacher," Sunny told Old Saul.

"I know. I saw it in his eyes. I feared it when I read his name on the slip of paper. But I trust that God knows what He's doing. He has plans for Noah. For all of us."

"What if Noah doesn't want to follow God's plans?"

"When God laid choosing a successor on my heart, I prayed long and hard. And I've been praying ever since I read Noah's name aloud. I think that Noah is listening to God, has always been listening to him. A man who is sensitive to God would take killing men harder than a heedless man. Do you see?"

Sunny pressed the man's hand. "Yes, Noah takes everything seriously." And then Dawn came to mind, pulling herself up using Noah's pant leg. Sunny grinned. "Except when Dawn makes him happy."

"The blessing of children. A child's love is so genuine and without reservation. And we don't have to do anything to reap it. A true boon."

"So my past . . . doesn't mean I can't be a preacher's wife."

"No, I think it will make you a kind and understanding preacher's wife."

The way he said the words, she thought he really meant them. She glimpsed herself as forgiving and being able to show forgiveness to others.

The older man patted her hand. "God's at work in Noah. Just love him and respect him as I know you do." The older man's eyelids drifted down. "I'm sorry, but I need to rest now," he murmured.

Sunny rose. "Thank you, Old Saul." She bent and kissed his cheek. "You've given me peace about my past."

She turned to fetch her daughter and head home. She would pray the whole way and let God handle this—this was certainly more than she could work out. She had found some answers, but the answers just seemed to raise more questions, one of which plagued her most of all.

Would Noah be there when she got home?

Noah finally glimpsed the thin smoke of his fire above the surrounding trees. From ahead he heard his dog bark in welcome and run forward through the brush. Exhausted, Noah waited for Neechee to reach him. When she did, he stooped down to receive her joyful wiggling and wagging. She licked his hands and his chin and barked, almost appearing to smile. "You're my girl, Neechee. Yes, you are."

The dog's affection helped him steady a bit more. *How long have I been gone?* He gazed at the sun that now had sunk well past its peak.

He still carried a solid chunk of iron in his gut. His head ached. His mind felt like newspaper soaked in water, limp and easily torn. How far he had walked before he'd turned back, he didn't know. But he'd been walking for hours now.

Hunger had finally turned him toward home, feeling used up.

All he wanted was to sit down at his own table and lift Dawn onto his knee. Sunny might want to talk but if he didn't, she would let him be. It was one of the things he most appreciated about her —she could be quiet with him.

He rubbed his temple with the flat of his hand and tried not to think about that little slip of paper that had turned his life upside down. He trudged the last half mile toward home, forming a simple apology to Sunny for leaving so abruptly. He couldn't think past that, how to confront this thing that had broken and shattered him.

He forded the stream, stepping on rocks one by one while Neechee splashed beside him. Then he passed his fenced garden, noting the green shoots had grown at least another inch this week. How could he even think of leaving this place? He'd done too much to make this place home. But what would people say when he refused Old Saul? The chunk of iron in his stomach weighed heavier.

He stepped into his clearing. The oxen grazed, tethered to their stakes. But his horse was gone.

"Sunny!"

He hurried to the cabin and pulled open the latchstring. The faint scent of salt pork and beans hung in the air. The pot still hung high over the banked fire. But no Sunny. No Dawn. Neechee whined at his feet.

"Where did they go, girl?"

Noah stood in the middle of his cabin. For that moment he stood alone, bereft, exposed to God.

Help. I need her. I need them. Help me.

He sank onto the bench and held his head in his hands. The old scenes of battle raged through him—cannon roaring and shaking the earth, bugles, drums blaring, black powder fog choking and twisting, angry faces screaming and cursing. The tumult overwhelmed him.

Neechee barked and ran out the door. The soft sound of horse hooves came. Noah wrenched himself from the past and hurried outside. He ran to help Sunny down and lead the horse to the lean-to. Dawn slept in the sling peacefully. With an arm around her he walked Sunny into the house and then lifted the baby into his arms.

The love he felt for the child and her mother swept away everything like a spring flood. "I love you, Sunny. And I love this child." He couldn't have held back the words if he'd tried.

Sunny threw her arms around him. "I love you, too. Oh, Noah, I've wanted to tell you for so long."

He turned from her and gently stowed the child in her hammock.

Then he turned back to his wife, his dear wife.

For a moment shyness caused him to hesitate. Then that, too, was swept away. He must be near her, hold her. He felt his love for her flow through him, forceful, demanding. "Sunny," he said, his voice becoming husky.

She buried her face against his shirt. "I was so worried," she said.

He lifted her chin and bent his lips to hers. "My sweet Sunny, my sweet wife." He thought to kiss her gently but yearning swept him up in its current.

She clung to him and kissed him back.

He breathed in her lavender scent and fresh strength flowed through him. What he had been powerless to change had come right. He lifted her into his arms and carried her toward the ladder to the loft. "Sunny, my sweet, please . . ."

She smothered his entreaty with a kiss, a kiss that breathed into him her love and gave him life.

Sunny, my sweet wife.

Chapter Sixteen

In the loft of the quiet cabin Sunny lay in Noah's strong arms—her husband's loving arms—replete. She didn't want to move or speak, fearful of disturbing their perfect peace. Nothing separated them in this moment, one she would treasure all the rest of her life.

"I'm sorry, Sunny," he murmured.

She couldn't think of what he was apologizing about. "For what?"

"For just leaving like I did. You didn't deserve that."

With the back of her hand she stroked his rough cheek. She loved the stubbly feel of it. "I was worried. I didn't know what to do." Then fear swirled cold in her stomach. Better to confess what she'd done right away. "I went to see Old Saul."

"All by yourself?"

She loved the concern she heard in his voice. "Yes, he was the only one who could help. He was the only one who could change things."

Noah kissed her temple. "My brave Sunny." Then he stilled. "Did he have a way to let me out of this?" The thought of what had been asked of him still defeated him, but here, now, with Sunny in his arms, he could face it.

"He said he'd pray about it." Sunny paused. She must tell him all. "I told him about my past."

"Why?" Noah increased his hold on her.

"I didn't think I could be a preacher's wife after what I'd done." Shame warmed her cheeks.

Not for the first time Noah wished he could make up for the life she'd been forced to live. The idea that men were free to sow their wild oats with impunity but a woman must stay pure or be ostracized had never made sense to him. The

311

double standard was cruel, heartless and the woman always paid the price.

"Sunny, I don't think like that." He kissed her soft ear.

"I know." Her gratitude prompted her to snuggle even closer. "Old Saul told me about David and . . . I can't remember her name . . . it's in the Bible."

"Bathsheba. About their adultery?"

"I can't believe that something like that is in the Bible."

Noah laughed harshly. "There's worse than that in the Bible. God doesn't pretty up what people do to each other and to themselves."

Sunny ran her fingers through his hair. She sensed the hurt in his tone had more to do with him than David. "Old Saul said that God forgets our sins and wipes them away. 'As far as—' "

" '—the east is from the west, so far hath He removed our transgressions from us.' " He'd heard it since he was a child. Why didn't he believe it?

Again Sunny heard the pain and regret under the words. "I don't understand it, either. But I'm going to have faith that God has forgiven me. Noah, we can't hold on to all the bad things that have happened to us. You're a good man—"

He tried to interrupt.

She pressed her fingers against his lips. "You are a good man, not a perfect man."

He tried to interrupt her again.

She kissed away his words. "Look at me, Noah," she demanded.

He obeyed her, amazed a little at her fierceness.

"Most men looked at me and saw a cheap harlot. But you looked at me and saw a wife, a woman you wanted to have with you, by your side. When I look at you, I see the most honorable, most kind, man. You're hard on yourself, Noah. Do you know more than God?"

That stopped him. "What do you mean?"

"If God says He forgives us, do we know more than He does?" She held her breath, hoping this would connect in his mind, too.

Noah rested his head against hers. "I wish I could feel that."

She still had trouble believing in forgiveness herself. "It's trusting God. Maybe it just takes time."

"What did Old Saul say about this . . . I mean, me being chosen?" Noah's heart thudded with dread.

"He says he's praying about it and wants to talk to you." She gently stroked his face.

Then Dawn called out from her hammock below, "No-No!"

Noah chuckled low in his throat. "Somebody's awake."

Sunny loved how Dawn's waking up amused him. She stirred, feeling languid, loved, complete.

"Take your time, Sunny. I'll get her up."

She listened to him, rustling down the ladder and over the half-log floor. She stretched and sighed with satisfaction. *Oh, Lord, please let this continue, this new harmony.*

She rose and got herself together. She hoped she'd added enough water and salt to keep the stew from drying out completely. Noah must be hungry. She, however, was filled to the brim.

The next afternoon Noah rode into the clearing at Old Saul's place to face this thing. This thing that had shaken him to his core yesterday. He and Sunny had agreed they would not leave Pepin. They'd put too much into their home and their community. So Noah must find a way to do this thing—or bow out gracefully.

Contrasting with his despair just twenty-four hours ago, Noah could not recall feeling as good as he did today. The final barrier between his wife and him had been breached and he couldn't stop the joy inside him. And last night with Sunny snuggled against him, he'd slept without one nightmare. With this thought he called out, "Hello, the house!"

Lavina opened the door and stepped outside. She smiled. "My father-in-law said he thought you'd stop by today. Come right in."

Noah dismounted, hitching his horse to a low branch. Inside the door he doffed his hat and let his eyes adjust to the dim interior, preparing himself.

"I'll leave you two alone to talk. I have a garden that needs weeding." Lavina left them, shutting the door after her.

Noah gazed at the old preacher as if seeing him for the first time.

"I'm glad you're here. Come sit beside me, son."

In that startling moment Noah felt as if he'd come home from the war—at last. This proved to be the welcome he'd been longing for, the one his own father had not been able to give him.

Noah swallowed down the emotion this sparked and went to sit beside the narrow bed. "Old Saul, I'm grateful you treated Sunny so kindly."

"You have been blessed with a special, very sweet woman. Hearing what she went through hurt me for her."

"It's not right, the way she was treated before." Noah's voice sounded low in his throat.

Old Saul reached out.

Noah accepted his hand.

"Have you come to start learning from me?" Old Saul asked, searching his eyes.

Noah had come to try to get out of this new responsibility. But with these words his heart leaped.

His name had been the one chosen. Did God know what he was doing? Noah's uncertainty didn't disappear, but he could approach this now. "Yes, I've come to start learning, but . . ."

Old Saul raised his eyebrows in question.

"I think there should have been two of us. More like the apostles—they picked two."

"In a way. But you're right. We will hold a second drawing. Better to have a deacon to help you. Did you bring your Bible, son?"

"It's in my saddlebag." Noah realized that this revealed that on some level he must have decided to accept his new responsibility even though he hadn't thought that true. This added to the strength growing inside him.

"Bring it in. We'll pray and read some passages about pastors."

So began Noah's education to become the next pastor.

God, You chose me. Now get me ready.

A triumphant shout rose in Noah's throat and joined those around him. The last piece had been set in place on the roof of his barn. Though panting and perspiring, the men around him beamed. Old Saul sat on his rocking chair in the shade, his feet propped high on a footstool Noah had crafted for him.

The old preacher clapped his hands momentarily and then let them fall. This show of the older man's weakness saddened Noah. Not long ago Noah had unloaded much of his feelings about the war to Old Saul. Just getting them said aloud to a man who understood had been healing.

Gordy clapped Noah on the back. "Well, one barn down and seven to go!"

Noah grinned. "You're always such a cheerful cuss."

Much to his surprise Gordy had been chosen by lot as the first deacon for the Sunday meeting. Now Gordy and Noah met weekly with Old Saul, learning about the Bible and how to pastor. Noah looked forward to these sessions.

The women came forward to admire the new barn. The structure only needed a door and bar to latch it, both of which Noah would craft himself. He looked around for his wife, but didn't see her. "Where's Sunny?"

"She's with Neechee," Nan said with a smile as big as the sky. "Neechee's already birthed one pup."

"Why didn't somebody tell me?" Noah squawked. He turned and pelted toward his cabin. Hoots of laughter followed him.

He stopped at the open cabin door and doffed his hat and wiped away his sweat with his pocket handkerchief. "Sunny," he asked as he entered, "how's our Neechee doing?"

"Just fine." Sunny held up a chubby brown-and-white pup. "This is number one." She nodded toward another pup, which the mama was grooming. "And I think there may be a number three." Sunny had laid an old ragged shirt of his before the fire and that's where Neechee lay.

Noah knelt by Sunny's side and stroked Neechee's head. The dog whined her pleasure at seeing him, then went back to licking clean the second pup.

Before long a third pup slid forth, and Neechee was done.

"I guess this means that the little Ojibwa boy will get his pup," Gordy said from just outside the open door.

"And that means," Noah said, as he turned, proudly holding one pup high, "that you and Martin will each get one, too."

"This is a big day," Gordy pronounced. "The first barn done and three pups born."

From behind Gordy came the sound of cheerful congratulations from others who were resting from their labor on the benches and chairs outside.

Dawn woke where she'd fallen asleep on her blanket on the floor near Sunny. The baby knuckled her sleepy eyes.

"Look, Dawnie," Noah said tenderly. "Puppies."

The little girl looked astounded and crawled quickly over to Neechee.

Still kneeling, Noah laid the pup back by the mother and then drew Dawn to stand beside him. "These are our puppies. Pup-pies," he repeated.

Dawn looked puzzled but then bounced up and down, bending her knees. She clapped her hands.

"That's right," Sunny said. "Today is a day for clapping hands." She clapped her hands, too.

Noah chuckled and clapped his, his heart lifted high and singing. He would never forget today, ever. God had been good to him. He knew that now. And he was immeasurably grateful.

Epilogue

With her shawl wrapped around her, Sunny stood in the chill autumn afternoon. Isaiah had come to say goodbye and to claim Miigwans's puppy. Tomorrow at dawn, the young man would be heading north to help Sam White and see how Bid'a ban was faring. Sunny felt joyful and sad at the same time.

Noah stood beside her with Dawn in his arms. "I wish I could go with you."

Sunny knew what he meant. She wished she could see her friend again. How could she and Bid'a ban have bonded so deeply in such a short time? "Maybe someday we'll go visit them."

Recognizing the longing in her tone, Noah brushed her cheek with his lips. Then he handed her Dawn and lifted the leather bag of gifts they and their friends had gathered for Bid'a ban— fabric and buttons and needles and thread and other little items that would travel light but be of use to her.

Onto the young man's shoulders Noah positioned the sling he'd fashioned for Isaiah to carry the pup. Then he went to Neechee and bent to pet her. "It's time for your last pup to go to his owner, Neechee. You remember Miigwans. He'll take good care of your little one." He lifted the pup and stowed it in the sling. "You be a good traveler, okay, little pup?"

Neechee rose to her feet and barked as if in farewell.

Isaiah patted the pup in the sling and murmured to it. "He'll be good company for me. Well, I best be off. Mom cooked a big dinner at noon and is baking me a cake for my last supper at home."

Sunny hugged Isaiah and petted the pup. "Be good, both of you," she teased, lightening the mood.

Noah shook hands with the young man and bid farewell to the pup. Then he stood with his arm around Sunny and watched the lad ride down the track and disappear around the bend of trees. From Sunny's arms, Dawn waved bye-bye. Neechee barked but remained at her master's side.

"I'll miss having the last pup here," he said at last.

Sunny turned to him and gave him a smile. Leaning close, she whispered, "I think we'll have another little one around here come next summer."

At first he didn't understand her. But when she placed his hand on her abdomen, he grasped the news. His heart skipped a beat.

"You mean it?" This was too good to be true. A child?

She nodded and then leaned her head on his chest. "Are you happy?"

"There aren't words," he murmured as his heart exploded with joy. He kissed her fragrant hair and tucked her closer.

Dawn objected loudly to being pressed against him so tightly. "Pa-pa!"

He lifted the child from her mother's arms. "Papa, is it? Now you know who I am?"

Arms wide, Dawn threw herself against him in one of her impulsive hugs. "Pa-pa!"

Noah drew Sunny under his arm and he stood with his family, bursting with love and gratitude. Never had he imagined such blessings.

Thank You, God, a thousand times, thank You.

Dear Reader,

I hope you've enjoyed Sunny and Noah's story. Sunny was a character in the book *Her Healing Ways*, the last in my GABRIEL SISTERS series. When I finished writing that book, Sunny's character just wouldn't let me fail to tell her story. And then in my mind I saw her in the meeting-house and Noah stood up and proposed. And I was off—typing as fast as I could.

I set this series, WILDERNESS BRIDES, in Wisconsin, now my home state. And I chose Pepin because someone very important was born there—do you know who?

Laura Ingalls Wilder was born in Pepin in 1867. Pepin is where *Little House in the Big Woods* took place. You may have noticed the Fitzhugh family —Charles, Caroline and their daughters, Mary and Laura. Yes, they are patterned after the Ingalls family. And yes, the Ingallses left for Kansas in 1869, the year this story takes place. But the Ingallses weren't done with Wisconsin. Maybe you'll see the Fitzhughs return in the next book . . .

You've already met my next "Wilderness" bride, Miss Ellen Thurston from Galena, Illinois, the daughter of a wealthy family. Now, what drove her to leave home—and who will she fall in love with, I wonder?

Lyn Cote

Questions for Discussion

1. Why do you think Noah decided to ask Sunny to marry him?

2. Can you think of any reasons that Noah's father and he didn't get along?

3. The Civil War was a bloody war, around 600,000 men died, more than any other in our history. The toll this took on the survivors—families and soldiers that returned home—is almost unimaginable. How did Noah show the aftereffects of the war?

4. How did Noah's healing begin?

5. What was Sunny's worst fear?

6. What caused her to face this fear?

7. Had you ever heard of the Ojibwa tribe? Did you realize that Native Americans had served in the Union and Confederate Armies?

8. Why did Sunny have trouble believing God had forgiven her sins?

9. Have you heard of what used to be called the double standard? This is very evident in this story. Can you give me an example?

10. What do you think of Ophelia's mother? Why do you think she acted the way she did?

11. Noah became a leader even though he didn't want to. What qualities did he have that drew him to the forefront?

12. Quakers or Friends are pacifists and were conscientious objectors in the twentieth century. Why do you think Noah decided he must go to war?

About the Author

Lyn Cote and her husband, her real-life hero, became in-laws recently when their son married his true love. Lyn already loves her daughter-in-law and enjoys this new adventure in family stretching. Lyn and her husband still live on the lake in the north woods, where they watch a bald eagle and its young soar and swoop overhead throughout the year. She wishes the best to all her readers.

You may email Lyn at
l.cote@juno.com

or write her at
P.O. Box 864, Woodruff, WI 54548.

And drop by her blog,
www.strongwomenbravestories.blogspot.com,
to read stories of strong women in real life
and in true-to-life fiction.
"Every woman has a story. Share yours."

Center Point Large Print
600 Brooks Road / PO Box 1
Thorndike ME 04986-0001 USA

(207) 568-3717

US & Canada:
1 800 929-9108
www.centerpointlargeprint.com